THE COUNTRY COUSIN

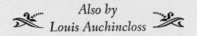

Also by
Louis Auchincloss

The Indifferent Children
The Injustice Collectors
Sybil
A Law for the Lion
The Romantic Egoists
The Great World and Timothy Colt
Venus in Sparta
Pursuit of the Prodigal
The House of Five Talents
Reflections of a Jacobite
Portrait in Brownstone
Powers of Attorney
The Rector of Justin
Pioneers and Caretakers
The Embezzler
Tales of Manhattan
A World of Profit
Motiveless Malignity
Second Chance
Edith Wharton
Richelieu
I Come as a Thief
The Partners
A Writer's Capital
Reading Henry James
The Winthrop Covenant
The Dark Lady

Louis Auchincloss

THE COUNTRY COUSIN

Houghton Mifflin Company
Boston 1978

Library of Congress Cataloging in Publication Data

Auchincloss, Louis.
    The country cousin.

    I. Title.
PZ3.A898Co [PS3501.U25]   813'.5'4   78-7233
ISBN 0-395-26687-4

Printed in the United States of America
    P 10 9 8 7 6 5 4 3 2 1

124496

For Joyce Hartman,
Friend and Editor

Then Space — began to toll,

As all the Heavens were a Bell,
And Being, but an Ear,
And I, and Silence, some strange Race
Wrecked, solitary, here —

EMILY DICKINSON

PART I

AMY

❧ 1 ❧

AMY HUNT ALWAYS associated the long cold winter of 1936 with her passion for Herman Fidler. She saw herself in the big bay window of the living room of Cousin Dolly's apartment on East 80th Street in Manhattan, looking down on the mottled black and white of the slushy snow. People hurried east and west, pushing against the cutting wind, scarfs muffling their faces, heads down in charging posture. The dark oblongs of car roofs moved slowly down the street, turning uncertainly on the skiddy corner like blocks pushed by a huge invisible infant. Behind her was a fire in the grate under a Whistler etching of the Grand Canal, a bright crackling fire before which Cousin Dolly was reading a volume of Emily Dickinson.

"What are you looking at, Amy?"

"People."

"'Menagerie to me, My Neighbor be—'" Cousin Dolly quoted.

"How lucky we are not to be out!"

"You mean how lucky we are to be *in*. Don't put things so negatively, child."

"I suppose Herman and Naomi won't be coming now. The weather's much too mean."

"It's a good excuse not to call on a poor old aunt. Whom Naomi hates, anyhow!"

"Cousin Dolly, you mustn't talk like that. Naomi is very fond of you, really."

"In a pig's eye. Brr! Listen to that wind. Get me a spot of whiskey, child, to warm me old bones."

Herman wouldn't come. It was too dark, too cold. It usually was. But did it matter? Wasn't it as well when he didn't? When she had him, in her mind's eye, to herself, and could deliberate if he was really handsome or only handsome to her? Perhaps he might have been handsome if one could somehow bring out the handsomeness. It might have been lurking behind the rounded contours of his bland, pleasant face, or in the pale depths of his tranquil blue gray eyes, or under his thick, short, soldierly brushed hair. Just as there might have been a latent strength in the well-built figure, so smoothly wrapped in dark tweeds, which moved about the cluttered rooms of Cousin Dolly's apartment with feline grace and silence. Herman was like an intensely domesticated animal, but Amy wanted to imagine that he had still the capacity to turn, to snarl, to lift a paw, to strike. She had to admit he did not do so. His conversation was polite, topical; his gestures, in lighting his wife's eternal cigarettes, in fetching a shawl for his aunt, were controlled, efficient, deferential.

Once, only once, at a Sunday lunch, had he seemed to confirm Amy's suspicions of the wilder creature under the rich, muted colors. He had been talking of a Caribbean island where he and Naomi had spent a winter holiday.

"You could walk miles down the beach without seeing a soul. And wade into that sapphire water to be alone with the fish. I used to swim for hours. Last summer, in Southampton, I could hardly get accustomed to a bathing suit again."

"You mean you swam in the nude down there?" his aunt demanded. "I hope nobody saw you!"

Amy's mind had become at once a cubist painting of thighs and buttocks and shoulders and a long male spine against a marine background of fins and seaweed.

"You ask if anyone was looking, Aunt Dolly," his wife intervened sharply. "There *were* some gangling teen-age girls who used to run down the beach to hide behind the dunes and catch glimpses of nude bathers. Don't look at me that way, Herman. *I* saw them. And so did you. That was why his lordship stripped!"

Naomi Fidler delighted in rubbing her personality against others to produce the effect of a long fingernail rubbed on a blackboard. Yet she was not a bad-hearted woman, Amy thought. She might have been almost pretty had she not scowled so often, pretty as big strong blond blue-eyed females can be, even when they pervert their naturally healthy looks by silly hats, clanking jewelry and too high heels. Naomi exaggerated everything: her anglicized accent, her strident laugh, her floor-tapping stride; she seemed intent on confirming the poor impression that she suspected people had already formed of her. Cousin Dolly had once said that the reason Herman was so gentle with people was that he always suspected that they might have just been insulted by his wife.

But that evening when Cousin Dolly was reading Emily Dickinson and the Herman Fidlers had not arrived the discussion continued, after Amy had brought her employer's whiskey.

"I don't know why Naomi always feels she has to come with Herman," Dolly grumbled. "Even if, as you say, she doesn't actually hate me, I certainly bore her to death. She makes that clear enough! Not that I mind, God knows."

"I'm the one who really bores her, Cousin Dolly."

"You, my dear? Don't flatter yourself. She hardly recognizes your existence. She sees you as a kind of upper servant. I know a snob when I see one."

"But I *am* your employee."

"You are family, dear. And closer to me by far than Naomi. I know why she comes. She's jealous!"

"Jealous?" Amy felt that she was riding in a closed car through a plague-ridden city. Someone, some hand, some reaching dark hand, threatened to break a window. "Jealous of whom?"

"Jealous of me, of course! She can't bear the fact that Herman is fond of his old-maid aunt. She may not find him any great prize as a husband, but small as he is she wants him all. She won't spare even a smitch. That's the trouble with the American heiress. She has no occupation, nothing to do at home, so she broods about her husband. In Europe, they go in for adultery. It may be better!"

"Cousin Dolly!"

"Well, Amy, I love Herman — you know that — but, between ourselves, is he a man to make a life out of?"

Amy shook her head silently and returned to the window. They did not live, any of them. They played with life: Cousin Dolly muttering over a symphony, a poem of Emily Dickinson's, a slant of afternoon light; Herman, glancing in the mirror to see that his tie pin was straight and furtively combing his hair in back. And Naomi thinking of her ankle, her well-shod foot, her high heel and how it tapped, tapped on a rugless floor, expressing her high birth, her money and the tartness of her wit. Why did love see such things? Why could not love be blind?

But Amy . . . well, Amy wanted to be like a sharp Anglo-Saxon monosyllable amid sonorous Latin adjectives. Amy was alive; Amy throbbed. For what was life but wanting to live? What was art but the expression of personality, and what was personality but the evidence of life? Why did people read the journals of Queen Victoria, the novels of Charlotte Brontë, the poems of Walt Whitman? Because, for all their egregious bad taste, their slop and their sentiment, personality poured out of them. Amy did not have to care that she was poor and plain and twenty-seven, a dependent country cousin, a paid companion, an upper servant. For all the while *she* was the one who took the world into a vision that endowed it with the pulsating colors of a Gauguin!

The dark street was beautiful; the room behind her was beautiful; the fire crackled gorgeously. Ah, those governesses, those dependent relatives of Victorian fiction, those demure, gray creatures, those heroines of *Mansfield Park,* of *Agnes Grey,* of *Jane Eyre!* It was good to be alive, even in 1936, even at Cousin Dolly's.

◦≈ 2 ≈◦

THERE WAS ONLY one likeness of Dolly Chadbourne in the apartment, a framed photograph which stood on the rarely played grand piano. It showed her as a young woman. The hair was blond, instead of blond gray, and combed straight back over the scalp into a knot behind. The strong face and features suggested something finely sculpted in a coarse material.

The tall figure was draped in a kind of toga and turned partly away from the camera. The eyes had a romantic, faraway gaze. Even then she must have thought of herself as a sensitive plant in a rock garden.

In her sixties, when she rescued Amy from poverty and nervous collapse, there was little outward survival of such fragility. She was stout and solidly built; she wore no make-up and affected mannish suits and low-heeled shoes. She smoked constantly and would stare intently at her interlocutor, shoving her massive, rounded chin forward and exuding clouds of smoke from behind clenched teeth. Yet the impression that she gave was not always that of a masculine woman. There was a depth of femininity in Dolly. It came out in the evening when, despite the clash with her severe black leather pumps, she adorned herself in richly colored satins and velvets trimmed with fine lace. It was heard in her tone when she talked about Keats and Shelley and, above all, Wagner, her beloved Wagner. She had a well of sentimentality which tended to overflow with her evening cocktails.

"Are you still expecting them?" she asked Amy, who had returned to the window. The latter's preoccupation awoke her possessiveness. "Why do you care? Herman's not *your* nephew. He and Naomi aren't interested in any of the things that we are. What's beauty to them? What's music or art or poetry? Herman's life is stocks and bonds, and Naomi's is bridge parties."

Amy had retreated so far into her fantasy that she found it difficult for a moment to return. "Herman does watercolors, you know. They're quite charming."

Dolly grunted. "A Sunday painter. If he really cared, he'd give everything up and just paint."

Amy remembered a Sunday afternoon in the early fall when she had been invited by Herman, after lunch at Cousin Dolly's, to walk with him and Naomi and their two little girls in Central Park. Naomi would have never thought to include her, but Herman had a small, sure fund of kindness behind his calm and placid front. It had been a warm day, and he had produced his pad to sketch the sailboats on the pond near Fifth Avenue. Naomi had taken the girls on to the Mall. Sitting by Herman on the bench as he worked, not venturing to speak, not even daring to glance at his drawing as it progressed, she had been briefly but perfectly happy. Secure in her privacy, she had transferred herself to a red velvet studio where she posed for her portrait, where he concentrated, intent on his work, until, abruptly, looking up as if he were seeing her for the first time, embarrassed, even mortified, then brilliantly clear, sensing in their instant communion that she would *have* to understand him, that they were bound to understand each other, that, really, nothing else mattered, he asked, with a charming, an almost boyish smile: "Amy, I'm sure you won't mind if I ask you to pose in the nude?" God! What the human mind was full of! She turned back abruptly to Cousin Dolly.

"What's wrong with being a Sunday painter?" she asked. "Isn't it an outlet? Shouldn't everyone have one? Think of all the beautiful things I see and hear with you, Cousin Dolly. They fill me up and up. Sometimes I wonder if I won't burst!"

"*I* haven't."

"But don't you ever feel that we ought to *do* something ... that it might be the obligation of a person as talented as yourself, as gifted ..."

"What are you trying to say, Amy?"

"Well ... that we ought to give some of it back?"

"Back?"

"By writing something. Or painting something."

"Oh, no, dear, that's not my line at all. I have too much respect for art to add my daubs to the pile. The poor old world has no need for any more ugliness."

"I suppose that must be true," Amy said ruefully. "I used to send short stories to the magazines. But they all came back. Perhaps it's just as well."

"If what you've written has pleased you, that should be enough. You don't have to be publishing all the time. Look at Emily Dickinson. She didn't. She showed her poems to friends. She put them in letters. And she was a happy woman, too, despite all the idiots who talk about her being psychotic. Her life was a poem; she made it an art."

"But suppose her poems had never been published? Wouldn't that have been a great loss to the world? And to you, Cousin Dolly?"

"Of course. But she knew they'd be published one day. She kept them carefully. She didn't really distinguish between writing and reading. It was all part of the same process. The process of communicating beauty. Gielgud's Hamlet, Flagstad's Isolde, Nazimova's Mrs. Alving, what's the point of any of them if you and I aren't there to receive? People used to believe the world was helped by monks and nuns who simply prayed. Because God required worship. Well, my function is to worship beauty!"

Dolly was well into her second cocktail. It seemed to Amy that her passivity was beginning to corrode her discrimination. Wasn't the woman who had had the acumen to buy Picasso and Braque in 1912, who had applauded the Armory Show and welcomed the music of Stravinsky, losing herself in the person who wept through the death scenes of *Traviata* or *Bohème*? But Dolly now took the offensive.

"If you want to write, why don't you write your own story? Didn't you tell me it was a Victorian novel? People have always liked them."

Amy looked back out the window. A novel? Hadn't she already lived one? The penniless orphan; the clerical, prosy father; the restless, social mother who had "thrown herself away" on a man of the cloth. The dowdy, shingled rectory in a Hartford suburb; the paternal stroke; the loss of the library job; the fiancé on relief who took to drink. What a recital!

But Herman Fidler was actually walking into the drawing room. He had come after all, and without his wife. Dolly was asking where she was.

"She's gone to stay with her mother in Florida," he replied. "Left this morning. But why do people always immediately ask: 'Where's Naomi?' You'd think we were Siamese twins. If a man is seen anywhere today without his wife, it's taken for granted he's up to some mischief."

"Well, how do we know you're not?" Dolly retorted gruffly.

"Because I'm calling on my dear old aunt!" he exclaimed, leaning down to kiss her affectionately. "It's as much as I dare do in these days of male servitude. I can't expect the liberty my father and grandfather enjoyed."

Amy now pictured Herman in a gray waistcoat with a tall gray hat and a black band. He had the figure for harmonious blacks and grays, for pearl studs, for spats. She could see his gently gazing eyes, his bland quiet face, in one of those big picture books of the Mauve Decade, on top of a coach, at a hunt ball.

Dolly suddenly winked at her, and Amy wondered with a

brush of panic if her thoughts had been read. "Is it women who rule the roost now, Herman, or just wives?" Dolly demanded.

"Women, Aunt Dolly. We men have lost the battle. All we can do is hold a little area below Canal Street. Everything else — the amusing things — the arts, the ballet, the opera, society, they're all in your domain."

"Isn't that because you men have abdicated?"

"What do you think, Amy?" Herman's diffident, curious eyes were turned to her. "Don't women rule?"

"Well, I suppose in your world, where people have money, money talks. If a woman has it, she rules. But in my world, where we have to make a living, it's very different."

"But, Amy, that's just it!" Herman exclaimed with a surprise which nonetheless gratified her. "That's just the point, isn't it, Aunt Dolly?"

"Oh, I don't agree with either of you," his aunt retorted with a sniff. "A woman's advantage has nothing to do with any of this. It resides in her finer sensitivity. People get what they deserve in this life. You men get your money. *We* have our sensations. Do you think I'd swap?"

The front doorbell announced more callers. It was Miss Bayard — Miss Caroline Bayard and her sister, her shadow. Amy felt the instant relief of being able to slip back into the shade to the seclusion of her thoughts and love.

"Hello, Dolly! Why, you're having what the young people call a 'cocktail.' "

"I'm having a little drink to keep me old bones warm, Caroline. Join me."

"Bless you, dear, I wasn't referring to your drink. A 'cocktail' is what the modish call a cocktail party these days."

Caroline Bayard was descended from a sister of Pieter Stuyvesant. She was small and imperious, with a long nose and snapping eyes; she reminded Amy of Lady Catherine in *Pride and Prejudice*. She had a way of putting both hands on the top of her cane as she addressed the room, like a British character actress playing a dowager. Her sister, Mrs. Bayard Jones, was as dim and self-effacing as Miss Bayard was vivid and assertive. She had been married, according to Dolly, to a fortune hunting wastrel, but so obscurely and so long ago that she might as well have been an old maid, too. Her nervous darting eyes and poking profile seemed, like her calling card, to be trying to thrust a depreciated Bayard before a bankrupt Jones in a desperate search for lost gentility.

Amy went to the sideboard to mix Miss Bayard's old-fashioned. It took several minutes to put in all the fruits required.

"I hope you'll forgive my fingers," she murmured as she plucked the ice cubes from the bowl and dropped them into the assembled drink. "Nellie seems to have forgotten the tongs."

"I can wait till you get them," Miss Bayard replied, staring at the proffered glass without taking it. Amy flushed and carried it out to the pantry where she flung it angrily in the sink.

"Miss Bayard doesn't want to be poisoned by my fingers!" she exclaimed to the maid.

Nellie handed her the tongs without expression. "If Miss Bayard knew half the things that went on when she wasn't looking, she wouldn't eat or drink."

When Amy reappeared with the tongs to mix another drink, Miss Bayard was holding forth on a favorite topic.

"Of course, he was nothing at Groton or Harvard. Good looking, but in a weak sort of way. And amiable, I suppose, as Cousin Luke Kip used to say. Certainly his mother has always been a respectable woman. So what happened to him? The polio! The world had smashed *him,* so he was determined to smash the world." Miss Bayard illustrated her point by socking her fist into her opened palm. "His world, anyway. Well, you've got to hand it to him; he's doing a fine job of it!"

Mrs. Jones saw fit now to place her own little offering on the high altar of her sister's Republicanism. "My son Bayard tells me that the men at his Flag Society say he's Jewish. That his name was changed from Rosenfeld."

But, poor creature, she had trespassed on a sacred domain. "Emily, you're talking through your hat! The Roosevelts came over as we did, in the seventeenth century. A bit later but still far enough back. Do you forget that our great-uncle, William Aspinwall, married a daughter of Isaac Roosevelt's?"

"*Isaac!*"

"Emily, you're being ridiculous! Biblical names did not mean one was Jewish. Our own grandmother was named Rebecca. Tell your son Bayard that these patriotic organizations won't do. They're always too middle class — it must be his Jones blood that attracts him to them. No, Franklin Roosevelt must be regarded as a rotten apple on a good tree. To some extent Theodore was that, too, although at least he was a Republican. But I can see by Dolly's frown that she disapproves. I daresay in musical circles the New Deal is venerated."

"It is at least considered in the light of a social experiment," Dolly retorted.

"I cannot understand how anyone brought up as you were can be taken in by left wing claptrap. How do you expect to eat, Dolly, when the wealth has been redistributed?"

"I suppose I must look for the miracle of the loaves and fishes."

"Very amusing, I'm sure. But there are some things even you can't laugh away, Dolly." Miss Bayard glared about the room in search of the radical infiltration which had corrupted her hostess. Her eyes rested upon Amy, who trembled. How was it possible that she even existed for Miss Bayard? What power was there in that long, thin snout to detect in the shrinking girl in the corner dissent, carnal fantasy, passion? But of course! Anyone who would touch her ice with dirty fingers . . . "And the young people! I hear they're all New Dealers. Is that so, Miss Hunt? Are you one?" Amy opened her mouth, but no sound emerged. "How about it, young lady? Are you in favor of redistributing the wealth?"

"I'm afraid I take very little interest in politics, Miss Bayard."

"Amy is a dreamer," Cousin Dolly suggested defensively.

"*That* would hardly disqualify her from being a New Dealer! But may I at least console myself that she doesn't want to see you and me, Dolly, reduced to selling apples in the street? While our heritage is used to support drunks and bums!"

"Now, Miss Bayard, aren't you going a bit too far?" Herman protested mildly. "You can't really claim that all the unemployed are drunks and bums."

"They're *lazy*, Herman! They don't know what real work is."

"Do you, Caroline?"

"Dolly, you talk like a Bolshevik!" Again Miss Bayard glowered at Amy. Why did she suspect *her*, of all persons, of radicalism? And yet as Amy thought of the tall, ancient Rolls-Royce with the long low black engine hood that awaited below to transport these withered females safely through darkness and ice on the ineluctable rounds of their duty-pleasures, and of Miss Bayard, erect in the back seat, glaring ahead at the traffic and shouting instructions to the chauffeur through the electric speaker clasped to her lips like a captain on his bridge in a storm, she wondered with a beating heart if she might not dare to become, for a moment at least, what Miss Bayard thought she was. She glanced at Herman. His eyes consoled her. Did they egg her on? They did!

"*Do* you believe in handouts, Miss Hunt?" Miss Bayard repeated.

Amy felt as if she had been gagged and bound while the rapacious old virgin fumbled in her clothes for secreted weapons. As Miss Bayard seemed to reach toward her heart, something tore. Amy heard her own voice in a hoarse whisper.

"People must live, Miss Bayard. These are fearful times."

"And don't you think *I* know that?"

"Forgive me if I wonder."

"I'll have you know, young lady, that I'm chairman of the board of Turtle Bay Neighborhood House!"

"Then you should have learned compassion. You are cruel. You are hard!"

"*Well!*"

Herman snickered at this, and the house lights seemed to flash on, as if her act were over. But it was wrong, all wrong! That snicker made Amy part of the fun and games, a diversion on a dull visit to an aunt. She jumped up now and fled to her room. She would have remained there all evening, without any dinner, had Cousin Dolly not sought her out.

"May I come in, Amy?" She entered when she heard no answer and came over to the bed where Amy was stretched, face down. "That's all right. Lie there, dear. They're all gone now. Caroline Bayard's an old bitch. She always was, even when she was a young one."

Amy began to sob. When words came at last, they came in

a torrent. "It's no use, Cousin Dolly. It won't work out. I've tried, but it won't. You must send me back to Connecticut. I have a few leads there. A few old family friends who might be able to find me something. I've failed you here. There's no reason I shouldn't hold my tongue when Miss Bayard is here. What business is it of mine if she's a mossback? That's her privilege, isn't it? She's not asking anyone for a salary or to be supported. She's not pretending to perform any services for anyone. God made her independent, and she *is* independent. If I can't learn my place, I should go!"

Dolly's brief silence exhibited her patience. "Have you quite finished now? May I speak?"

"Oh, Cousin Dolly, what is there to *say?*"

"There's this to say, dear. You have a heart, a tender heart, one of the tenderest, and that should get you through."

"To what? To more suffering? More anguish?"

"You can't know joy until you're capable of anguish. After that the joy will come."

"Where? How?"

"Watch me. Watch your old cousin. You'll find that I can find joy, real joy, in a sonnet of Shakespeare."

"And what do you *do* with your joy?" Amy demanded in sudden fretfulness, sick to death of the old argument. "What good does your joy do the world?" Dolly's smile faded, and Amy recoiled at her own brutality. Couldn't she get herself out of the life of this harmless, half-cracked old woman without smashing her few illusions? What else did she have to live by?

"Every bit of joy adds to the joy of the universe," Dolly insisted. "We do something for the poor old world when we're simply happy."

"But Cousin Dolly, how can I live so . . . inwardly? Haven't you ever . . . ?" She hesitated.

"Say it."

"Been in love?"

Dolly rested her head against the back of her chair and closed her eyes. "I thought I was. Once."

"Can you tell me about it?"

"You'd really like to know?" Dolly was silent for so long that Amy thought she might have gone to sleep. But at last she began to talk, her eyelids still lowered, her tone low and grave, as if she were speaking to herself. "It may surprise you to hear that I was not totally without allure as a debutante. I was big, to be sure, but I had high spirits and was considered a good sport. I made people laugh. And I loved to dance, even if I was a bit rambunctious, in a whirling waltz. I probably sweated, too." Here Dolly chuckled suddenly and opened her eyes. "Yes, I'm sure I did. But young people liked me, young men, too, the nicer ones, anyway, and there was one in particular who began to pay me decided attention. He was very sweet and good, a bit smaller than I, but he had a gentleness, a charm. He wasn't literary or anything like that — he was a Yale man — but he was earnest about all the things a young man should be earnest about: his college and his country and his future career. He became really attached to me, and it wasn't for money or social position. He was much stronger in those departments than I — indeed he had a horrid old mother who thought he could do a sight better than tomboy Dolly Chadbourne. But he didn't care what she thought, and he proposed to me, and I accepted him. I supposed that I was very happy and very much in love with Alec — that was his name — and that we would have a wonderful life together. My parents approved, and all seemed fine until . . ." Her eyes closed again.

"Yes, Cousin Dolly?"

Dolly started and resumed her tale. "Until I had this most frightful fit of depression. A kind of panic, really. What was I going to *do* with Alec when I had married him? Oh, I suppose you've heard that young virgins in my day weren't told the facts of life, and it's true that some of them didn't learn them till the wedding night, but *I* knew. I was a great reader, and, besides, my sister Roz had told me all about *her* wedding night. No, it wasn't ignorance but the idea of Alec in bed with me that seemed suddenly scary. And then I was afraid there was something terribly wrong with me, so I went to Mother. I would have gone to Roz but she was abroad. And Mother... well, how can I describe Mother? You never knew your great-aunt Mildred, did you? Well, she was just the opposite of me. Very small and neat and prim and dignified, with a cool temperament. And she suffered from migraine headaches. Dr. Weir Mitchell, a great favorite in those days, used to prescribe bed rest and there was always a hush in the house, and the maids would whisper: 'Ssh, Miss Dolly! Your mother's resting.' But Mother could be very firm and definite, too, and when she had heard me out, lying there in bed, as you are, staring at me, she said in a voice which admitted no dissent: 'My daughter, if you are not sure, absolutely and unconditionally sure, that you and Alec are right for each other, you owe it to him to end your engagement. Marriage at best is a tricky proposition. With the least doubt, it may be disastrous!' "

Dolly looked at Amy in silence now, her face expressionless. She might have been calling on her to witness the depths of her parent's folly or simply affirming the inscrutable essence of the world's mystery.

"So you gave him up?"

"I gave him up."

"And did you regret it?"

"I don't know."

"What happened to him?"

"Oh, he was a great success. He became a Morgan partner and married the sweetest girl. He died last year — prematurely, at least by my count."

"And that could have been your life."

"As you see."

"Were there other men, after him?"

"No, because I wouldn't let there be. I didn't trust myself."

"Oh, Cousin Dolly, I'm so sorry!"

"Don't be, child. As I've told you, I've had my joys. And sorrows, too, that were a kind of joy because they had to do with love, love of friends." Amy was afraid she was about to weep, but instead she gave one of her unexpected little snickers. "Love even of relatives." Dolly had a way of combining snickers with tears. "And I don't want you to go back to Connecticut, Amy. I want you to stay here with me, and learn to live. You will find that you can. Life is not going to pass you by. And don't worry about my dying . . ."

"Please, Cousin Dolly."

"Don't. I can't leave you anything from my trusts, but the pictures and drawings are mine. I'll see my lawyer, Jamey Coates. I'll do a codicil and leave them to you. You can sell them. It won't be any fortune, but it will be a nest egg. Don't say anything, please. I'll give you twenty minutes, and then it will be time for my before supper drink."

And she left. But although Amy blessed Dolly for her kindness, what she had learned did little to lift her spirits. If with one hand Dolly unlatched the gates of captivity to give her a dazzling and unbelievable — and unbelieved — glimpse of future liberty, with the other she pulled her back to herself to lock her in an embrace that Amy estimated with a shudder might last both their lives.

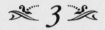

THE SMALL SOCIETY that called on Dolly Chadbourne or dined with her before the music or play was divided into two groups. First there was the group that Amy mentally dubbed the "hangers-on," although it included some who were by no means dependent on Dolly for their meals and tickets: breathless, dowdy, overdressed old maids, always in ecstasy over something ethereal; dark little widows, usually grim; singers, musicians or actors, of obscure fame, for the most part retired or out of work; an occasional young person, always hungry, sometimes a student or schoolteacher. Second, there was the vastly more formidable group of Dolly's "old New York" world, the relatives and family friends, like Miss Bayard, who kept up with her, in the rigid fashion of their class and generation, no matter what Bohemian airs she might affect. Some of these, of course, were related to Amy: they were civil to her but little more. The blood connection had been diluted by the humbleness of her employment.

Of all Dolly's relations the Fidlers were the closest. Rosalind Fidler, "Roz," her widowed older sister, lunched or dined at the apartment twice a week. She was large and firmly built, like Dolly, but despite her gray hair and big, equine features, she was the handsomer of the two, and certainly the better dressed. Mrs. Fidler was a more integral part of Manhattan society than her sister; she served on the boards of the Colony Club and the Colonial Dames and was secretary of a ladies' committee at St. Luke's Hospital. She liked to affect a rather masculine air of "no nonsense" in her daily dealings with people, but no woman could have had a greater love of gossip. Dolly used to describe her as the "Saint-Simon" of New York.

The congeniality between the sisters largely overcame their differences of opinion. Mrs. Fidler, who talked brusquely out of the side of her mouth, her hands usually engaged in some nervous activity, such as snapping shut or open her purse or moving small objects to and fro on a side table, deplored Dolly's aestheticism and artistic friends, emphasizing, by way of contrast, the virtues of being a mother, a clubwoman, a dispenser of charity. Dolly, in her turn, scoffed at Roz's worldliness and conventionalism, telling Amy privately that her sister had sacrificed a first-rate mind and imagination to the exigencies of the "limited" world of the Fidlers. But both could laugh at the antics of the Bayard sisters, which formed the subject of conversation toward the end of a dinner of four at Dolly's before the opera two nights after Amy's scene with Miss Caroline.

"Who does Caroline Bayard think she is to give herself such airs?" Mrs. Fidler demanded. "Of course, the Bayards are all right, but her mother was a Hone, and we all know the Hones started in the auction business. I shouldn't wonder if they had a Jewish origin. And the way she treats poor Emily! As a vestal virgin might treat a sister priestess who'd run off with a gladiator."

"You should have seen Amy stand up to her, Ma!" Herman exclaimed. Naomi Fidler was still away, visiting her mother in

Florida, and he obviously relished the attention that he received as the only male at table. "The old dragon was completely routed. All she could do was breathe out smoke and lash her tail."

But Mrs. Fidler's glance at Amy was not approving. "I trust that Amy did not forget that she was talking to an older lady."

"Amy said nothing for which there had not been ample provocation," Dolly intervened emphatically.

"I hope so. You remember how *we* were brought up, Dolly. No matter how extreme the opinions of the older generation, we had to hold our tongue. I recall when you were sent to bed without supper for contradicting Grandpa Chadbourne when he said that those striking workers in Pittsburgh deserved to be shot."

"Well, good for Aunt Dolly!" Herman cried. "I guess Amy has inherited the family spunk. You'd have been on her side if you'd been here, Ma. She simply represented mental light against mental darkness. There was no choice!"

Amy flushed and looked down at her plate. She had liked even less the second look that Mrs. Fidler had flashed at her. Was it possible that Herman's mother considered that his warmth of tone in favor of her sister's paid companion implied some disloyalty to his absent spouse? It was horrible the way reality kept poking its blunt fingers into her fantasy! If she lost her sense of borders, she would lose her sanity. Why did Herman have to talk so? She hastened to correct his mother's misapprehension.

"You mustn't believe him, Mrs. Fidler! I really said very little to Miss Bayard."

"It's true, Roz. Under all the circumstances Amy showed considerable restraint."

"Of course I know how Herman exaggerates things. I'd hate to hear what he says about *me*."

"You, Ma? Do you think I'd dare say anything about *you*? Why, I'd be tarred and feathered! Everyone's always telling me what a wonderful mother I have — so good, so even tempered. I sometimes wonder if it isn't their way of making a snide crack at Naomi."

"It seems to be *your* way of doing just that," his mother retorted.

"Is it making a crack at Namoi to imply that she lacks your even temper?"

"If she shows occasional impatience, it may be because you try her. That's what I mean by your exaggerations, my boy!"

"As if I could exaggerate Naomi's temper! It would be like exaggerating Vesuvius in eruption!"

Amy resumed the study of her plate. She knew that Mrs. Fidler detested her daughter-in-law, but she also knew that such matters, in Roz's code, were never discussed before outsiders. And Amy was still an outsider.

"I have nothing to do with such comments, Herman," his mother said coldly.

"Shall we go to my room to get ready, Roz?" Dolly suggested tactfully. "Amy, why don't you take Herman into the den and give him a snifter of the old Chadbourne brandy? That should keep him quiet."

The sisters rose, and Herman followed Amy out of the dining room.

"What's the opera?" he asked with a sigh.

"*Salomé*."

"Again? God! We went to it last month."

"Well, your aunt says she has to take the box when Mrs. Dunn offers it, or she won't get it again."

"Oh, well, *Salomé, Aïda, Gioconda,* what's the difference?"

"You don't like opera?" Amy handed him his brandy.

"Who was it who said: '*On s'y ennuie, mais on y revient*'?" It's an escape. All those silly plots and lilting tunes."

"What do you have to escape from, Herman?"

"What does anyone have to escape from? Life."

"But I should have thought yours was too full of interesting things."

"What sort of interesting things?"

"Well . . . real things." She turned away, embarrassed by his mocking look. "Your work. Your home. Your charities."

"You interest me, Amy. *Real* things?"

"Why aren't they real?"

"Well, I suppose they might be to someone else. But take my work. I go to an office downtown where I sell stocks and bonds. I'm supposed to know a lot more about it than I do, so I'm always scared of giving customers a bum steer. And business is lousy, so I have a lot of time to sit around being scared. Of course, I should be reading market reports. But half the time I don't. I'm worried sick and bored to death, so I read fiction. But I don't even read good stuff because that would look too blatantly unconcerned. So I read trash. Whodunits."

Amy tried to make herself understand, with a pang of humiliation tempered by awe at this sudden candor, that the only reason for such revelations was not her importance to him but precisely its opposite. What was Amy Hunt but a domestic receptacle into which anything could be dropped?

"I suppose we all have to earn our living."

"It's not even much of a living. Without Naomi's income we couldn't possibly live as we do. And if you think it's easy to be dependent on a rich wife, you're wide of the mark. Naomi's always throwing it in my face that I ought to earn more. Do you know what she said to me the other night at a bridge party? As she passed my table, she leaned down and pretended to whisper in a voice that everyone could hear: 'If you lose again tonight, Herman, I shan't pay.' "

"Oh, no! She couldn't have!"

"Oh, but she could, Amy. Another time, I overheard her down the dinner table saying: 'What Herman earns doesn't pay the cook.' "

"Surely that's not true!"

"No, of course it's not true. But it's true that Naomi pays more bills than I do. And even that I wouldn't mind if she could pay them all. But she can't. She's madly extravagant. And for all her pretended toughness, she's always being taken by tradespeople. I don't know where it will end, Amy."

"But, surely, with your mother and aunt . . ."

"I won't starve. Maybe not. But that's about all I can count on. And to people brought up the way I was, not starving may be worse than starving."

Amy shuddered. "But there must be balancing factors in a life as full as yours. Your children, don't they make up for other things?"

"Lila and Sally? They're at the silly age: nine and eight. They giggle and whisper all the time. Oh, they're good enough girls, but they don't even hide the fact that I bore them to tears. A daddy's function will come later: to provide a coming out party, and woe to him if he can't do that! And what was the other thing you mentioned? Oh, yes, my charities. Well, I sit on the boards of a small private hospital and an ancient lending library, both because my father did. I know nothing about hospitals, and I hate all things medical, so I vote the way the chairman votes. We're always unanimous, anyway. As for the library, it's the only cultural institution in the city that can't spend its income, so there are no problems there."

"You could find organizations that need you more!"

"Yes, but I'm not looking. I have troubles enough of my own."

They heard Dolly's voice now from the living room: "Children! We're ready to go."

Amy loved *Salomé*. She loved the wild, weird, haunting arias. In her fantasy she danced before Herod; she dropped her veils, one by one, and when she called for the severed head of the Baptist, there was a twisted ecstasy in the premonition of the violent death that would follow the pressing of her lips against his cold dead ones. When the great gold curtains fell on the soldiers crushing her and Salomé with their shields, and the lights went up she sat dazed, even after the others had risen to applaud the curtain calls, to turn to the lobby, to seek coats.

"Look at Amy!" she heard Dolly's voice. "She's still in Galilee. Come, dear, it's time to collect all those veils you cast." Amy jumped up, mortified, and hurried to the anteroom to find Dolly's coat for her. But when she returned with it to the box, she was frozen by the sound of Dolly's voice saying: "Herman, you great lout, why don't you be a good cousin for once in your life and take Amy to the Plaza for a nightcap? The party's on me. That poor child never gets out."

"I'd be only too delighted, Aunt Dolly. How about it, Amy?"

"Oh, no, Herman, please no, thank you ever so much! You're very kind, but I'm tired . . . and I have a headache, and . . ."

"Well, that's too bad. But never mind. We can always do it another time."

"Stuff and nonsense, she has no headache! And one drink

isn't going to kill her. Go ahead, children. Enjoy yourselves!"

And so it was, fascinatingly, even rather horribly, that Amy found herself with Herman Fidler, at a table at the Plaza bar, before two large glasses of Irish whiskey. She glanced nervously about, not to see if she was recognized — for who that ever came to Cousin Dolly's would go to a bar at midnight? — but to see if he was. And he was, too, for he nodded pleasantly across the room, with perfect equanimity. But was it perfect equanimity? Might it not have been savoir-faire?

He talked, she had to admit, without giving the least sense of apprehension. He reverted at once to the earlier topic of himself.

"Do you know something, Amy? It did me good to talk the way I did after dinner. It made me do some real thinking during that silly opera. I thought: do I have to keep on doing all the things I'm doing? I mean, is there some kind of law that requires it?"

"And is there?"

"Of course not! It's just that life has a way of closing in on you when you aren't looking. It's like a jungle. You can clear out any part of it you want, but if you don't keep it mowed . . . bingo, it grows right up again!"

Amy's silence was intended to concede the truth of this.

"Of course, Naomi is my jungle."

It seemed to her most improper that they should discuss his wife in a bar. Reaching about nervously in the alarm of her mind, she snatched for a neutralizing factor. Reality had to be put back in its place.

"I know that she's as beautiful as a jungle," she replied, with a deliberate fatuity. "But I shouldn't have thought her so sinister."

"She's not really sinister. She simply grows over any space

that is not cut back. It's her nature. Every concession I make is at once turned into a constitutional right. I go one summer to her mother's in Southampton; I must go every summer. I have a lucky windfall on the stock market; that becomes my minimum income. I buy her a sapphire ring for Christmas; I must do the same next year. I spend my life painting myself into corners."

Amy hoped that the topic of downtown, where at least Naomi never went, might be safer. "But you don't have to go on being a stockbroker if you don't want to, surely? Naomi doesn't expect that, does she?"

"No. She doesn't give a damn about that. So long as I stay in New York and earn at least what I'm now earning, and don't do anything mortifying like becoming an undertaker or a dentist, she doesn't care what I do. But what else *can* I do? I'm not trained, and, besides, I'm thirty-three."

"I wonder if it's fair to assume that Naomi wouldn't live anywhere else. Didn't I hear you tell Cousin Dolly that you'd have been happy as a teacher? Wasn't there some idea of Dr. Drury asking you to come back to St. Paul's?"

She saw the look in his eyes that she had learned to recognize at any mention of that school. It was introduced by a slight flash of something like surprise that anything so brilliantly irrelevant to the dullness of daily life should even be mentioned. This was followed by the brief complacent beam of the dreamer who knows that his dream will soon be interrupted, but who intends to enjoy it while he can. Herman must have been happy in that part of his life as few schoolboys are. Somehow St. Paul's and its vigorous, idealistic headmaster had inspired him as representing the good life — a vision of which his after-existence had supplied no duplicate.

"Oh, that was long ago. Yes, he wanted me to come back and

teach. There was an opening in math, a subject I liked. And I could have helped with the new art gallery. I've always loved painting. But he wouldn't want me now."

"You could write him and ask."

"Yes, I could." Herman seemed to be turning the idea over gingerly, touching it, almost furtively, like an object on a shop counter that he knew he could not afford. Then he finished his drink abruptly and waved to a waiter, pointing to the empty glass. "Hell, can you imagine Naomi with the faculty wives of a boys' school in Concord, New Hampshire?"

"With a slight effort."

"Oh, Amy, she wouldn't be able to abide them. You know it! And they wouldn't go for her, either. It would never work."

"I don't think you challenge her enough. She might respond better than you think."

"Yes, that's Mother's idea." Herman shrugged moodily. "She and Aunt Dolly work on the theory that if I would just punch Naomi in the jaw a couple of times, she'd simmer down and want to bill and coo. Like Katharina in *The Taming of the Shrew*. But what they don't realize is how vulnerable Naomi is. She's tense, horribly tense. She might crack wide open and spill all over the place. Her father committed suicide, you know. In nineteen twenty-nine, when he thought — erroneously, I'm glad to say — that he had lost his shirt."

Amy stared. "But you can't really think she'd do herself in if you simply changed jobs!"

"No, no, don't misunderstand me. I only mean that she's not stable. You should see the terrible scenes she pulls over nothing at all."

"Maybe she enjoys them. Lots of women do."

"But *I* don't!" Herman's tone was fervent. "Everyone thinks

I'm henpecked. They never stop to consider that I might simply hate scenes."

"Mightn't that be the definition of a henpecked man?" she asked with a boldness that surprised her. "One who hates scenes?"

He smiled wryly. "You're a clever girl, Amy. Life would be a lot easier if there was some of your common sense in my household."

"Girls in my position can't afford the luxury of nerves. At least not of showing them."

"Well, I wish there had been someone like you around in my deb party days." He actually went so far now as to place a hand on hers and to squeeze it! He looked at her sadly, with his gentle brown eyes. "Do you believe me when I say that, Amy? I wish there had been."

Half in panic, half in anger, she jerked her hand away. What did he think he was doing? What sort of a game did he think he was playing? Couldn't he see that in the world of facts and colors in which he lived and had his being, there was no place for the pale little yearning dependent body that she was? No, she belonged back with the governesses, the poor relations of old English fiction. She was Fanny Price, she was Jane Eyre, except that she lacked the spark, the temper. Who was the Baroness Ingram of Ingram Park but Naomi Fidler? *Her* scenes, her temper, her very bitchiness, might have been part of her sex appeal — might even have been necessary to arouse a man like Herman.

"I never went to any parties!" she exclaimed, almost in tears. "And it's too late for me to start now. I shouldn't be sitting in a bar drinking with you. I had better get back to Cousin Dolly's."

He was obviously mortified by her brusqueness, but his

manners were too good to allow a protest, and, as Dolly lived only twenty blocks from the Plaza, Amy was home in as many minutes. But when she closed the front door of the apartment behind her, after their almost speechless and embarrassing taxi ride, she felt a proper fool. She went to bed and dreamed of Herman locked in a cell like John the Baptist while she gazed down at him through the bars of a trap door.

≈ 4 ≈

AMY DID NOT SEE Herman again before his wife's return from Florida. It was agreed that the Fidlers were to dine with Dolly at a small party to celebrate her birthday (she would never admit which one), and on the night of this festivity Naomi arrived early and alone.

"A happy, happy, Aunt Dolly. Can I get myself something?" She stepped briskly to the drink tray. "I've come ahead of the others to have a little private chat. No, Amy, don't go. You might even be able to help."

Naomi had had her blond hair cut and reset, and the tighter cap which it formed over her round head made her large eyes and nose seem even more threatening. Her birthday greeting to her hostess was almost insultingly perfunctory. Obviously, she wanted to get right down to some business which would be disagreeable — perhaps, to her anyway, pleasantly disagreeable. Drink in hand she came over now to sit by Dolly.

"I've heard some funny things since I've been back. About Herman."

"What kind of things?" Dolly's tone at once reflected the challenge in Naomi's.

"Wait. The reason I come to you first is that I know he sees a lot of you whenever I'm gone."

"And what's wrong with that? Ain't I his adoring aunt?"

"You are. Undoubtedly. But what I want to find out is whether you've had reason to suspect that anyone *else* adores him. I'm not one of those foolish wives who think they own their men. Or even that they have special insights into their characters. I realize perfectly that there are sides of Herman that I don't know, and don't even want to know. There's a Fidler side and a Chadbourne side. Perhaps it's the Chadbourne side that I'm concerned with tonight."

"Why that in particular?"

"Because there's a vein of sentimentality in the Chadbournes." Amy marveled at the clear, precise articulation of Naomi's hostility. How did she dare to speak to an older relative in that way? "That's all very well in the women. They can take it out in art and music and such things. But when it comes to the men, watch out!"

Dolly picked up a miniature of a young man with a pale forehead and curly black hair. It was of the 1830s and, like so many miniatures of that period, it was trying hard to be Byronic. "Everett Chadbourne," she murmured in a dreamy, whimsical tone. "He was in love with the singer, Aldini. He followed her to every opera house in Europe. Of course, when she finally married him, she made him miserable. She became stout and cross and grew a mustache. But he always saw her as Zerlina or Norma or Eurydice. Yes, you're right, my dear. There *is* a strain of intensity in the Chadbournes. Perhaps even in Herman. It is wiser to give it rein. We are not people to be tied down."

"I hope you don't consider adherence to the marriage vows as being tied down, Aunt Dolly."

"I don't enter into particulars," Dolly retorted majestically. "I simply say this: that we were country gentlemen long before we were businessmen. We antedate Wall Street. We may even have preserved one or two aristocratic qualities. It is doubtful, I admit. Herman seems pretty well brokerized." Here Dolly gave vent to the little snicker that was always on hand to dissipate her most serious moods. She liked to pretend that there was an irrepressible imp in her which might pop up at any moment, even during a funeral service where her grief was genuine. "The aristocrat abides by his word. But he has his secret places. Oh, yes, there's a bit of the poet, a bit of the Shelley in us." Perhaps the vision of Herman was too much for her here, for she added: "A wee bit, anyway."

"Well, if you consider it Shelleyan to keep some little slut on my money, I think it a curious use of the word!"

As Dolly glared sternly now at her antagonist, Amy imagined her strong arm reaching for that flung glove. "I should think you might have the grace not to use such language before Amy."

Naomi glanced at Amy with a faint surprise. "Oh, Amy. She knows all our secrets."

"Amy is a young, unmarried woman!"

Naomi's second glance disposed briefly of Amy's age. "You're not up to date, Aunt Dolly. They know everything these days. Amy doesn't mind, do you, Amy?" Amy murmured something inaudible. "Let's put it directly, then. *Is* there another woman, Aunt Dolly?"

"I don't use such vulgar terms. Other than whom?"

"Of course, I don't mean yourself or Mrs. Fidler. I quite understand the fetish about blood relations that Herman shares with all the Chadbournes. It's positively Chinese! No, I mean an unrelated woman."

"Do you think he would have told me?"

"He might have. He might even have boasted of it!"

"And why, if such were the case, would I divulge his confidence?"

"Because you might have the wisdom to perceive that, armed with the knowledge, I would be in a better position to save a marriage whose preservation, you must believe, is in his best interest."

"Must I?"

"Aunt Dolly, you can't be so immoral as to want me to divorce him? And have him lose his children, as well as his support!"

"I don't go into that, Naomi. I know nothing of Herman's domestic situation. Or to what extremities it may have driven him. You're knocking at the wrong door, my girl."

"Very well, Aunt Dolly. At least we know where we stand."

Dolly seemed to be debating if dignity did not require her to drop the matter now. But in the end so simple a thing as curiosity prevailed.

"What is it that makes you suspect him?"

"While I was in Florida he was seen out on three different occasions with a girl. Once in a restaurant. Once at the ballet. Once at the Plaza."

Amy felt giddy. It was as if she were watching the stage, not from her usual place in the dark orchestra pit, but from behind the scenes and way high up, with a gnomelike man who was manipulating the lights. Now he was grinning at her wickedly. He moved as if to push her over. She would fall!

"The same girl?" Dolly demanded. She did not so much as glance at Amy.

"Well, I assume it was the same girl. Herman's not that much of a Lothario."

"Maybe it was a customer. Maybe they were talking stocks and bonds."

"Maybe."

"Can't a man and woman go to a public place together without being lovers?"

"Undoubtedly."

"Maybe he doesn't find enough amusement at home."

"Naturally, it would have to be anyone's fault but Herman's!"

They were interrupted now by the arrival of the subject of the discussion with his mother. Herman, in his filial way, had stopped to pick up Mrs. Fidler and bring her to the party. Amy jumped up, as usual, to mix the drinks. With her back to the other four she was able to hide some of the tumult of her embarrassment and to take in, with a stab of violent relief, that Naomi had chosen not to pursue the topic, as she would have been quite capable of doing, in the face of her husband and mother-in-law. More permanent safety was assured by the arrival of Miss Bayard and Mrs. Jones — who had magnanimously elected to overlook Amy's former rudeness — accompanied by Dolly's lawyer, James Coates.

The latter was always an agreeable addition to one of Dolly's gatherings, though why he came to them Amy never quite knew, unless it was to get away from the old parents with whom, as a bachelor, he continued to live. Of course, Dolly was presumably a good client, but "Jamey," as he was known to all, was far too important an attorney to have to cater to such relatively small fry as the Chadbournes. Not yet forty, he was already the managing partner of the downtown firm of Coates, Lane & Coates, and although he had followed in his father's footsteps there, it was generally acknowledged that his own had needed no precedent. He always struck Amy as being rather too pleased with himself, but also as having a good bit to be pleased with. He was short and a trifle plump, but agile in his movements; he had fine wavy chestnut hair with a few becoming stripes of premature gray and a pleasant, smiling countenance with large, greenish, brilliant eyes. He was precise in his articulation, even a bit fussy, and he had a great reverence for tradition and the "good old way" of doing things. But for all of what Herman, jealous of the respect which his success evoked at Dolly's, called his "old maidism," he had a personality and a brain which dominated their small assemblies.

At dinner Miss Bayard returned to her favorite subject.

"The trouble is that Roosevelt — you needn't rise — has interrupted the natural fluctuation of the stock market. I was talking the other day to one of our greatest bankers, and he quite agreed. In a capitalist economy you have to put up with the downswings if you want to enjoy the ups. A great president would have taught us to bear the rigors of the depth of the depression and then led us in triumph back to the peak!"

Miss Bayard glared about the table and adjusted the shawl over her shoulders as if she were clasping together the skins which protected her from a freezing winter climate.

"That bottom might have been too deep for some of us, Caroline," Dolly demurred. "You might have found yourself in the company of some rather strange deep-sea fish."

"With red fins," Jamey suggested.

"You think there would have been a revolution, Mr. Coates?"

"I think there would have been grave trouble. How far it would have gone I cannot say."

"Well, have we no army? No national guard? No police? Or are we too decadent these days to stand up for law and order?"

Amy had noted that it was never Jamey Coates' way to let himself be caught in the crossfire of general issues that Dolly's friends so loved. He would retreat to a specific issue of which he had special knowledge, knowledge that was apt to be salted with hints which alarmed, even as they titillated, his audience.

"You might all be interested in a bit of news which I heard in Washington last week," he announced in his confidential tone. "I had it on a high authority that the President is preparing to do something drastic about the Supreme Court. He is said to be furious about the invalidation of so much of his legislation."

"And what will he do?" demanded Mrs. Jones. "Throw the poor old men in prison?"

"Oh, I guess we haven't quite come to that yet," Jamey replied with a chuckle. "He will simply ask Congress for the power to make additional appointments."

"He's going to stack the Court?" Herman cried.

"I believe that term would express his purpose."

"But the Constitution will not permit it!" Miss Bayard exclaimed. "The Constitution prescribes that there shall be nine justices."

"You must permit a carping lawyer to pick you up on that, Miss Bayard. The Constitution actually prescribes no fixed number. We started with six justices. Since then the number has been changed to five, seven and even ten. But, of course, you are right in essence: there *is* a grave Constitutional question raised by the President's motive. I am told that he will seek the power to appoint an additional justice for every one on the present Court who is over seventy."

The table at once burst into scandalized reproach.

"Is it criminal to be seventy?"

"Isn't age the source of wisdom?"

"Does Roosevelt want a court of babies?"

"He's a madman!"

"Ladies, ladies." Jamey raised his hands in smiling deprecation. "Let me say at once that I agree with you that the proposed legislation is abhorrent to our Constitutional balance of powers. It must be defeated. We, who have benefited from the mature glory of such minds as Marshall's and Holmes' cannot admit that age of itself disqualifies. Why, look at Mr. Justice Van Devanter. He's as sound as he was twenty years ago. When he was in town for the meeting of the American Bar Association last week, he put us all to shame with the pace he kept up. You remember, Herman. You saw him at my table at the Plaza Monday night."

"Oh, was that Justice Van Devanter?"

"*You* were at the Plaza, Herman?"

"Is that so strange, my dear? Aunt Dolly suggested that I take Amy there for a nightcap after the opera."

"Oh!"

It all happened at once. For just a second Amy was conscious of the yellow glare of Naomi's eye; then the latter was talking to Mrs. Jones. Had Dolly noticed? She gave no sign. Why in the name of God, Amy asked herself desperately, had she not *told* Naomi before dinner, when she was asking? Because it would have made what Naomi believed untrue? Was *that* her reason? Now she could only twist and turn, trying to wake up. It was no use. Her nightmare seemed to have engulfed the whole table to her vision, even Herman and Jamey, still innocently talking about judges and decisions and faraway, unreal things. Amy could not have uttered a word. Fortunately no word was expected of her.

A further trial, however, awaited her. After dinner Dolly, perhaps in defiance of Naomi's implied criticism of her Plaza "treat," insisted that the "young people," Herman, Naomi, Jamey Coates and Amy, "go dancing." It was in vain that Herman pleaded a hard day at the office and Naomi an early engagement the next morning; Dolly would not be refused on her birthday, especially as it was to be her party. They should take the car; they should go to La Rue. They had all, thank you very much, simply to "scat." Only Jamey managed to be civil about the unpopular expedition, though he probably wished to go even less than the rest.

"I must say, Miss Chadbourne, you always have some pleasant surprise in store for one."

He chatted away in the car, while Naomi stared sullenly out the window. He asked Herman's opinion on stocks and bonds, and Amy's about operas and concerts. He tipped the chauffeur and told him not to come back, that he would see everyone home, and he instructed their waiter at La Rue to bring a bottle of champagne and put it on his, not Herman's, bill. No sooner had this arrived than Naomi suggested in a flat tone:

"Suppose you two gentlemen sit at the bar for a few minutes. I have a bone to pick with Amy."

"What kind of a bone, darling?"

"Herman, please do as I say."

"But if it's something about my aunt or the family . . ."

"Jamey, will you take my husband away, please!"

"Come on, old man. We're obviously not wanted here."

When they had gone, Naomi turned her glittering gaze upon Amy.

"I think I should make it quite clear at the beginning, Amy Hunt, that I shall be wanting my husband back."

❧ 5 ❧

THE REASON, known only to himself, that Jamey Coates came so often to Dolly's apartment was to see Amy, or, more accurately, to look her over. He had long ago made a resolution that he would be married by the age of forty, and he was now thirty-eight. There was ample time still, but less to be lost. Of course, he was perfectly aware that in the eyes of his family and friends, not to mention his law partners, Amy would seem an unlikely candidate, but he had had his disappointments, and they had taught him that there might be virtues in quiet, modest, dowerless women. He had also learned a lesson by observing Herman and Naomi Fidler. Amy, seemingly discreet, intelligent and unspoiled, was certainly worth serious consideration. Perhaps the time had even come to ask her for what, had he not been a graduate of Groton School, he would have called a "date."

He found it difficult sometimes to realize that so much time had already elapsed since he had reached thirty, the age which he had regarded as the earliest at which a prudent man could marry. Four of the eight years that had since passed had been devoted to an abortive friendship with Sally Lane, a girl whom he had known all his life and whose father, the Judge, had been a senior partner of Coates, Lane & Coates. Sally was a good, plain, sensible "outdoors" girl who never seemed to lose her good humor and who was always willing to do the things that Jamey liked, either mildly cultural or mildly athletic. They knew the same people, and she called his parents Uncle Percy and Aunt Iris. But when he at last put the question to her, after a family anniversary party and a good deal of champagne, when his parents had gone to bed and he and Sally were sitting alone in the library in 36th Street, her answer had come as a shock.

"Oh, no, Jamey, this kind of thing won't do for us at all. I've never thought about you that way, and I doubt you really have about me. Tonight it's probably the wine. Or was it your mother's idea? 'Good old Sally, just the girl for Jamey'? But you and I are too good friends for that. Let's keep it that way."

It had been impossible to resent Sally's tone, but Jamey had been sorely embarrassed. When, only a few months later, she had, rather surprisingly, married an attractive lawyer, almost as successful as himself, he had tried to recover some of his lost dignity by sending an expensive wedding present. He resolved, at any rate, to gain by the humiliating experience and to be guided more by his senses in the future.

The next girl that he courted was the very opposite of Sally. Alexandra Godwin was as flighty as she was pretty, as giddy as she was gay. She had not married, at twenty-seven, because she was not really interested in anything but parties and drinking. An amiable soul, she had no desire to take advantage of anyone, least of all Jamey, despite Iris Coates' conviction that, being a "pauper," she was after his money. Jamey played about on the fringes of her hedonistic existence for three years, until he was almost in love with her, and then shed a few bitter tears when she ran off with a nightclub singer, of greasy good looks and bad character, who, she wrote him, was quite good enough for her. She later killed herself.

Jamey had not become the lover of either of his proposed mates. Indeed, he had not become anyone's lover, at least on the western side of the Atlantic. Only on summer visits to Paris did he indulge his need for the opposite sex, and then only in the most expensive and hygienic professional establishments. At home, where he continued to live with his parents, his conduct was above reproach, except to the large, socially unimportant group of his male contemporaries, who deemed it unhealthy. It was generally believed in east Manhattan society that Jamey Coates was a "mother's boy," and this despite the fact that Iris Coates was certainly not demonstratively fond of her younger son, making little secret of her preference for his brother, Augie. But then had it ever been essential for a mother's boy to be adored by his mother? Was maternal domination not a trap into which any son, loved, despised or merely tolerated, was at liberty to stick his foolish head? The only thing that really puzzled fashionable New York was how Jamey had survived as well as he had. For that he was a success and Augie a hopeless flop was acknowledged by all but Iris.

It was Jamey's private theory that the reason he had survived such unblushing favoritism was precisely that it was so blatant. Iris Coates not only felt that it was natural for her to attach all her maternal love and pride to her handsome first-born; she expected Jamey and his father to kneel with her before the altar which she had reared for her cult. The unfortunate younger son could not even remember a time when this had not been the case, when the grinning muscular Augie, with his shining olive complexion, his inky, curly black hair and Alexander the Great profile, had not occupied the center of household attention both in East 36th Street and on the dunes of Southampton. Indeed, it sometimes seemed to Jamey that the very stillness and order of his parents' houses, the glinting darkness of the brownstone with its gently creaking stairs, its rustle of bead curtains, and the airy lightness of the big bare shingle cottage by the sea, had been created for the sole purpose of dramatizing by contrast the exuberant animalism of Augie Coates. What were the clucking maids, the shadowy butler, the beaming parents, the goggle-eyed kid brother but acolytes throwing up their hands at the miracle of his athleticism, his godlike maleness? If Augie smashed an old Venetian decanter, if he rode his bicycle through the maternal rose garden or backed the old Pierce-Arrow over the emerald Southampton lawn, it seemed part of a rite, a fulfillment of a natural function.

At Groton and at Yale, Augie's low marks and disciplinary infractions were regarded by his parents as simple tragedies when they were not monstrous injustices. Jamey's brilliant academic record and spotless conduct card, on the other hand, were received with parental complacency, perhaps even with a faint hint that such excellence might smack of middle-class grubbing. Poor Jamey could not be captain of the school football team, nor could he stroke the freshman crew, so the world of grades was left to him, like the church to younger sons in feudal times. Grades perhaps were all very well, but they were not quite "real," were they?

How did his parents get away with it? How did they justify this obsession with primogeniture? What warranted them in putting on such aristocratic British airs? Jamey, who preserved a little boy's respectfulness, at least in his outward demeanor, who called his father "sir" and leaped to his feet when his mother entered the room, tore them to pieces in his angry fantasies. Were they not Yankee burghers? Had Percy's grandfather, the immigrant, not worked as a boy on a loom in Glasgow? Wasn't Iris the daughter of a dry-goods merchant? Where was their castle, their park, their priest, their hunt? And yet he could never quite rid himself of the impression that Percy Coates, with his high brow, his smooth pink face, his faded tweeds, his long slim figure, his easy posture, suggested nothing so much as a peer. Standing on the veranda in Southampton, watching the twirling lawn sprayers, patting his ancient Airedale, or even sitting on a campstool before an easel, he exuded a relaxed superiority which made all of Jamey's intellectual endeavors seem frenetic. And Iris, with her messy auburn hair, her pale, etiolated skin, her high, blue-veined forehead, her long, tapering nose, her distant, gray green eyes, her unfashionable, wide-brimmed hats, her habit of scarves, her stately dowdiness, might have stepped out of a novel of Edwardian high life. Why was poor Jamey, who had saved their law firm, preserved their investments and taken care of their taxes, always made to feel that he was a bit of a bore?

It was Augie who kept him from open protest. Without Augie's restraining, hypnotizing smile, without that broad arm clapped firmly over Jamey's shoulder, the victim might have writhed under his mother's steely stare and cold evaluations, might have challenged the sincerity of his father's breezy approvals and carelessly assumed airs of impartiality, might even

have gone off to build his own life. Augie held him under his
spell, the simple spell of love. Augie was fatally charming in
his acknowledgment of his own stupidity, in the frank way that
he deplored his vulnerability to drinks and women, in his playing down of his gallant war career, his months in the trenches
when Jamey had still been a freshman. Augie told everybody,
even Percy and Iris, who never seemed to hear, that "little
Jamey" was the genius of the family, that if the Coateses ever
amounted to a hill of beans in the future, it would be the doing
of this youngest scion. And now, when Augie at forty was
unemployed and unemployable, twice divorced and frankly
alcoholic, and Jamey was managing partner of the reconstructed
family firm, when it was evident to all the world that Iris' fixed
belief in her oldest son was sheer infatuation, Augie's unaffected
pleasure in his brother's success, his pride in Jamey's achieve-
ments, robbed the latter of even the dusty satisfaction of daydreams of revenge. Indeed, Jamey still sought to win his mother
by his own deserts. For Augie had had only daughters by his
two dissolved marriages, and Jamey cherished the secret dream
that it might be his good fortune to produce the first grandson
and to repay Iris' failure to appreciate her younger son by his
magnanimity in calling the boy August Coates.

But first he had to find a bride. If with Sally he had been too
concerned with the qualifications of position and character, and
with Alexandra too obsessed with mere physical attributes, might
it not still be possible to combine the two? If he could find a
girl of good character and adequate attraction, and one who
could love him, should not that be enough? He was not in
the least put off by Amy Hunt's humble position in Miss Chadbourne's household. He noted that she was a lady, and he
approved of her meekness and modesty. He also approved of

her spirit. The girl could be pushed so far and no further; she had a just sense of her status and of her rights. He seemed even to make out that there were depths of feeling in her, the idea of which was exciting. Suppose one day it were to be directed at him?

It also pleased him that Amy was virtually isolated from males of a suitable age. Her appeal was of a subtle kind; her pale skin and dark hair and intense brown eyes were not such as to attract the casual passer-by. She seemed a flower "born to blush unseen," unless he were to pluck her. He should have plenty of time to make up his mind. And then, when it *was* made up, when he had finally spoken, could he not imagine the thrill of her gratitude, the deep vibrating love which such a girl might feel for a man of the great world, a man who presumably could look to the richest debutante, who had reached down to raise *her* to his side?

Jamey realized, of course, that this attitude was old-fashioned, outdated, Victorian — something from a poem by Elizabeth Barrett Browning: "The chrism is on thine head — on mine, the dew." But that simply meant that it could not be safely expressed in today's world. So long as he was silent, he need not be accused of condescension and could continue to enjoy the titillation of his inward drama. The only danger of his situation was that he had Amy so much to himself that he might never get around to intensifying their relationship.

Deliberately now, on visits to Dolly, he found occasions to talk to Amy alone. He would arrive early at one of Dolly's little dinners or linger on after the other guests had gone. One night, when Dolly had retired, he remained for an hour to tell Amy of a case his law firm had just won. A greedy widow and a shyster lawyer had failed in their effort to surcharge the Manhattan Bank with heavy losses in the husband's estate. To his surprise, Amy seemed not overly impressed.

"I suppose the widow was greedy, if you say so. And I can easily believe that her lawyer was a shyster. You know the facts, and I don't. But even if she'd had a better claim and been represented by more respectable counsel, wouldn't you still have been for the bank?"

"Of course, Amy. I'm their lawyer."

"But aren't there ever times when you'd like to be free to choose your own side?"

"No, I like the Manhattan Bank. The men who run it are great guys. Really, they are. There's a lot of rot talked about bankers. I find them, on the whole, to be gentlemen."

"I don't question that. It's the business of being a lawyer that I sometimes wonder about. For a man of your brains and talents, anyway. Don't you ever get tired of having to present just one side of a question? Don't you ever want to present it all? Don't you sometimes yearn just to get at the plain truth?"

"But, my dear Amy, to quote Pilate, 'What *is* truth?' We lawyers believe that to have the different sides presented by the best advocates, before a qualified and impartial judge, *is* the best way to dig truth out."

"Perhaps it is, pragmatically. But I was thinking of the individual. Of you. Life is so short. I'd rather be Jamey Coates than Jamey Coates representing the Manhattan Bank."

"But Jamey Coates *is* Jamey Coates representing the Manhattan Bank!"

"Maybe that's what I'm afraid of."

Jamey was a bit dashed by this on his walk home that night. Amy's opinion of his role at the bar was evidently a good deal lower than he had assumed. His wife in his fantasies had always revered the corporation lawyer. But he was not going to be such a fool as to be the slave of fantasies. He would rather believe, he told himself briskly, that a woman with an independent mind would be a greater help. After all, if he could not ultimately persuade a girl as intelligent as Amy that his vision of the lawyer's role was the right one, was he the lawyer that he thought himself? And had there not been a consolation in her phrase about his brains and talents? No, it had not been a wasted evening.

Whenever now there was a legal document for Dolly to sign, no matter how routine, he would take it to her apartment himself. He would arrive after work, armed with his paper — an admission of service in a trust accounting, a power of attorney, a tax return, an insurance form — and if Dolly grumbled that she couldn't afford so high-powered an attorney for such trivial matters, he would reply:

"I charge you nothing for the service, Miss Chadbourne. It's my pleasure. I only admit to very special clients that I am also a notary public."

One evening, when Dolly had gone to her room after signing papers, Amy sat watching Jamey as he conformed the copies. He suspected, with a faint discomfort, that she might be smiling inwardly at the satisfaction which he took in such ministerial functions, placing the stamp precisely under the signature, affixing the seal with too much pressure.

"I thought you were a corporation lawyer," she observed. "Why do you bother yourself with Cousin Dolly's taxes?"

"Because I like to keep in with people. I don't want to turn into a dry corporate man. Wills, trusts, estates, those things are all tied up with people and their passions and greeds."

Amy's expression was skeptical. "Are those things really

connected with people? Aren't they more connected with property? Aren't one rich old lady's bonds pretty much like another's?"

"Amy, your tone! As Miss Bayard would say, you sound like a Bolshevik."

"Well, she may yet turn me into one! If *her* passions and greeds are the things you observe in trust law, I should think it would send you rushing back to the corporate department!"

"She's really a harmless old creature."

"If you want to keep in with people, couldn't you work for someone less rich than Miss Bayard?"

"We lawyers need fees, Amy."

"Oh, *need*. What do you know of need, Jamey?"

Her tone was softer, sadder. She had never spoken so boldly, or yet so kindly, to him before. Was she thinking of something else? Or was she simply *distraite*? Or was she contemplating the gulf between them? Did she find it unbridgeable? Too much so even to dream of bridges? As he gathered up the paraphernalia of his notarial competence he thought that he had never felt such a surge of warm feeling for a girl before. It was time to ask her for a "date." On the very next visit.

⚜ *6* ⚜

To Amy, sitting at La Rue and taking in, like a hypnotized bird, her table companion's yellow viperine stare, the silent minute which followed Naomi's challenge seemed to spread out to engulf the whole evening in a muffled darkness shredded by strange lights. She was filled with a dread that she would have to leave her quiet seat in the darkened pit and climb up at last on the lighted stage where the others were waiting for her.

"Well, Amy?"

Still she did not answer. It was too important. She had to have time. If she were going to stand up under those lights and declaim, would it be acting or would it be that thing that she had not yet done: living? She might have been an animal tamer, with a silly, jaunty high hat, in rhinestone-studded boots, holding a long, white whip which she had never cracked, which she did not even know that she *could* crack, about to enter the cage and mingle with the big cats which she had until then only observed, goggle-eyed, through bars. Would they leap and tear her? Certainly Naomi was snarling.

"Have you lost your tongue?"

Oh, if it were only Naomi, she could cope. But how did she know it would stop there? Wasn't Herman, too, a kind of cat, however lovable, and besides Herman, Cousin Dolly? And if they sprang on her, to consume her, mightn't it be that they required, as a kind of vitamin, to be sure that they were alive — and they were not sure of it, either, for all their growls and lurid stripes — the very essence of Amy Hunt? How did she know really that *she* was the one climbing up on the boards or pushing her way into the cage? Maybe they were peering over the footlights to join her in the darkness or dashing themselves against the bars. Because she, Amy, had the elixir, the force, whatever it was that they had to have!

At last she heard her own voice. It was low, surprisingly controlled. "Herman was once kind enough to buy me a drink after the opera. At his aunt's suggestion. Why do you make so much of it?"

"Because you concealed it from me! You both concealed it!"

"What was there to tell?"

"It's a matter of deduction. And I know how to deduce. Like one of those paleontologists who can reconstruct a whole dinosaur from the bone of one toe. But what do you think you can possibly hope to get out of Herman . . . except possibly a roll in the hay?" Naomi pursed her lips in disgust. "You surely don't expect him to leave the wife who supports him for a penniless servant?"

Amy at first did not know how to deal with such rudeness. But after a moment's reflection it struck her that it might be liberating, even, in a curious way, exhilarating, to try. The lines now came to her. "Maybe a roll in the hay would be enough."

"Don't be revolting."

"Is it *I* who am revolting? Do you know what you make me think, Naomi? That you're so bored with life you're looking for a little excitement."

Naomi's eyes bulged. "*I'm* the one looking for excitement?"

"Why else would you deduce so much from so little?"

"Oh, I don't say that Herman isn't looking for some cheap thrill that he hasn't the guts to seek among his equals."

"Herman has said nothing and done nothing that he couldn't have said or done in an opera box."

"Very well. If that's the case, you shouldn't mind giving me your word that you will not see him again. Alone, I mean."

Naomi seemed to feel she had made a great point with this. But Amy was beginning to relish her new speaking part. Naomi had already exhausted the potentialities of her role. Understudies, choruses, messengers were free now to speak their parts.

"Why should you believe my promise?"

"I've told you: I know how to deduce. I size you up. I see

through you. You might borrow another woman's husband, but you wouldn't dare break a promise. You're too much of a puritan!"

"I'd like to think that was true."

"Will you give me your word, then?"

Amy found that she hardly hesitated. "No!"

"No?" Naomi paled. "Why not?"

"Because I love him!"

So far Naomi had been like a child playing in rough surf and with little cries of pretended courage and pretended fear. Now she looked up to see a mammoth breaker, which seemed to have materialized out of nowhere, curling its ominous razor tip above her.

"You tell *me* that?" When Amy simply remained silent, Naomi cried, "What do you intend to do about it?"

"Oh, I don't *do* things, Naomi. I exist. I feel. You're the one who's concerned with doing. I just am, that's all."

"But you plan to do a lot more 'amming,' I take it."

"I plan nothing."

"Are you sitting there, Amy Hunt, and telling me that you wouldn't steal my husband if you possibly could? That you have no designs on him?"

"The designs seem to be all yours."

"I think you ought to know that without my money he would be in no position to support you. Particularly as I should expect him to provide for the children. That alone should take all he's got."

Amy began now to feel something like confidence in her role. "Can you really believe, Naomi, that if Herman and I loved each other, we would allow any such sordid consideration as money to stand in our way?"

"I'll never divorce him!" Naomi almost screamed.

"Why should I care? Do you imagine the empty title of wife would mean anything to me?"

Naomi clapped her hand over her mouth as Herman and Jamey now rejoined them. But her silence was only for a moment.

"Amy says she's in love with you!" She flung the words in her husband's startled face. "Have you been leading her on, you hound? Have you been taking advantage of the poor girl?"

"Amy, what have you been saying?" Herman cried. Amy, looking at him, had a quick impression of whiteness, of blankness.

"Only what is true!" she responded in a voice that struck her, in her now leaping mood, as all of silver. "I have loved you ever since I came to work for Cousin Dolly. Why should I be ashamed of it? Could I help it? I never expected anything or asked for anything. I was good. I was quiet. I suffered by myself. But then your cruel wife had to come and gouge the secret out of me. Well, let her take the consequences! Why should *I* respect any rights of hers after what she's done? If there's any feeling at all on your part for me — and the only reason I say that is that it's hard for me to believe I could feel what I feel *just* on my own — then I encourage it. I welcome it, my darling!"

When Amy saw the look of dumb astonishment in Herman's eyes as they sought hers in bewildered inquiry, she felt suddenly sick. How could she, of all women, be such a bitch, a bitch such as even Naomi had never aspired to be? She opened her lips again to deny it all, to plead some kind of bad joke, or, better yet, to cry out that she had simply been seeking a brief revenge for Naomi's unjust suspicions, when another look in Herman's eyes struck her speechless. Was it kindness? Sympathy? Once again that night her world reeled. Was her love *true?* Was fantasy fact?

"Naomi, you're the one responsible for this shocking scene. Have you no consideration for anybody's feelings?"

"Of course not, you big boob! Suppose you tell Amy that she has misconstrued your cousinly attention. And suppose you make a point of going to Aunt Dolly's only when you're with me!"

When Amy now turned to Jamey Coates, she understood why he was such a good lawyer. His eyes were directed down at the tablecloth, and his clear brow expressed no visible concern or emotion. He might have been in a courtroom, listening to the lawyers in a litigation unfamiliar to him, before his own calendar call.

"Jamey, will you do me the great favor of taking me home?"

"Certainly, Amy."

In the taxi Jamey looked out of the window and said nothing. Presumably he was too embarrassed to talk. As the reaction set in from her extreme intensity, Amy felt suddenly irritated by his aloofness.

"I suppose you're terribly shocked. I can hardly blame you."

"It's not my business."

"I remember what you said about keeping your hand in with people. After tonight I should think you'd be glad to go back to your corporations. Who would have thought that Miss Chadbourne's lowly companion would so forget herself?"

Jamey turned to her now, and his pallor, even in the dim light of street lamps, struck her. "Why do you take it out on me, Amy? I've always wanted to be your friend."

"But you don't anymore."

"Why do you say that?"

"Because you've found out what a terrible person I am!"

"I don't agree. I think you're a very nice one."

Amy started to sob, and they finished the ride in silence. At the door of Dolly's apartment house she murmured an almost unintelligible "thank you" and hurried from the car into the building. She would not be "coped with" by Cousin Dolly's lawyer! She would not be straightened out like a rumpled sheet. It was kind of him, perhaps, but too much had happened, and she was very tired . . .

Alas, Cousin Dolly was still up. Her guests had gone, and she had been drinking alone.

"Go away with him," she said in a thick voice, waving a glass at Amy in a wide arc. "Go away with him, and to hell with her. Don't worry about the money. I'll pay."

"Do you mean Herman, Cousin Dolly? Whatever put such an extraordinary idea in your head?"

"I saw how she looked at you tonight when she heard about you and him at the Plaza. I saw the hate in her eyes! Save him, girl. Save my boy!"

"Cousin Dolly, you've got it all wrong. Herman doesn't want to do anything like that. He's perfectly happy with his home and children, and . . ."

"Don't forget Uncle Everett and Aldini," Dolly interrupted huskily. "They were miserable, but at least they lived. It was like *Tristan*. Love and death. Aren't they the same?" And she hummed something that Amy took to be the *"Liebestod."*

"But Tristan and Isolde drank a love potion, by mistake. You may remember they behaved quite respectably before that."

"Respectability. Humph! What's respectability where love is concerned?"

"But if I went off with Herman, how could I look after *you?*" Amy was suddenly so exhausted that she thought she would not be able to stand. The evening had curled itself up and hit her over the head like a rolled rug. How late did she have to keep up the scene?

"Love. What do young people today know of love?"

Dolly's eyes closed, and Amy went to wake up Nellie to help get her to bed.

⚔ 7 ⚔

HERMAN FIDLER had learned at Yale, in a course in ancient law, that in certain German tribes inheritances passed through the female line. He wondered if in old New York the same rule might not have obtained. His mother and Aunt Dolly had inherited their money from their mother, who had inherited her own from hers. Indeed, to find the first male accumulator Herman had to look back all the way to a great-great-grandfather who had had the good luck or the sagacity to hold on to a large farm in what had ultimately become Union Square. The fortune that he had so derived, modest by the standards of later Goulds and Fisks, had been widely distributed among his many descendants, but there was still enough of it left in Herman's branch to support his mother and aunt in what would have been considered an adequate style by any whose eyes were not constantly dazzled by the reflection of a grander past. Everything in his mother's brownstone, as in his aunt's apartment, seemed to suggest to its owner that it had been purchased for a larger habitation.

There was a busy, buzzing sense, throughout Herman's memories of his childhood, of decisions made by women. Women were loud, assertive, restless creatures; they were apt to be large and to wear large hats. They were always giving orders to children, to shopkeepers, to schoolteachers, and to a lesser breed of subservient women: nurses, cooks, chambermaids. Women seemed always to know what one was doing and were apt to tell one to stop. And men? Well, men went downtown or to clubs, or they exercised. Besides, they were not supposed to be interested in children.

Yet there was never a time in Herman's youth when he had not been aware that the dominance of women was precarious and that at any moment the male animal might reassert his natural sway. Mr. Fidler was unquestionably the supreme arbiter of the household — whenever he wished to be. This portly, red-complexioned gentleman who was always fiddling with the heavy gold objects on his watch chain, which his son vaguely identified with the things that adults called "responsibilities," could raise his voice to a pitch that made all female cackles at once subside. But for the most part he was content to be served and flattered. He was like a magnificent tawny lion, yawning lazily on a high rock while below him the females chased the buck and the gnu, scouted for fresh hunting fields and brought up the young. Only when the game was carried in did he descend, leisurely, majestically, serene in the knowledge that none of his mates or offspring would dare so much as to sniff the meat until he had consumed his fill.

Herman regretted the change of attitude in his own generation. Nothing seemed more sacred to his contemporaries than "love," and love was supposed to be based on mutual understanding. But where was the mutuality? Herman suspected that women had stolen a march on men by establishing as an early axiom that they, the subtler sex, had always understood their former masters, so that now, in the new enlightenment, it behooved the latter to knuckle down and learn their spouses' whims and fancies. Certainly Naomi's oft-proclaimed taunt: "You don't understand women!" was based on the unchallenged, the quite taken for granted proposition that she knew him, poor boob, to the core.

Then why had she chosen him? For there was no question that, from the beginning, the choice had been hers. From early days at dancing school, in the mirrored ballroom of the Colony Club, she in velvet, he blue-suited, through dances at St. Paul's and proms at Yale, it had been clear that this mechanically smiling, aggressively dancing, strong-armed and strong-minded girl of the rather billboard prettiness had marked him for her own. There were times when her muscles and firmness seemed to reject all erogenous thoughts, but there were others, he had had to concede, when these same qualities had struck him as feline, passionate, throbbing, when he had had an image of Venus behind the awkwardness of the noisy debutante. Perhaps what it boiled down to was that Naomi may have wanted his body and only that. From the beginning he had suspected that he bored her. It was as if she actually resented his putting his own sex appeal in the way of the Lochinvar whom destiny might have otherwise sent to rescue her from the stuffiness of her own antecedents.

And after ten years of marriage it was still that way. The regularity of his habits continued to irritate her; his compulsion to have his suits pressed after only two days' wear; his workbench, where he made crude toys for a settlement house and which Naomi had relegated to an unused maid's room in the basement of their apartment house; his summer seascapes which he painted so unvaryingly; his constant reading of detective fiction; his devoted visits to his mother and aunt. Yet Herman suspected that Naomi derived an actual sexual satisfaction out of the frustration engendered in her by his love of routine, and that this added a certain angry zest to their lovemaking. She was a difficult woman to satisfy, and there were nights when Herman yearned for peace and quiet, yet he had to admit that his physical needs were well taken care of. In ten years' time he had not been unfaithful once. He sometimes wondered if he could have managed it.

Amy's declaration at La Rue had struck him at once as a vital event, something for which he might for a long time have been unconsciously waiting, something miraculous, something which simply could not be ignored. Looking into the dark eyes of that pale girl he had a sudden wrenching vision of life as it might have been. Imagine! Imagine coming home to *that!* To someone who was willing and happy, nay, anxious, vehemently anxious, to place all her quiet subtlety, all her wit and shrewdness, all her loyalty and intensity, at *his* disposal! He had hardly thought of Amy to date, except as a mild but agreeable addition to the amusements offered by his amusing aunt, and as the source of a few random sexual fantasies, such as any girl might have created in him, but it had taken only a minute for him to make the adjustments for which he now saw he had long been ready. His mind rushed ahead into a tumult of visions: he was alone with Amy; he was embracing Amy; he was watching the gratitude irradiate her adoring eyes; he was slipping the blouse off her rounded shoulders; he was kissing her; he was . . .

"The poor girl is all turned around. She doesn't know if she's coming or going. I can't really blame her. Give me another splash of that champagne. We may as well drink it up, as long as Jamey's paid for it." It was Naomi talking, still at La Rue, after Amy and Jamey had gone. Her tone was brisk, but not unkind. What Herman principally sensed was its note of relief. Had it occurred to her already that he might be in love with Amy? Well, if it had, he might be! He filled her glass splashingly and then his own. "That's enough! Don't spill it. Well, my dear, I guess you don't know your own powers. Not, I suppose, that it took so much. Poor Amy must be starved for a man, cooped up all day with your crazy old aunt in that hot-house atmosphere, listening to all the yackety-yack about music and art and ancient scandals and *l'amour, toujours l'amour!*" Naomi rolled her eyes derisively to the ceiling. "Small wonder that the poor deluded creature, exposed to such drivel, should start building castles in Spain. I wonder she didn't go off long ago with one of the elevator boys."

"Thanks!"

"For what?"

"For making it so clear that if Amy's in love with me, it's only because she's in heat."

"Well, you must admit that living that way is not a healthy state."

"Oh, I admit nothing. I simply note that you begrudge me the smallest component of masculine appeal. Herman Fidler, the elevator boy, anything in pants, what's the difference?"

"Well, how do *you* see it?"

"Very simply. I see that a young lady of irreproachable virtue and modest demeanor has been so overcome by my personal charm as to transcend the limits of decorum!"

Naomi's tense, immobile face became suddenly pink with surprise. She opened her mouth to retort, but something arrested her. When had he talked back to her like that before? "Well, of course, I know that you're not unattractive," she said, almost placatingly. "After all, didn't you attract me?"

"Perhaps you were in the same state of desperation in which you find poor Amy."

"Oh, Herman, come off it! I was young. I was popular. And if I say so myself, I was damn good-looking. You can't compare me with that poor drowned rat, living off your aunt's charity!"

"I wish you would stop disparaging my conquest."

Naomi seized upon the pretended humor of this retort as a chance to make peace. If they could joke together about Amy, their marriage might be safe. "Oh, I'll concede she's a vamp, just what Hollywood has been waiting for, anything you like, if you'll only agree to go easy on the poor girl. Don't subject her to any more temptation. Of course, you've got sex appeal, you big boob! You know it; I know it; everyone knows it. But tell the Tarzan in you to stay out of Amy's jungle until she gets hold of herself. How is she going to mind her thatched hut with you strutting about, pounding your big hairy chest?"

"That's better." And Herman proceeded to finish the bottle.

When they got home, Naomi wanted to make love, but for the first time he refused without pleading either that he was tired or that he had had too much to drink. "I'm not in the mood," was all he said. Naomi was angry, but it seemed to him that she actually made an effort to control her temper. While he lay awake, hours later, listening to her snores, he enjoyed the unique sensation of feeling no guilt at leaving her unsatisfied.

For the next few weeks there was a kind of truce between them. Naomi gave up her references to Amy, but she seemed to be always watching him to see if any would be forthcoming from him. None were. He retreated into habitual silence, at home, even at the office. Sitting at his desk in the glassed-off compartment which looked out on the crowded room with the ticker-tape machine, he would gaze out of his window at the sooty spire of Trinity Church and try to make sense out of a senseless life. He had always found it difficult to believe that God could inhabit a church in the financial district. But if God was everywhere, might He not even be there? Even in Trinity?

Religion had played no role in his life since his days at St. Paul's. He had left God and his angels behind, hovering over those long gray school buildings and over the rusty red chapel, casting their beams like winter light along the marble slabs with the names of dead boys. Herman had always felt that the "real" time in his life had been at boarding school, when all the proportions had seemed just right, when his serious looks had been suited to an early maturity, his athletic aptitude to campus sports and his mild wit to the school paper. But above all his soul had responded to Dr. Drury's impassioned preaching. Life had had purpose then! The idea of dedicating himself to God and of living for his fellow men had been no idle one. Herman had had no greater ambition than to become a teacher at St. Paul's.

What had happened? What had disillusioned him? What cynic had taught him doubt? Nothing and nobody. It had all simply dripped away in his four years at Yale. He had had a circle of amiable friends, all from St. Paul's or similar schools; he had enjoyed famous courses: Tinker on Boswell, Phelps on Browning; he had been elected to Psi U; he had spent his weekends in New York. Naomi Fisher had been available to go dancing or to a show. What had gone wrong? As he thought back on it now, before the dark, thrusting spire of Trinity, the black, worn phallic symbol of the last male stand in Manhattan, it seemed to him that his college years had been veiled behind a great gauze of chat, mild, endless chat, long talks in rooms late at night, banter at parties, laughter, burbling, never stopping, and discussions always personal, anecdotal, about friends and girls and families and vacations and automobiles and sports. It seemed to him now that his friends at Yale had always been talking about people, the same people, their relatives, their backgrounds, making gentle fun of the strictness of the older generation, its severity, its empty formality, its comfortless houses, its pointless display. And yet beneath the spoofs had there not been a sharp little pride to be part of so definite a stratum, a subdued reverence for elders who, after all, for all their angularities and oddities, were responsible for making their offspring stand out a bit from the dusty mass? There had been no rebels in this group, no philosophers. There had been some with more ability and some with less, but few had sought greater opportunities than their fathers offered. Herman had gradually accepted the idea that God belonged in prep school, to be put aside with childish things.

So Christ had melted away, God had melted away, and there was nothing to put in His place but a series of duties, "responsibilities," more or less cheerfully accepted. It was not, after all, so hard to be a gentleman, particularly when there were so many generations of gentlemen behind one. Herman's father had told him that if he became a broker, a seat on the Exchange would in time be his. Naomi had offered her resources and passion. The Racquet and Tennis Club had proffered exercise; Brooks Brothers, clothes. In Southampton, in Newport, he could go to the beach and paint his endless seascapes. Surely ninety-nine percent of all humanity born since the building of the pyramids had been less fortunate. Herman had gained the whole world, and what had the price ever been but just a soul? And then the world, as worlds do, had begun to slip away. The devil never kept his bargains, if indeed he ever made any. The depression had removed all chance of Herman's seat on the Exchange. Naomi's father had gone out the window, and his own had died of a stroke. Money worries began to crumple the crisp corners of the Fidler life. Naomi became shriller. She could have no more children after the second daughter; Herman would never have a son. He wanted a son. Why? He was patient, inert. He had the feeling that he would live indefinitely, in pressed flannels, with polished shoes. His seascapes showed more water and less sky. The horizons blurred. As he looked about his world, he saw that his case was not unique. It was even banal.

Only at Aunt Dolly's did he feel the flicker of life. It seemed to him that she was the richer for all the things his mother was forever pointing out that she lacked: a spouse, offspring, a regular occupation. Aunt Dolly, who was to all the Chadbourne clan the very symbol of artistic preciousness, of social uselessness, of "non-living," struck him for perhaps these very reasons as the one individual who might have a tiny glimmer of ultimate truth. He liked to hear her round condemnation of accepted things, her scorn of family values, her passionate faith in the arts. He did not much care for the opera, but he liked the fact that it was important to her. There was nobody at Aunt Dolly's who was going to ask him awkward questions about stocks and bonds. She encouraged him, on the contrary, in his weekend painting and watercoloring which she did not scruple to call his "true vocation." She even joked, or half joked, about his becoming another Gauguin and going to the South Seas. It was a pleasant fantasy.

He jumped up one morning to walk to the window and stare down at the hustling sidewalks of Broadway. Amy's declaration — why was it not his signal? Why was it not the message on the road to Damascus for which he must have been waiting? Why could God not take the form of a girl as well as an angel? He rubbed his eyes. Of course, she did not really have to be God or even an angel. That was the sheerest cant. He did not believe in such things. But might she not be the force of life, or art, a signal to the flesh, the heart, that he was not, after all, quite dead? He turned now and walked to the office of John Rappelye, big, dark, hirsute, his oldest friend, a perennial adulterer.

"John, do you still have that little apartment on the West Side? The one you told me about?"

John leered. "An apartment? It's a couple of rooms. I hope you don't go round telling people."

"Be my pal. Are you using it now?"

"You want the key?"

"Very much."

John handed him a key with an address tag and winked. "The rest of the week is yours, fella. The cleaning woman comes Thursday at noon."

"I'm grateful."

"I wouldn't have thought it of you, pal. Congratulations!"

When Herman left his office that evening he went to the Hudson Club to dine alone. The clubhouse, a vast square white Roman palazzo designed by Stanford White, was a favorite refuge. Amid marble and red plush, in silent huge chambers hung with gilt-framed portraits of ugly men under ceilings sixty feet high, he felt as if all the opulence and power of Renaissance Europe protected him from the women of his world. That the feeling was quite illusory he was also aware. He was not even surprised when, after his second martini, a page told him that he was wanted on the telephone.

"Herman! Aren't you coming home?"

"No, I thought I'd dine here tonight." The gin had made him bold.

"Are you crazy? We're dining at the Rappelyes!"

"Oh, I'd forgotten." The liquor, the club, Amy herself faded.

"Well, come home now. You have to dress!"

"I'll be there," he muttered and sullenly hung up.

❧ 8 ❧

THE HOUSE OF the John Rappelyes, on lower Park Avenue, was proof that the best Victoriana, perfectly maintained, could be handsome. The bewildering accumulation of tassels, of curlicues, of oddly shaped mahogany commodes, of paintings of Roman festivals by Alma Tadema or of disingenuous angels by Bouguereau seemed to gleam and glitter in the dimly lit interior like jewels in a dark velvet case. Presiding over it all, fresh, expansive, smiling, yet with some of the rigidity of a "royal," Sandra Rappelye seemed to be taking with cheerful sobriety her duties as representative of all that was oldest and best in a dwindled and deteriorated society.

"Ah, Herman and Naomi, my dears, at last! A party's never quite a party without you two."

Herman wondered if she knew of her husband's infidelities. There had to be a sense of injustice behind a backbone so straight. A world that was greeted with such a forward good will must have been a dangerous world. Glancing about he saw that they would be eight: John's old deaf mother and Sandra's big, bony unmarried sister were matched with Bayard Jones and Jamey Coates. Were the Rappelyes trying to catch Jamey for the sister? Fat chance!

"What a gathering!" Naomi hissed in his ear. "It's the kind of party you'd read about in a *Saturday Evening Post* story about old New York."

Herman felt detached, not only from Naomi and her eternal dissatisfactions but from the party itself, as he moved across the room to take the undesired, vacant seat beside old Mrs. Rappelye. He had had too many drinks at the Hudson Club, before and after Naomi's call, to do much talking, and his host's mother could be counted on for a monologue.

"Coming to sit with me, Herman? You always did have such good manners! Or did Sandra tell you to? I'm really blessed in my daughter-in-law. She not only takes care of me; she pretends it's a pleasure! Is Naomi like that with your mother? Not exactly? Well, that's too bad, but it's too much to expect more than one Sandra. How *is* your dear mother? And Dolly? Still as keen on music and art as ever? Well, that's what comes, I always say, of not marrying . . ."

Herman thought of Naomi's remark about the party. It was always a tenet of their group that writers who purported to describe it floundered helplessly in a mire of misunderstood nuances. In much the same manner upper-class Londoners and Parisians had sneered at the aristocrats in Trollope and Balzac, even at those in Thackeray and Proust. But wasn't society anywhere fairly easy to comprehend? Old Mrs. Rappelye with her

simple values, Bayard Jones with his shrill, defensive snobbish-
ness, Naomi Fidler with her rudeness and emotional insecurity,
and himself — with his dullness? And yet, he reflected, it was
also true that John Rappelye was a financier of near genius, and
certainly Jamey Coates was supposed to be a great lawyer. A
man who wanted to paint should never oversimplify . . .

"Will you take me in to dinner, Herman, please?" The old
lady had risen.

John Rappelye followed his mother and Herman closely into
the dining room and actually poked the latter slyly in the ribs.
"No need for that key tonight, I guess," he whispered with a low
chuckle.

At dinner Bayard Jones, an emaciated male caricature of Miss
Bayard, divulged to the table the latest rumor from Washington,
picked up at his Flag Society.

"They say King Franklin the First has great plans for us. In
two years' time the inheritance tax will go up to ninety percent!
Except there will be a deduction for philatelists. The Roosevelts,
you know, have their fortune in stamps. It looks so harmless,
doesn't it, to receive a present from Mussolini in the form of a
rare issue? Whereas if il Duce were to write them a check . . .
well, that would be a bit crude, wouldn't it?"

Herman recalled a dinner dance two years before when
Bayard Jones had created a sensation by proposing a toast "to
the damnation of Roosevelt." Herman and half the party had
remained seated while the other half, including Naomi, had
enthusiastically drunk it, but now he despised himself for not
having jumped to his feet and denounced Bayard publicly.

The rest of the table tolerated Bayard in what struck Herman
as a rather tribal manner. He was a fool, but he was their fool.
His attitudes were at least recognizable as cartoons of their
own.

"I don't suppose things are quite as bad as Bayard makes out." John Rappelye gave vent to his host's laugh, a deep, rumbling sound, as from subterranean plumbing, full, clogged, yet ineluctably in motion. "But I think we all recognize that there's some truth in it. What Roosevelt and his boy geniuses are doing is simply gnawing away at the backbone of the nation. For what is that but our past and our traditions? And who are the guardians of those but our old families? And how are they to keep their heads above water without a bit of property passed down the line? Think of those old mansions in the South which have been in the same family for five or six generations!"

"Most of them have been bought by Yankees," Herman put in, his heart quickening a beat as he sensed the instant antagonism around the table. "And how in New York can we justify ourselves by the pretense of keeping up appearances? How many of us live in the houses of our parents, let alone our grandparents? Certainly, Naomi and I don't. Jamey's parents built theirs. Bayard lives in the Hudson Club. And you bought this house, didn't you, Mrs. Rappelye? It's still in its first generation, even if you eventually leave it to Sandra and John."

This tirade, ending as it did with so untactful a reference to the old lady's ultimate demise, created a pained silence. Herman reflected with a mild exhilaration that he might as well have broken wind. He drank off the wine in his glass in a gulp, dreading the inevitable wearing off of his club cocktails. Sandra's brief glance at the butler warned him that the bottle would not stop at his place on its next round.

"You don't have to live in the same house to keep up a family style," old Mrs. Rappelye intervened in a high, quavering tone. Of course, her deafness had not spared her the one comment of the evening that would have hurt her feelings. "We take our things with us to new abodes. There are paintings in this room that have been in our family for almost two hundred years. The Copley, for example. Some property has always been necessary if one is to keep one's head up in the world. I remember, when I was a girl at school in England, hearing it said that Queen Victoria would ask, when it was a question of creating a new peer: 'Can he keep it up?' Oh, yes, John is quite right. There must always be inheritances. I suppose Mr. Roosevelt will wait till his mother dies before eliminating them altogether!"

"Well, it's not just money and things." Sandra turned to Herman with a look of only the mildest reproach. "It's all the good that people do with them. And it takes a couple of generations for a family to learn how to give money away properly. Where would our hospitals and colleges be without private charity? What about our museums and zoos and botanical gardens? And what about the opera?"

It was like Sandra, Herman reflected, to put the whole silly argument on a noble basis. But, really, how could one go along with it? How could one go along with the ridiculous idea that their group stood for anything at all? That the sum was more than the total of its inane parts? "Andrew Carnegie made his own money and gave it away," he pointed out bluntly. "It didn't take him two generations. And anyway I don't see what that has to do with the argument. The government can support the arts and hospitals."

"Oh, Herman, don't be such an ass!" Naomi's patience had been thoroughly exhausted by three weeks of the novel experience of keeping her temper. "Everyone knows the government throws its money away. What's got into you tonight, anyway?"

"What's got into *me*?" Herman turned to stare boldly at his wife, elated at once by her challenge and provocation. "Nothing's got into me. What's got into the rest of you? All I'm professing is a little basic Americanism: the simple idea that people might be equal, or at least *start* equally. I think a man who makes a fortune by the sweat of his brow — or by using what's behind it — ought to be allowed to keep it. But I'm blessed if I see why he should be allowed to enshrine it in perpetual trusts to maintain a posterity of fops!"

"Herman, you sound like a Bolshevik!"

"Really, my friend . . ."

"Surely, he's joking!"

"If you don't like this country, old man, why don't you go live in Moscow?"

"Come, come, let's not be too hard on Herman." Jamey Coates, the perennial advocate, now took control of an outraged courtroom. "As a matter of fact, his tax philosophy would be perfectly acceptable to many of our self-made men. The real trouble with it is that it wouldn't work. Most of Uncle Sam's revenue derives from the income tax. So little comes from inheritance taxes that Herman's proposition might well fail on constitutional grounds."

"Oh, do explain that, Jamey." Sandra smiled at him gratefully, trying to pick up the pieces of her shattered party. A dull topic was just what she needed, and what was better than the Constitution? "Tell us why it would be unconstitutional."

"Because Congress has the power to impose taxes only for the purpose of raising revenue. If the real purpose behind a tax is to destroy a class, it could be invalid."

"But the government always needs money," Herman insisted. "A tax that raises any revenue at all shouldn't be thrown out just because it has some other incidental good effect."

"And you would call the elimination of inherited wealth a good effect?" demanded John Rappelye. "You astonish me, Herman!"

"Maybe not all of it. But most of it."

"And where would that leave *you*, I'd like to know?" Naomi now exploded. "Just what in the devil's name would *you* expect to live on?"

"How like a woman to put the whole issue on a personal basis," Herman retorted, emboldened by the gleam of alarm that he now caught in Naomi's eye. "But, all right, let's be personal. Let's put the issue of survival squarely on the table. There are four men here. What would they do without inherited wealth? Let's go around the table."

"Herman, you're tight!"

"I really don't see why we have to be quite so personal."

"Ease up, old boy!"

"Let's change the subject."

"Wait a minute, wait a minute." Herman rudely raised one hand in the air. "My wife put the discussion on this basis, and I'm going to answer her. Now let's take our host. John could make a living in any sort of society. He is a magician at making values appear where they are not, and that might make him useful even in Moscow. Or maybe I should say, especially in Moscow. And Jamey here . . . well, when was there a civilization where a brilliant lawyer couldn't persuade people that they couldn't do without him? Imagined wealth for imagined poverty; imagined solutions for imagined problems; yes, John and Jamey will always be with us." Herman chuckled pleasantly as he faced the assembled hostility. "And as for Bayard and myself — we can always run elevators."

"Speak for yourself!" Bayard cried with a squeak of fury.

"Herman, if you don't pull yourself together and at least try to act like a gentleman, I'm going to take you straight home!"

At this Sandra turned to Jamey and proceeded to engage him in private conversation. It was clearly a signal, and the three other women, trained in the discipline of parties, at once followed her example. Herman found himself firmly involved with Sandra's sister in a discussion of her summer camp for poor children. He knew that he was being "handled," and he spent the rest of the meal listening, with an occasional nod, to the gurgling stream from his neighbor's unfathomable well of small talk.

He had expected to sober up during dinner, for, as he had anticipated, no further wine was poured in his glass, but the effect of his earlier dosage proved unusually persistent, and as soon as he had swallowed a glass of brandy in the library, where the gentlemen had withdrawn after Sandra had risen, he knew that he was intoxicated. John Rappelye had tactfully taken the irate Bayard Jones to a corner to show him a folio of prints of ancient flags, and Herman was left with Jamey, whose reserved, mechanically smiling expression was that of the professional specialist in family problems.

"I'd go easy on that if I were you, old boy," he observed as Herman helped himself to another glass of brandy.

"Do you think anything I could do now would make a worse impression?"

"Oh, my, yes. What's happened so far is easily repaired."

"Don't believe it!" Herman shook his head in gloomy conviction. "In our world a man is never forgiven for stepping out of character. I've always been known as that nice Herman Fidler, so dependable. But now I've shown myself to be unreliable. That is never forgiven. If I were Reggie Sanders I could get sloppy drunk and pee on the carpet, and nobody would really mind, because that's what Reggie always does."

"I doubt he'd get away with it here."

"He might. He has the formula. Establish early that you're unreliable, and that becomes in itself a kind of reliability. Society abominates the unexpected. Twenty years from now, even if I've been Jesus Christ in the whole interim, Sandra and John will always ask, when they hear that *I* was at a party: 'Did he behave himself?' Decades of a blameless life will go for nothing! I'll always be that sorry drunk."

"Herman, you're being ridiculous."

"Well, what of it? I won't be coming here again, anyway. Jamey, if you ever feel the impulse to marry, lie down till it passes away. At least if it's a girl from our world."

"I wonder if that isn't good advice," Jamey replied, frowning in a sudden mood of gravity. "Do you really mean it?"

"Why shouldn't I mean it? You have no idea how lucky you are. You have a profession that you love. It's more important to you than any man, woman or child. And it *should* be, damn it! A man who builds his life on a woman is building on sand."

"A mistake that I'm not likely to make!"

"Why, Jamey, you sound as if you'd been disillusioned by a woman. Have you?"

Jamey brushed it aside. "No, no, it's all book learning with me. But, Herman, if you're bored, you can always change your job. You can . . ."

"I'm going to change more than my job. I'm going to change my life!"

Jamey's eyes at once narrowed. The managing partner of Coates, Lane & Coates sniffed a threat. Herman knew well which side the lawyer would take if two clients, himself and Naomi, fell out.

"What precisely do you mean by that?"

"I'm going to run off to Samoa and paint, like Gauguin. I'll take a savage woman — 'she shall rear my dusky race'!"

"You joke, of course."

"Don't be too sure. Do you remember the line: 'nothing in his life became him like the leaving it'? Well, there's more than one way of leaving."

Jamey's expressionless stare indicated to Herman that at last he was being taken seriously. Indeed, it was the first time that he ever had been taken seriously by Jamey.

"Very well, Herman. If we're going to lay it on the line, let us both be frank. If you leave Naomi, you will encounter the united opposition, not only of her family, but of your own."

"How do you know that?"

"Because I know how your mother feels about such things. When your cousin Lansing Tower left his wife last year, she told me: 'If Herman ever does a thing like that, I'll change my will and leave every penny I have to his daughters. Remind me, Jamey!' "

Herman's jaw dropped. "You mean Ma thought I *might*? I didn't believe she thought I had the guts!"

"Your mother meant what she said, I'm sure. And I have little doubt that she would persuade your aunt to take the same attitude. Miss Chadbourne is basically a conservative, for all her love of art. Remember that they both have the power to appoint their trusts among the issue of your grandmother. And your daughters are just as much your grandmother's issue as you are. Don't think, either, that you could obtain an allowance from your children's property. You would almost surely be deprived of their custody. You couldn't even depend on your salary. I think you can imagine how John Rappelye would decide if he had to choose between you and your mother-in-law's account."

Herman looked at Jamey with astonishment. He had had no idea that the lawyer so hated him. But of course! Bachelors of that age, when they were not avowed homosexuals, were always jealous of husbands and fathers.

"You've thought it all out, haven't you, Jamey? You're the watchdog of wealthy women. Small wonder you haven't married when you know so intimately what they're like!"

"Stay with us, Herman. We hold all the cards. And yours isn't a bad life, as lives go."

"It isn't a life at all . . ." Herman hesitated. It was as if the door in the slowly flying plane had slid open, and there he was, the first up, feeling the heavy pound of his heart under the strapped parachute. "Jamey, if I leave now, will you see Naomi home?"

"Where are you going?"

"Away."

"How far?"

"Far enough."

"Let me go upstairs and get Naomi. It's only fair to hear what she has to say first."

"No. I don't want to talk to her."

"You mean you don't dare?"

"Interpret it any way you like. You're the family lawyer."

Jamey seemed beside himself. Herman had never seen him in such a state. "If you do this thing, Herman Fidler," he said in a low, hissing tone, "I'll ruin you. So help me God, I'll ruin you!"

Herman stared for a moment in sheer surprise at this suddenly furious man. Then he rose and hurried from the room.
In the hall he tore his coat from a hanger, leaving his hat, and
bounded down the stoop to the snowy street. A taxi took him
to Times Square, from where he telephoned his aunt's apartment. It was Amy herself who answered.

"It's Herman. Could you come out and meet me now?"
Before she could answer he gave her the address of the bar.

"Herman, what are you talking about? How can I leave
Cousin Dolly?"

"Let me speak to her."

"She's gone to bed! She has a cold."

"Well, then, she doesn't need you. And I *do*. I've left
Naomi."

"Herman! You can't have!"

"But I have. I've left Naomi and my children and my job
and my future. I'm alone and desperate. If you don't come
down here and talk me out of it, I may jump in the East River.
No, I guess it'll be the Hudson. It's nearer."

"You're intoxicated!"

"Not very. Just enough so I might really do it. And it'll be
on *your* head. The girl who wouldn't come. Who couldn't
leave an old lady safe in bed in an apartment with three maids.
The girl who was too shy — at twenty-seven! The girl who
wouldn't lift a finger to save the man she said she loved. *Some*
love, Amy Hunt!"

"Oh, Herman, please. Oh, my God!" There was an agonized
pause. "Where did you say the bar was?"

Herman repeated the address and rang off.

✠ 9 ✠

AMY WAS VERY desolate after the scene at La Rue. There were moments in each day when she hoped that she might be about to sense some revival of her old vitality, but then, inevitably, like the small remote ache of the first stage of a fatal disease, the feeling of desolation would shiver back. She had a sense of having gone to bed one person and awakened another, a worse one. The new Amy Hunt — perhaps the real Amy Hunt — was a liar and exhibitionist. More importantly, she was not any longer that most indispensable of beings, by Chadbourne standards, a "nice" person.

It seemed to her, now that she had been expelled from the quiet Eden of her old personality, an Eden of small green walls and neat petunia plots, that everything in her former life must have rested on the pillars of what she had deemed her own essential decency. It was that which had enabled her to hold her own with Cousin Dolly, with Mrs. Fidler, even with the terrible Miss Bayard. It was that which had given her the courage to stand up to Jamey Coates when she disagreed with him. It was that, in the last analysis, which had made up for her social obscurity, her inability to become a writer, even her lovelessness. If she had nothing else to believe in, at least she could believe in herself! What else had kept up the spirits of those Brontë governesses, those dowerless Austen heroines? She had learned this principle in the last years of her parents' lives. The Reverend Lamar Hunt had been a sweet, soft-voiced, prissy little man, a Trollopian cleric born decades after his time, who might conceivably have been a bishop in 1875 but who could not even hold onto a small but fashionable rectory in a suburb of Hartford a half century later. Sermons addressed to peccadilloes in mellifluous tones did not commend themselves to parishioners in the jazz age. Before his death at fifty Amy's father had even lost his faith. One morning he awoke to find it gone, like a shiny gold-plated cuff link missing from the top of his orderly bureau. He took Amy into his confidence. For his wife, given over to bitterness at the way in which events had justified her family's disapproval of her marriage, had little interest in spiritual matters.

"Your mother's god is the god of the Chadbournes," he told her sadly. "He has no concern with the likes of me. And why should he? If I can't even sustain a feeble faith in *him*? But I'll tell you something, Amy. Nothing need make a man ridiculous. I may be a poor sort of creature. I find it difficult to persuade people of the things I believe in. Or of the things I used to believe in. Which would seem to make me a symbol of futility. Like a lacy valentine with a red heart which contains no message of love! I have caused your mother to make needless sacrifices. But I am still a man. I am not ridiculous because mankind is not ridiculous."

Amy had not forgotten that moment. It seemed to her that behind the sloping shoulders, behind the black satin covering the round paunch, behind the sad, watery eyes and the brave little smile, she had a glimpse of the saints and martyrs. She had many thoughts about her father in the brief remaining span of his life, but never again did she condescend to him.

In her mother's widowhood, which lasted only three years, she learned to revise another opinion. Eleanor Hunt was determined to bring her daughter back to the world of her own origins. They would skimp pathetically for ten months of the year in order to be able to afford exiguous rooms in the eaves of fashionable watering place hotels for July and August: Northeast Harbor, East Hampton, Nantucket. Amy suffered at the snubs that they received, but her mother seemed equal to anything. She was admirable in her determination and in the brave show that she assembled from the use of all her few assets: the faded, graying loveliness, the cultivated musical voice, the rather regal stance enhanced by the very dowdiness of broad-brimmed hats and large cultured pearls. It was all so useless and so pathetic! Nobody was going to pay any attention to an oversolicitous, impecunious widow with a diffident, speechless daughter, nobody, that is, but other widows in the same hotels, sometimes, to be sure, rich ones, but whose friendliness and hospitality took a quick leave of absence whenever the unattached males of their family called on them. The most that Eleanor could obtain for her daughter by all of her card-dropping and telephoning, by all of her picking up of bare acquaintances in lobbies and dining rooms, was an invitation to a ladies lunch or a ladies tea, or to a concert or charity raffles.

It was all vaguely ennobled by a death from lung cancer of whose approach Eleanor was fearlessly aware.

"Remember," she would tell Amy fiercely again and again, "Dolly Chadbourne is your best chance. She has never liked me, but she has family feeling, and, after all, we are first cousins. When she hears I'm gone, and under what circumstances, she will find it pathetic, and she may do something for you. Whatever it is, take it, Amy! I've had little enough from the Chadbournes. They owe you something!"

It had seemed to Amy that her parents had proved themselves superior to the world which had defeated them. They
had given her a faith in the durability of character in a chaos of
poverty and jeers. Somehow or other good old simple "niceness"
might be proof against illness, against death itself, even the
cruelest death by cancer, even death that obliterated and ex-
tinguished the soul. How could "niceness" survive in the void,
in the dark, in the interstellar spaces? Well, perhaps just because
it could! But now niceness appeared to have fled.

Herman, since the night at La Rue, had not come to his
aunt's, but Naomi came. She not only came; she was demonstratively pleasant. Obviously she wanted to convince Amy
that her husband in no way reciprocated her feelings and that
consequently no jealousy was required. One evening she
arrived while Jamey Coates was calling on Dolly.

"How is Herman?" Dolly asked her at once.

"Oh, Herman's never been better." Naomi glanced signif-
icantly at Amy. "He's going salmon fishing with John Rappelye
over Easter, and there's nothing that makes him happier. If I
were jealous of anything, it would be of a fish!"

"He never comes to see his old aunt anymore."

"Well, don't you think that, just for a bit, that may be
advisable?" Naomi, pleased with the opening which Dolly's
tactlessness offered her, actually winked at Jamey. "If you
know what I mean, Aunt Dolly. And I think you do."

"I have no idea what you mean, Naomi."

"Must I cross my *i*'s?"

"And dot your *t*'s. When have you not?"

"Well, after what happened in a certain nightclub I thought
it might be easier for all concerned if my husband didn't come
here for a while. Was I wrong, Amy?"

"Not at all."

Amy had thought that she was beyond caring what Naomi said or thought, but she found that she minded having her speak so before Jamey. The latter's behavior, however, was perfect. He did not alter his expression; he seemed to take no sides. His head was slightly inclined as he accepted an explanation of Herman's absence, which he had never questioned. But on his last visit to Dolly's the week before, he had not availed himself, as on previous occasions, of the opportunity to talk to Amy alone. She had had the distinct impression that he would have found it embarrassing to be alone with her.

"Oh, you're referring to what took place that night when you all went dancing," Dolly said with a sniff. "That was just a lot of foolishness. Amy was putting it on. She told me all about it afterward. Were you taken in by it, Jamey?"

"Not for a minute, Miss Chadbourne."

Naomi's mouth was open with surprise. "You knew Amy was acting, Jamey?"

"And very competently, too."

"Did you think *I* was acting?"

"No. I think you took the bait, Naomi. Just for a minute, of course. Amy is very clever. And gifted. But after a bit you saw through it all."

"Did I? Oh!"

In the silence that followed, Amy felt her desolation illuminated by a sudden flare of hope. Jamey surely did not believe that she had been acting, but did he *want* to believe it? And if so, why? Did he perhaps care to see her as she had seen herself, as a decent person? And suddenly it became very clear to her that she valued Jamey's opinion, valued it highly. The lawyer had become the judge before whom she would now like to rest her case — if she had one. Behind the façade of Jamey's mannerisms, his briskness, his near unctuosity, she sensed a latent power.

"Is that true, Amy?" Naomi was asking her. "It was all a joke? Hardly in the best taste, I think."

Amy was about to say yes, it had been a joke, to put everything back as it had been, when a door seemed to blow open noisily in her mind to disclose a new area of desolation. Was she now going to become a third person, yet another character, and one who made mock of every serious thing, including her own love for Herman? No, oh God, no, there had to be an end to this!

"No! I wasn't acting!"

The pained silence was broken by Naomi who rose abruptly.

"Well, I guess I'd better be off. We're dining at the Rappelyes, and I have to arrange the girls' evening. Will we see you there, Jamey?"

"Yes. How nice. I'll go out with you."

Alone with Dolly, Amy pleaded a headache and went to her room. It was in a very turbulent state of mind that, four hours later, she received Herman's telephone call. She had fallen asleep, still dressed, on the chaise lounge when she heard the distant ringing of the telephone in the hall. For a long time it rang and rang, and she had a confused sense of the porter's knocking in *Macbeth*. Then, suddenly, realizing that nothing ever awakened Dolly and that the maids were out of earshot, she jumped up and ran to the hall. For a moment she surveyed the ringing instrument with a kind of horror. Why was it so persistent? What terrible news had it to give her? She snatched it up.

When she hung up, she had still not made a commitment, but

she knew what she was going to do. For her mind, racing down a long pebbly beach of indecision, skipping over incoherences like rock piles, could now put together the new drama that was forming, that *she* had formed. She had started as a Brontë governess; she was ending as Hedda Gabler! Well, the least she could do was to play her part. That she was no longer a nice person was made even more manifest by the horrid fact that she had felt a little crawly thrill down her back at the idea of spending the rest of the night in the bed of a man she did not love. She fled from the apartment before she could change her mind.

But there was another shock for her in this night of revelations. When she got to the bar, she saw rising and coming toward her with arms outstretched and a small foolish smile on his bland face, not only a man whom she did not love. She saw a stranger.

❧ *10* ☙

WHEN JAMEY HAD moved the offices of Coates, Lane & Coates from a shabby old building on Liberty Street to a trim new edifice on lower Broadway, there had been considerable grumbling among the older partners, a good deal of talk about "cheap modern design" and some mutterings about quarters which had been good enough for Judge Lane being good enough for Percy Coates' "boy genius." But Jamey had smiled his way through all opposition. Times had changed, and clients were no longer charmed by walruses behind roll-top desks who kept them waiting for hours and then, like as not, called them damn fools. No, clients liked what they now saw and heard: long, wide beige corridors hung with Currier and Ives prints, the discreet muffled murmur of new typewriters, fine paneling and Sheraton desks glimpsed through half-opened mahogany doors, the discreet silvery bong of the Auto-call summoning lawyers to their telephones. Jamey had expanded an old and distinguished trusts and estates partnership, a loose medley of intense individualists, into a smooth, modern, coordinated corporation law firm, of twenty-five partners and twice that number of clerks, without, he liked to think, losing any of the grand traditions of an honorable past. If the portraits of deceased partners had been taken out of their old gilt casements, cleaned, stretched and fitted into bright steel frames, their subjects could still frown uncompromisingly down at the smooth purr of telephones, the click of high heels in the corridors and the glossy magazines in the reception hall. Jamey prided himself on having got the best of two worlds.

Best of all he loved his own large corner office, with the commanding view of Trinity Church, dark and high and noble, below the north window. The sober Gothic of Richard Upjohn's masterpiece symbolized to Jamey the rationalism of his era, as opposed to the mystic dreaming of the Middle Ages. Not that he found Trinity more beautiful than Chartres. Of course not. That would have been ridiculous. But Trinity would never have tolerated the burning of heretics, the pulling out of tongues of those who denied the virgin birth. Trinity was sensible; Trinity was kind; Trinity loved work and order and neatness. Trinity did not even mind the discharge of carbon monoxide from Broadway, the profusion of dirt, for it could

always be cleaned. What if people said it was the tabernacle
of a burgher's god? Didn't God care for burghers, too? Or did
He care only for wiseacres, journalists, academics? Jamey would
sniff at the idea. If God did that, He made a great mistake,
for they cared nothing for Him!

Some of his partners had male secretaries; most, young
women. Only Jamey had a "mother." Mrs. Glennan, a widow
of sixty, wide and bland and soft-eyed, had been Judge Lane's
secretary, and she worshiped Jamey for having made her his
after the Judge had died. She had dreaded the suttee of being
dismissed to the "pool" of typists who worked for junior clerks.
She could hardly believe her luck in being once again, and so
soon, secretary to "Number One."

"Mrs. Fidler called," Mrs. Glennan told him on a Monday
morning. She was sitting before Jamey's desk, book in hand,
ready for the dictation that his buzzer had told her to expect.

"Roz or Naomi?" He liked to refer to clients familiarly, to
show that he trusted her not to do so.

"Mrs. Herman. She said to call right back. Shall I ring her
before you dictate?"

"No. Let her cool."

"And just how do I get her to do that?"

"Isn't that your job, Mrs. G? I thought you were here to
protect me."

"Not against yourself, sir."

"And what is that supposed to mean?"

"Simply that if you keep giving her the run-around, the way
you've been doing lately, you may lose a client. And with that
client, a brokerage house. And with that brokerage house, the
whole Chadbourne clan which this firm has represented for
a century!"

Jamey looked up in astonishment at the plain, ample creature in inappropriate bright red before him. Her little eyes, almost lost in the expanse of her brow and cheeks, sparkled with their own daring.

"Why, Mrs. Glennan! Do you really think I'm handling the case that badly?"

"I don't think you're handling it at all!" she exclaimed, and now he made out the glitter of sudden tears in her eyes. "Something has come over you, Mr. Coates. Forgive me for saying it, but if *I* don't have your best interests at heart, I wonder who does. If you want me to hold my tongue, just say so at once."

"No, no, Mrs. G. Please go on."

"It won't take long. Here is Mrs. Herman Fidler, a faithful wife, a devoted mother, shamelessly abandoned by her husband who takes up with his aunt's companion, his own cousin! Both families, Mr. Fidler's as well as Mrs. Fidler's, are unanimous in denouncing him."

"Well, there may be a question about Dolly."

"Miss Chadbourne, sir, if you'll pardon my term, is a known eccentric. What she thinks about it has nothing to do with the price of eggs. The point is, Mr. Coates, that you should be suing the teeth out of Mr. Fidler and naming that hussy as corespondent!"

"And what makes you think that I won't do that?"

"What are you waiting for? Everyone knows the facts. People are beginning to say you have a softness for Miss Hunt. I hate to say it, sir, but they are. Why else would you delay? The two of them are living together — shamelessly — in the Village."

"It's true." Jamey, appalled by her speculation, hastened to deal with her second point. To calm his now jumping nerves, he walked to the window to look down on Trinity. "It's perfectly true. But I have hesitated to take any step that might destroy the last chance of reconciliation. Even if that chance is a slight one. Mrs. Fidler is losing nothing by my delay. I have already been at some pains to establish the facts of her husband's cohabitation with Miss Hunt — the hussy, as you call her." Jamey pursed his lips in distaste. "The managing clerk has reported to me that our detective will be able to verify the relationship in court. So long as Mrs. Fidler does not condone the offense by resuming marital relations with her husband — which, under the circumstances, seems hardly likely — she prejudices none of her remedies by waiting."

"But can you imagine any chance of reconciliation? She even described Mr. Fidler to *me* on the telephone as a snake!"

"True, Naomi is very angry. Hell hath no fury, as we know. But I think a lawyer's duty in these matters is very delicate. So many of us like to come slamming in, calling names, making hot denunciations, breathing fire and brimstone, so that the smallest chance of peace is at once obliterated. And you see, Mrs. G, that is precisely the way *I* started this case. I allowed myself to explode at Herman when he told me he was leaving Naomi. I insulted him. I may even have goaded him into it!"

Mrs. Glennan's stare was uncomprehending. "But if he *said* he was going to leave her?"

"Ah, but did he really mean it? What business had I to allow my personal judgment, my personal morals, to intervene? I should have played along with him, persuaded him to put the decision off till the next day. But, no, I had to be judge, I had to be jury. I had to play God! I gave in to the luxury of showing Herman Fidler how much I despised him. And now, before I bring a divorce action that will shatter the happiness of a mother and two children, I have to pause to see if there is not *some* way that I can make up for my confounded interference."

"Bravo!"

Jamey turned from the window to face the tall figure of his father. Percy Coates always appeared as he wished to appear, a survivor in the dark shadow of the 1930s of the *belle époque*. His seventy-five years showed only in the black circles by his eyes and at the edges of his lips.

"Good morning, sir." Jamey stood almost to attention. "Forgive so hearty a statement of principle so early in the morning."

"Remember Talleyrand, dear boy. *Surtout, point de zèle.* Is there anything new in your poor brother's case? No, Mrs. Glennan, you needn't leave. You know the sorry facts only too well."

"If you'll permit me to say so, sir," Mrs. Glennan replied, pink-faced at the violence of passing from one extreme emotion to another, "Mr. Augie has been very much wronged. Drunken driving, my eye! That Roslyn cop has had it in for Mr. Augie ever since we arranged his last speeding ticket. I bet he was waiting in the bushes for Mr. Augie to come out of that party and drive off! Of course, he knew he'd have had a drink."

"*A* drink, Mrs. Glennan? What a loyal creature you are! But did this entrapment, as I suppose one might try to call it, justify my son in punching a police officer in the nose?"

"It was only a cuff, a push, really. An expression of natural impatience in a high-spirited young gentleman!"

"Shall we ask Mrs. Glennan to argue the case?" Percy Coates smiled sardonically from her to Jamey. "I think she might be more persuasive. More so, anyway, than your mother, who, by the way, thinks she should call upon the judge."

"Mother thinks she's a marquise under the old regime!"

Jamey exclaimed hotly. "That's all I need, to have her think she can bribe the judge by asking him to dinner!"

"Well, you'd better tell her yourself. Mrs. Glennan, will you get my wife on the telephone?"

Mrs. Glennan moved at once to dial the number. Jamey was never permitted to see his mother before leaving the house in the morning, so telephone conferences were frequently required. When his secretary handed him the instrument, he started talking at once.

"You must promise, Mother, to leave Augie's case entirely to me. I have already spoken to Senator Lawson, and he will be in touch with the district attorney of Nassau County. It is probable that we can swap a plea of guilty for a suspended sentence. But the matter is in the last degree delicate. The least movement could swamp the boat."

"Very well, James," the low, sedate voice came back to him. "Of course, while you're in charge, we must respect your judgment. I had thought that the judge might not understand the emotional strain that August has been under since his last terrible divorce. Surely a young man who has had such bad luck in marriage . . ."

"Young, Mother? Augie's forty. He's only three years younger than the judge."

"Is that so? Well, I don't see why they elect such children to the bench."

Jamey sighed as he visualized his mother's pale gray green watery eyes. She would be holding the instrument away from her, as if it were some small importunate animal. A cigarette would be smoking in the ashtray by her bed, its end stained with lipstick. Even now, when she depended absolutely on her younger son, she would not beg.

"Leave it to me, Mother. It will be arranged."

Jamey, hanging up, assured himself that he had no reason not to be proud of his high ethics. He would have tolerated no tampering with justice by a corporate client. But with small people, with lesser folk, one's standards had to be more benign. In the shadowy world of the fixed traffic ticket, the evasion of jury duty, the tax frauds of domestic servants, a certain realism was expected of a gentleman. Galahads in trivia were bores.

"Augie will be all right," he assured his father. "If you can only induce Mother to leave well enough alone."

His father left the room now, as did Mrs. Glennan, and he sighed in restless relief at being alone with his torturing thoughts. He walked back to the window for another look at Trinity; he went to his bookcase to run his finger over the backs of his valuable collection of early English law reports; he closed the door; he crossed and recrossed the room.

It was like being in a boat that was dragging its anchor. He felt no movement, but a constant, uneasy sense of change. First, there had been the incredible scene at the nightclub. Yet the most shocking part of that experience had been to find that he was not more relieved that he was not committed. There he had been, considering — yes, actually considering — and in a smug, lordly way at that (face it!), offering his hand and heart to a girl who was all the while in the grip of a guilty passion for a married man, and yet he felt no relief at the knowledge that he had just been saved from any further risk of exposing himself. On the contrary, he felt as exposed as if all the world had joined in one loud bray of laughter at his expense! What was the sense of it?

The sense, he could only suppose, was that he had allowed his infatuation to get out of control. He had not thought that it could happen to him. He had perfectly recognized that the emotions aroused in him by his other candidates had been safely subject to his regulation. When he had read in Proust about the power of jealousy, he had rather turned up his nose. Did not such an obsession go with cork-lined rooms, with invalids, with homosexuals? Yet why, if he had not been jealous, should he so hate Herman Fidler?

Because he had wanted to be Herman Fidler! Yes, that was the incredible thing. He, Jamey Coates, a successful man, respected by all, had actually wanted to change places with a third-rate stockbroker, of no past and less future, married to a nagging wife, and *why*? Because Herman had been the object of the abandoned passion of Dolly Chadbourne's paid companion!

Jamey slammed his fist against the radiator, and the pain threw him into a reaction against himself. What did it matter if she was a paid companion? Was hers not a beautiful passion, a throbbing passion, one which irradiated all the grayness of life, which lit up its dark chambers, which burnt and crackled and exploded and made luminous fireworks out of a dreary stockpile of daily duties? Oh, God, supposing it had been *he* who had been the blessed recipient of that burst of feeling, would it not have made anything else, even in his lawyer's life, absurd?

But how could the girl be such a dunce? How could she be so besotted as not to distinguish between Hyperion and a satyr? For he, Jamey, *was* Hyperion, at least in brains and character, compared to a man as negative, as flat, as nerveless, as incompetent as Herman Fidler. How did such a man presume to reach out a lazy hand to take Amy Hunt as his due? Amy Hunt, whom Jamey Coates had wanted for his own wife! And whom Fidler thought only good enough to be his mistress! And when he was tired of her, what would he do but kick her ass out? And good enough for her, too! There were tears now in Jamey's eyes, tears that Mrs. Glennan could not help seeing when she came in with the mail. She turned at once to go, with tactless alacrity. Jamey almost shouted at her.

"I'm going uptown, Mrs. Glennan! I can't be reached. I'll call you later."

Twenty minutes afterward he got out of a taxi beside a four-story red brick house in Bank Street. He climbed the stoop and pushed open the front door to examine the panel of names before the house telephone. He pushed the button beside Herman Fidler's engraved card, which had a lonely grandeur amid the typed and written ones. Almost at once the buzzer sounded.

"Who is it?" came a voice, barely audible.

"It's Jamey Coates, Amy. May I come up?"

She replied with something that he took for an affirmative, and he climbed to the top floor. Amy, in the plain brown suit that he knew so well, stood by an open door. Her face was impassive. Behind her he could make out what appeared to be a studio.

"Herman's not in. I tried to tell you, but you hung up. He won't be back till six. He's sketching by the East River."

"Can't I talk to you?"

"Should you? As Naomi's lawyer?"

"It's still all right for me to talk to you. At least until you get your own lawyer. Herman so far has refused to."

"That's his affair, I suppose."

"Amy, you and I were friends once. At least I thought so. Won't you let me come in? Just for a few minutes?"

She seemed startled by his insistence. "But what's there to gain?"

"Perhaps nothing. But then there's nothing to lose, either. I want to appeal to you."

"You mean to my better nature?"

"You can decide that."

"You're going to ask me to give him up? Like the old father in *Traviata?*" She managed to smile, if rather bleakly.

"You can boo if I miss a note."

She shrugged now and stood aside. "Come in, Jamey. However much a lawyer, I'm sure you're still a gentleman."

"For that much, thanks." He followed her into the apartment. It occupied the back of the house and consisted of a large study with an easel, a couch, a few chairs, a kitchen table, a stove and a door which presumably led to the bedroom. Jamey averted his eyes from the latter to the unfinished canvas on the easel. It was a painting of Brooklyn Bridge. "May I look at it?"

"Of course."

He went over to the little picture and studied it. Like some of the other of Herman's things that he had seen, it was skillfully rendered, exact, uninspired.

"It's charming."

"But has it any 'oomph'?" Amy asked with unexpected detachment. "I'm not really sure that Herman was meant to be an artist. He has the technique, perhaps. Is that enough?"

"I can hardly be the judge of that."

"What will you be the judge of, Jamey?"

He turned now to look at her more carefully. There was nothing in the least Bohemian in her aspect. Her face seemed paler, thinner. It went with the new flatness in her tone.

"Are you happy?"

"Life has its problems. But that is nothing new."

It suddenly seemed to him a terrible thing that she should be unhappy. Yet surely he had come there, dreading to find her redeemed, as it were, by bliss! He could hardly bear to think of the waste. Who was Herman Fidler that he was allowed to blight so many lives?

"Damn Herman!"

"Really, Jamey. Is that what you call wanting to talk to me?"

"Give him up! Give it all up. Go back to Miss Chadbourne. Everything can still be patched up. Naomi will forgive him. Oh, Amy, please! Things can be the way they were before." He actually clasped his hands. "I beg of you, Amy!"

She was staring at him now with an astonishment that bordered on awe. "And what makes you think that I want things to be the way they were? Were they so wonderful for me at Cousin Dolly's?"

"Amy, marry me!"

She gasped. "Jamey, are you out of your mind?"

"I've never been saner or more serious."

"Is there nothing you won't do for a client?"

"It's not that. Don't be cruel. I love you! I was just about to tell you when all this happened."

"Marry *me!*" She shook her head incredulously. "A girl in *my* position? Without any character? What in God's name has gotten into you?"

"Will you think about it?"

For a few moments she stood in silence, her mouth half open. Then her body was shaken by what seemed a sudden sob. She turned her back on him. Several seconds passed. When she turned again to him she was in control of herself. Her tone was firm, almost peremptory. "You've given my ego a great boost. And just when it needed it. I'll never forget that. Never. But you must go now." She walked quickly to the door.

"I'll go if you'll promise to think it over."

She smiled, rather wistfully, he thought. "No, my friend. You're in no danger. What would you think of me if I were to walk out on Herman now?"

"But you don't love him. I feel that!"

"You feel nothing of the sort. Please go now. I'll tell Herman you called. And that's all I shall tell him. The rest will be between us. It will be a charming memory."

"It will be more than that!" Hurrying down the stairs, he did not look back. He didn't want to think or talk or even walk. It was true what she had implied. He was mad! It wasn't happiness. It wasn't even misery. It was madness!

๑ 11 ๑

AMY LEARNED TWO important things in the first two months of her life with Herman. To begin with, she learned that it was perfectly true, as she had read in novels but never for a minute believed, that one could share a bed and bathroom with a man without getting to know him much better. She had always imagined that the extraordinary, the rather terrifying intimacy of the sexual act, had to be accompanied by some degree of intensification in the mutual understanding of those involved. But Herman, after the moderate embarrassment of their first embraces, and when she had learned to be more at ease with him, seemed to take her as much for granted as he probably had his wife. He evidently expected her to know things about himself — his past, his habits, his wants, his needs — as if she had been with him all along, as if, indeed, she were a kind of extension of Naomi. She began to suspect that he simply needed a woman in his life, a mate, and that it did not matter much who that woman was — just so long, of course, as she was not cursed with Naomi's vile temper.

In the second place she learned that love, a great love, an undying passion, was not only *not* what she felt about Herman; it was not even what she wanted to feel. He was too sensible, too matter-of-fact, too ordinary, to put it bluntly, to be the subject of thrilling emotions. He even made that sort of thing seem rather silly. His inebriation on their first night together had liberated him to the point of expressing his desires with some appearance of ardor, but in the days and weeks that followed he had been much more restrained. He never told her that he loved her or asked her if she loved him. He must have been satisfied with her declaration at the nightclub. Amy found herself living with a man who was relaxed, friendly, neat and oddly contented with a brand new life in which he seemed to have cut all ties with his past, his family, his friends and his security.

Yes, that was perhaps going to be her third lesson: that Herman had not only given up much more than she had; he missed it less. She began even to wonder if he missed it at all. How could a man be so unconcerned about his daughters, his wife, his mother? It was extraordinary. Secretly, she found it a bit indecent.

Casual seemed the word best qualified to describe all aspects of their liaison. When not in bed she and Herman might have been college roommates. They did not quarrel; they shared the small tasks of cooking and housekeeping; they went quietly about their respective routines, he sketching and painting, she reading or trying to write. Amy sometimes wondered where her dream of passion had gone and almost blamed herself for losing it. It seemed rather gross to be even as mildly satisfied as she was with Herman's competent but perfunctory amorousness. He made love to her every other night, once, immediately after the light was out. When he had finished he would help her into her nightgown, cover her up, turn over and right away go to sleep.

It was certainly a strange existence. They had had no communication with the Fidlers or Chadbournes since the first few days of stormy telephone calls and recriminations. Even Dolly remained silent. Amy assumed that Naomi would eventually take legal action; she had spotted Jamey's comically obvious detective, but nothing happened. They had moved from John Rappelye's flat to one in Bank Street after a week, and Herman said he had enough money in his savings account to last them a year. Beyond that he simply declined to discuss the future.

At times she felt that she owed it to herself and to the gods of love to put a little more glamor into their adultery. She suggested that he use her as a model, and she posed in the nude. It did not seem to make much difference in their relationship, but at least he looked at her. One morning, as he was sketching her lower back and buttocks, they had a conversation that was almost intimate. Perhaps it was because she was facing away from him.

"If Cousin Dolly could see me now!" she exclaimed.

"You think she'd be shocked? But she knows that artists use models. Under the circumstances she would think it quite natural."

"You don't know her the way I do. She has no idea what is natural and what is unnatural. I'm beginning to wonder if she knows anything."

"Poor Aunt Dolly! You're hard on her."

"No. Because only a few weeks ago I was in the same boat." She heard his chuckle. "I wonder if that's a compliment."

"It's a simple statement of fact. I didn't know anything."

"And now you've learned? What?"

"Well, perhaps I've learned there isn't anything to know!"

His laugh was positively cheerful. "Amy, you're wonderful!"

She turned around to face him in exasperation. "Can't you ever be serious? What are you going to do with your life? Are you really so sure that you can be a professional artist?"

Herman's face at once assumed the stubborn look that she had seen him adopt when Naomi badgered him. Good God, had it come to that already?

"I've told you the plans I have," he said in a quiet, deliberate tone. "Such as they are. I'm not holding anything back. I'm going to stay right here in Bank Street for a year. I'm going to sketch and paint. I should be happy if you stayed with me. That is all. Absolutely all. If it doesn't suit you, you must make your own plans."

"But what will you do when the year is up? When your money's run out?"

"I haven't the least idea."

"And you don't care?"

"I don't care now. I may care then. I'm through with the future, don't you see? I probably don't have a future. Why should that spoil my present?"

Amy paused to reflect. She did not want to give him the opportunity to think that she was being bitchy because he didn't make more of a fuss over her. She was determined not to be another Naomi. "What about your children?"

"What about them?"

"Won't you have to earn money for them?"

"They have enough already. For all reasonable purposes. Did money make *me* happy? Or Naomi?"

"But won't you have to regulate your life so that they can visit you?"

"Do you mean I ought to marry you?" Herman's voice was very level; there was not the least acrimony in his tone. "I'll consider it. If Naomi ever divorces me. But I don't think either of us should feel in the least pushed or committed. The great thing is to be free. I've been a slave. I know what it's like. And if it's respectability you want, you should be able to do a lot better than me."

"With a ruined reputation?"

"Oh, come now. Don't be old-fashioned. This is 1936. The man who would be put off by one love affair wouldn't be worth marrying. You don't want an antediluvian stuffed shirt like Jamey Coates or Bayard Jones. You want a man."

"I like the one I've got, thank you very much. *If* I've got him."

"And he likes you. And nobody's 'got' anybody else. So why isn't everything all right, just as it is?"

"For the time being?"

"Well, what in God's name have any of us got but the time being?"

"Herman, you're not being fair. It's all very well for you to throw away the future. You've *had* a family, a good job, a social position. You've learned that you don't want those things. You can afford to shrug your shoulders at them. But what about me? I've never had them. How do I know I might not like them?"

"Well, you can still find them."

"How? Who is going to come courting me in a Village studio while I'm living with you?"

"More men than would come to Aunt Dolly's, I'll bet!"

The extraordinary thing about this prediction was that it was fulfilled the very next day. Jamey's remarkable visit and even more remarkable proposal left Amy thoroughly shaken. She was in a daze all that afternoon. When Herman came home, she told him merely that Jamey had called. She did not have to worry about her agitation because he did not notice her moods. He had learned from Naomi what not to look for in a woman.

"What did he want?" he asked.

"I suppose to discuss the terms of a separation."

"Well, he can go to hell! If Naomi wants to divorce me, let her go ahead and do so. She has her grounds. I won't defend the suit. And even she can't expect any more money out of me."

"I wouldn't bet on that."

"How can she get blood from a stone? All I have is five thousand dollars in my savings account. Ma has all the rest of the family dough. Every penny of it. Let her go to her."

"Couldn't Jamey get a judge to order you to go back to work?"

"Wouldn't he just love that! Jamey goes on as if God had appointed him the defender of public morals. He doesn't see that all his hatred of you and me is nothing but envy. He wants my balls, Amy, that's the long and short of it!"

"What makes you so sure he has none of his own?"

"Just look at him! And listen to him!"

But Amy had already done both these things. As she turned

away from Herman now, she thought with a new emotion of Jamey's glittering, damp eyes and the sudden harshness of his usually mellifluous tone. Was it quite inconceivable that Jamey, alone of all of them, might have possessed the quality of which she had daydreamed in the long afternoons at Cousin Dolly's? That passion, like Maeterlinck's bluebird, was to be found where one least expected it? She was suddenly appalled at the prospect of the disillusionment that might be in store for her. It was with relief that she remembered that tonight was the night when Herman "didn't."

The image of Jamey persisted in Amy's mind until he seemed to become an invisible but unwelcome witness to all that went on in the Bank Street studio. And to all that did not go on. For Amy was beginning to find that the time on her hands was growing in weight. Herman concentrated more and more now on his painting. He turned from his river and harbor views to small abstracts and would spend hours before his easel meticulously painting lines and circles in geometrical patterns. Although this kept him in the apartment his absorption made him seem more absent than when he had been roaming the waterside with a sketchbook. Her own writing had come to a dead stop. She had attempted a character sketch of Cousin Dolly, but guilt had blocked her.

"It's good," Herman told her, when she finally let him read the skimpy start.

"Oh, Herman, you know it's terrible!"

"Not at all. You've got the hang of her. Even though you don't say it, the reader knows the old girl drinks."

"But a writer should do something more than expose the foibles of actual people!"

"Should he? A writer's got to make a start, that's the real thing. Start with anything: Aunt Dolly or Naomi or even myself. Don't expect to write *War and Peace* in a few weeks."

She had to concede this was good advice. And she had to concede that he was showing a decent interest in her problem. He was not very much interested, to be sure, but why should he have been? He had his own work. Was it not up to her to develop her own? Ah, but that was it, that was her grudge, that he had led her to a boat and rowed her to a desert island which had nothing on it but fruit bearing *his* kind of fruit! There were moments now when the bleakest days at Cousin Dolly's seemed full of incident in contrast to her present.

She tried to take a correspondingly decent interest in his painting. She made efforts not to be envious of the fact that he so evidently enjoyed it. Was is possible that he had talent? It shocked her to reflect that she had hitherto taken for granted that he had none.

"Why do you never paint people?" she asked him one morning. He was standing back from the easel to study a white canvas crossed in black, like a window.

"I painted you."

"You painted my buttocks."

"Aren't they you?"

"Only a part of me, dear. Only a part."

"A part may be all that a painter needs."

"You still haven't answered my question."

Herman turned to look for a cigarette. "Are you really interested? Because if you are, I have a theory."

"Of course, I'm interested. Your trouble, Herman, is that you assume nobody *is* interested. The world is not entirely made up of Naomis, you know."

"Isn't it? Anyway, here's my theory. The only real artistic influence in my life was religion. When I was a boy, at St. Paul's, I was very religious."

"Why do you call that artistic?"

"Because religion was the only thing that ever touched my aesthetic sense. I never took any interest in art. Impressionism, post-impressionism, cubism, fauvism — they were all blanks to me. The only pictures that excited me were religious pictures."

"Well, what's wrong with that? If you'd never seen anything but Italian primitives, you could still get by. Not to mention the whole Renaissance!"

"As far as the painters are concerned, yes. As far as color and technique are concerned, maybe. Who could ask for greater teachers than Leonardo and Michelangelo? No, my quarrel is only with their subjects."

"But what difference does a subject make?"

"Aren't you begging your own question? Didn't you ask me why I don't paint human beings?"

"But religious paintings are full of human beings!"

"Ah, but what sort of human beings?"

Amy paused to think. "Virgins and Christ Childs. Saints and martyrs. Shepherds. Is that what you mean?"

"Exactly. Biblical subjects. Hebraic subjects. Apostolic subjects. That was all the painters were allowed, except for portraits. Now stop to think, Amy. What would you say was the one quality missing from all those Christian subjects?"

"Missing? How could I possibly tell you that?"

"Then I'll tell you. Magnanimity is missing. Human generosity is missing. There's not a smitch of it in the Bible. All those old prophets and apostles — they were too full of themselves and their angry God to think of their fellow man. Go to any museum. What do you see? Abraham sacrificing his son. Hagar and Ishmael sent to starve in the wilderness. Jehoiada violating a truce to slaughter Athaliah. Peter smitting Ananias for cheating about the collection plate. There's no end to it. Can you imagine a Socrates in the Bible? Or a Regulus?"

Amy stared. She was surprised that he had so thought it out. "But can't those still be great subjects for art?"

"For a believer maybe. But I no longer believe. When I lost my religion, I was left with a gallery of horrors. Adam casting the blame on Eve, and all for nothing! For himself, for his ego! Think of it, Amy. How could I paint such monsters?"

Amy shook her head gravely. "So that's how you saw it. Your whole world. Naomi, the Rappelyes, Miss Bayard. Oh, I begin to see it! I mean, I see what *you* saw. They were mean; they were dead. And there was no God to justify them. But what was I in that world? Why did you pick *me* out?"

"I thought you'd picked me!"

"And how could I blame you for that?" she cried in a sudden anguish of self-reproach. For a moment they looked at each other, startled, and then, with a shrug, he turned back to his easel.

Amy thought a good deal about his theory in the next days. It occurred to her that Herman was simply trying to put back into his abstract canvases some of the color that his sense of the colorlessness in people had stripped from his life. This was evidently wise, but what good was it going to do for her? The very things that had at first most appealed to her in their new existence: the informality, the freedom from pressure, from peoples' demands, began to seem flat, endless, without goal or point. Even their lovemaking, with its careful precautions against conception, had an air of purposelessness. And at the same time Cousin Dolly's more limited world, with all its jabbering old maids and widows, its terror of the smallest social change, its petty rules and fetishes, started to take on a vividness of color, enhanced by its very compactness, like a perfect miniature in a gilded frame. The world of Bank Street struck her now as a liquid spilled out on a plane; it flowed and flowed until it disappeared, whereas the Chadbourne community seemed to borrow life and loudness and even vigor from the very fact of being bottled up, from its own limitations, as it were. At least people *cared* in Cousin Dolly's New York, even if what they cared about was nonsense.

Herman's broad-mindedness, viewed in this new light, appeared as merely tiresome. In throwing overboard his inherited prejudices, he had made too clean a sweep. Taste and discrimination had gone out with the rest. In forming new friendships he looked no further than the neighborhood in Bank Street, to persons met in restaurants or bars. There were evenings when he was perfectly content to drink beer with the plumber who lived down the hall and who liked to talk endlessly on the evils of city sewage disposal. When she protested once that the plumber bored her, Herman was positively prim in his reproach.

"We have all been so acclimatized to artificial talk and artificial values that we imagine we must be bored when some poor guy merely states what's on his mind."

Amy did not agree. She was coming to the realization that in seeking the world of the novels in which she had so long reveled, she had plunged even more deeply into unreality. Herman found release in a social void. Just as his seascapes, his abstracts, never contained human figures, so his life seemed to need no friends, only a few acquaintances and her own bare body. She had thought of her life at Dolly's as a Victorian novel without a hero or a happy ending. Now she began ruefully to wonder if she might not be a Jane Eyre who had missed her Rochester. But who would have suspected him in a man called Jamey, the constitutional authority at Cousin Dolly's board? Who would have suspected that those mild brown eyes, which had beamed so benignly, so benignantly on Miss Bayard and Mrs. Jones, could be kindled to so hard a glitter?

One morning she received a cryptic note from Cousin Dolly in the mail. After staring at it, she tossed it to Herman who read it aloud in a mildly mocking tone.

"You two have left me in a cage of roaring lions. I have had to do what they told me to do. Unless you come home, Herman's share of the lucre will go to his pelican daughters. Forgive me, child! I could stand only so much."

"What in God's name do you suppose she means?"

Herman shrugged. "Simply that I'm to be disinherited. It's Jamey's idea. He gave me fair warning. I'll grant him that."

"Disinherited? By Cousin Dolly?"

"By her, by Ma. But to hell with them. I don't want their money."

"And does Cousin Dolly mean that if I go back to her, she won't do it?"

"Presumably."

"Shouldn't we give that some thought? I don't want to be the cause of your impoverishment!"

He gave her another of his level stares. That's your problem, dear. Not mine."

Never had she felt more the rejecting quality of his independence. "Aren't you even going to help me decide?"

"How can I? Do you want me to persuade you that a penniless lover is better than a rich employer? I can't, Amy. I don't even want to. You have implied several times that in suggesting our present arrangement, I took an unfair advantage of you. Very well. I can only stand aside when it's a question of its dissolution."

"Oh, Herman! If you would only say 'I love you!' If you would only say 'Please, darling, stay!' "

"Is that what you really want, Amy?"

It seemed to her, in that bleak moment, that she had left all of love, all of romance, behind in Cousin Dolly's apartment. "I don't know what I really want," was all she could honestly say.

✕ *12* ✕

DOLLY CHADBOURNE WAS unpleasantly surprised at the depth and permanence of the hole in her life made by Amy's abrupt departure. She had not realized the extent of her own dependence on the art of Amy's listening. Indeed, she would have said, had anyone asked her earlier, that Amy left something to be desired as an audience, that she was too guarded with her sympathy, too critical of small things, too afraid of seeming to admire. What Dolly did not fully appreciate, until her younger cousin had gone, was that Amy's great quality as a listener was precisely that she knew how to listen. Never once that Dolly could now remember had she had to repeat herself. The quiet, sober girl, who had sat for so many and such long hours with her, had taken in her every anecdote as completely as a recording machine. Too late, Dolly recognized what she had lost.

"If you opened the top of that girl's head," she moaned to her maid Nellie, "you would find the whole life of Dolly Chadbourne. No one has ever known me like that!"

And Nellie, to make matters worse, showed by her silence that she thoroughly agreed. It began to seem to Dolly, in the dreary weeks that followed, that the fun of concerts, of operas, even of reading, had become the discussion of these things with Amy. Was it possible that the girl should have obtained such a hold on her in a year's time? She even wondered if it might be possible to hire Amy as a companion on a daytime basis, while Herman was painting. She murmured something of this idea to Miss Bayard when the latter called to suggest the name of a companion to a recently deceased Bayard as a possible substitute. Miss Bayard's eyes widened to an incredulous stare.

"You don't mean you'd have that . . . excuse me, I shan't say it . . . that *creature,* under your roof again!"

"I don't consider myself the guardian of other people's morals, Caroline."

"But this would be more than that! You would be publicly supporting the cause of a fallen woman against your own niece-in-law. Dolly Chadbourne, I can't believe that even you would dare to throw down your gauntlet in that way against decent society!"

Dolly stared with a frozen detachment at the craggy features of her friend. Caroline Bayard might have been an idol in a Mayan temple; her big, bug eyes, her square chin, her short, rebellious hair, carved in malachite and viewed in a dimly lit temple, might have terrified the sacrificial victim into a trance which would have made his death less terrifying. But *was* Caroline that much of an anachronism? Were not such superstitions still rampant, if half concealed: the making of fetishes, the collecting of bones, the mumblings of toothless hags in the doorways of dark alleys, echoes of some ancient voodoo to drums? Dolly shuddered at the vision of Caroline, robed in white, waiting for her at the top of a pyramid with an obsidian knife.

"But there's such a thing as casting people out," she murmured, "when there might be a chance of redeeming them."

"Your nephew and that woman have cast themselves out. Were you going to make it a condition that she leave him before she re-enters your employ?"

Dolly had a sudden memory of herself and Roz walking with their mother down Fifth Avenue after a Sunday service at the Fifth Avenue Presbyterian Church and hearing the lovely, musical voice of their Aunt Sylvia Chadbourne crying: "Why, girls, girls, you look too lovely!" And Dolly had been about to rush forward to be clasped in the arms of this absurdly, this almost childishly youthful aunt, when she had felt the iron check of the maternal grip.

"Look the other way!" her mother had hissed fiercely, jerking both daughters back, and they had swept by Aunt Sylvia with a crudely executed "cut direct." It had been Dolly's and Roz's first hint of the marital misconduct which had brought down on poor, lovely, half-crazy Aunt Sylvia's head the enthusiastic wrath of a clan united only in hate. But Dolly distinctly remembered thinking, despite her distress at her aunt's pained and puzzled look, that if divisions had to be made, it was better to be with those who delivered, rather than with those who received, that glacial affront.

"I suppose I should make some such condition," she said

miserably. "I haven't really thought it out yet. The point is to keep both sides talking. That is what Jamey Coates says."

"Oh, we've heard about that young man, too. He's apparently dragging his legal heels. What on earth has that drab little Hunt woman got to make you all act so irresponsibly?"

"Your own family is not exempt, Caroline. You've known divorce, too."

"If you're referring to my poor sister, indeed we have. But her wretched spouse's name is never mentioned. Bayard was not even allowed to see his father after the divorce."

"I've never really understood why, when we get so little out of some family ties, we should take such violent pains to preserve them."

"The family, Dolly, is simply the sole basis of society!"

Roz Fidler was less pompous than Caroline, but even graver, when she dined with Dolly that night.

"Herman is going straight to the dogs," she announced in her brisk, no-nonsense tone. "I never saw anything like it. He has no remorse, no compunction, and even worse, no plans. He seems perfectly contented to go on with his silly painting until his last nickel has run out. After that, what? I suppose he'll go on relief."

"Have you seen him?"

"Once. I waited in a grocery store in Bank Street until I saw *her* go out. Fine occupation for a lady of my years! But I knew I'd get nowhere with her. Then I went upstairs and knocked, and Herman let me in. He didn't bat an eye. Cool as a cucumber. 'Hi, Ma! Have you come to see my etchings?' Well, I went in. Of course, they live like pigs. I told him straight off that if he didn't go back to Naomi, he'd never see a cent of my money. That it would all go to his daughters."

"Did he believe you?"

"I think so. But he didn't care. He didn't give a damn, Dolly! The thing that made me realize how bad things were was that I couldn't get him mad. He simply grinned at me. When I left, I'd gotten nowhere at all. But I *have* changed my will, and that brings me to the point. I want you to change yours."

"Mine!"

"Yes. I believe that he and Amy are counting on you. They probably figure that if they can't get something out of you while you're alive, they can make do until you die. I want you to exercise your power over Mother's trust so the principal skips Herman and goes straight to his daughters. You can do it, just as I did. Jamey Coates is very clear about that."

"But, Roz, what good will it do to starve the poor boy?"

"It will give me something to hold over his head. Once I can show him copies of my will *and* of yours, indisputable copies from Jamey's office, it may bring him to his senses. And if it doesn't, tant pis! I've done all I can for that boy. I believe that after a certain point one must move one's responsibilities down the line. Herman chooses to abandon a wife who's a neurotic and who comes from a neurotic family. He says that a man has only one life to lead and that he must lead it as it suits him. Very well. *I* have only one life, and it suits *me* to lead it for the advantage of his desperate wife and children. I think it more than likely that Naomi and her mother will go through every cent they have. *I* choose to take care of my granddaughters, thank you very much! And I appeal to you, Dolly, to help me."

"But suppose Naomi and Herman were to be divorced. Suppose he were to marry Amy . . ."

"I don't care. That's their lookout. Of course, you needn't

make any commitment to me. I know I can trust you. Remember that Mother would have expected the same thing of you. Jamey will call on you tomorrow. See him when he comes, that's all I ask. *Listen* to him!"

Jamey came in the morning, as Roz had said he would, with a codicil duly prepared, substituting Herman's daughters for Herman "as remaindermen of the trust under the will of Mildred Chadbourne for her daughter Dorothy."

"You seem pretty eager," she muttered with a grunt as she surveyed the brief, lethal instrument.

"Your sister told me you wanted it this way. Was she wrong?" Jamey seemed to be in a snappish mood, unusual for him.

"Well . . . no. Not exactly."

"If she was, just tear it up."

Dolly looked at him half resentfully. "Aren't you going to persuade me?"

"Why should I?"

It was not like Jamey to seem so uninvolved. Dolly had always known that he and Herman detested each other. "Of course, you're Naomi's lawyer."

"You know I am."

"And presumably you'd like to see Herman punished, wouldn't you?"

"I have nothing to do with that."

"But you know about my sister's scheme to force Herman back to his wife?"

"She has told me of it, yes."

"Do you think it will work?"

"I doubt it."

"Do you have any better ideas?"

"Yes!" Dolly started at the sudden bark of his answer. Now she noted that his eyes were actually glistening. "I *do* have a

better idea. Ask Amy to come back to you. Ask her to give him
up. Tell her what you and Mrs. Fidler have done. Tell her that
it's up to *her* to save Herman from financial ruin!"

"Oh, I see. Put the heat on her, not him."

"That's right! Herman, in his present mood, would simply
laugh at you. But Amy will not want to bring ruin on the man
she loves."

"I suppose I'll have to think it over. In the meantime, can't
we skip the codicil?"

"No, you'd better sign it now, Miss Chadbourne. Bait the
hook, by all means. It's much stronger to say 'I'll tear it up if
you come back' than 'I'll sign it if you don't.' "

"You've thought it all out!"

"Isn't that my job?"

"But you seem to take such a personal interest in it."

"I want to help Naomi. She's my friend as well as my client."

"Naomi." Dolly shrugged skeptically. "I can't imagine anyone caring that much about Naomi. But if I must sign, I suppose
I must sign. Where do I do it?"

"Wait. We need a second witness. One of my younger
partners, Fred Stiles, is meeting me here at six. I think I
heard the doorbell."

When Mr. Stiles came in, Dolly, as usual, indulged her
compulsion to play the clown and show her familiarity with and
contempt for legal formulas. Raising her right hand, she intoned
solemnly:

"I, Dorothy Chadbourne, being of sound mind and testa-
mentary capacity, do hereby affirm, despose, declare, assert, aver,
allege, propound and state, that this document or indenture or
paper-writing or instrument is, be and ever shall be a codicil to
my last will and testament. There! Will that do, boys?"

And she signed her name with a flourish. Jamey and Mr.

Stiles signed after her. After they had gone, she wrote her brief note to Amy and gave it to Nellie to mail. If Amy's and Herman's had been a real passion, she tried to console herself, she might have acted differently. If they had gone to Venice and written her beautiful letters, she might have been able to face her sister and Caroline Bayard. But how could one make a stand of any dignity in defense of a pair who occupied a room in a third-floor walkup in Bank Street and shopped together in the A & P for Kotex and toilet paper? Roz's chauffeur had seen them!

Amy did not answer the note. She simply appeared, suitcase in hand, on a late afternoon two days later. Nellie greeted her with a cry of joy and burst into the living room with the news. Dolly looked up rather apprehensively at the silent figure in the doorway.

"So you've come back," she said gruffly. "Do you know the terms? You're not to see him again. If he comes here, you'll go to your room."

Amy waited silently until Nellie had gone. "I agree to that."

An awkward silence ensued.

"Herman was willing to let you go?"

"Oh, Herman took it in his stride."

"He didn't make a scene?"

"Herman never makes scenes."

"You call that passion?" Dolly sniffed. "Is there no red blood in your generation?"

"I never said it was passion. I'm sure your friends and relations have given it a very different name. Let me go to my room now and unpack, Cousin Dolly. I'll be in to mix your drink at six."

Dolly, alone again, wondered uneasily if this self-contained creature had not already become a stranger. Might she not even be an intruder, bringing an alien wind into the temple of beauty? For if the artists who had executed Dolly's etchings and watercolors, if the composers who had written the operas and symphonies on her records, if the poets and novelists whose works filled her shelves, had enjoyed lurid sex lives, at least their publications had been the distillation of what was finest in their passions. Surrounding Dolly, these art works actually protected her from the intrusion of the purely physical. What came horridly now to her mind, in connection with Amy, was the passage in *Cymbeline* where Posthumous imagines Iachimo's success with his wife:

> *This yellow Iachimo in an hour, was't not?*
> *Or less; at first? Perchance he spoke not, but*
> *Like a full-acorn'd boar, a German one,*
> *Cried "O!" and mounted.*

That was the kind of bone on which Dolly sometimes broke an unsuspecting tooth in the feast of literature. Music, of course, was safe, and even pictures, for one could tell at a glance which ones offended, but a library was a stable of Trojan horses. And now Amy, once so discreet, so suitable, threatened to bring the acorned boar into the very center of Dolly's treasures! Ugh! She wondered if she could not hear already the grunts of bestial copulation.

Promptly at six Amy returned. Silently she mixed two cocktails and brought them over to Dolly's table. Dolly noted that Amy had brought one for herself. In former days she had not done so without asking leave.

"Is Herman painting?" she asked.

"Oh, all the time."

"What sort of things does he do?"

"Abstracts. Or designs. You might call them exercises in color."

"Has he a real talent, do you think?"

"I don't know. I can't judge."

"He used to do some rather pretty things. But I wonder if it's a gift to support a career."

"Cousin Dolly, do you mind if we don't talk about him? I think it might be better to close our minds to the whole unfortunate incident."

Dolly was not pleased by this. She had no desire to hear of Amy's intimate relations, but she had looked forward to discussing some of the more general aspects of the affair. What fun would it be to be closeted day after day with a girl whose personal disappointment had been encased in so prickly a defensiveness?

"Well, of course, if you don't want to talk about it, we won't. But you might remember that Herman happens to be my only nephew."

"And I do remember it. Which brings me to the one thing about him that I *should* like to discuss. Have you changed your will back? Have you canceled your disinheritance of him?"

Dolly stared, incredulous, at such boldness. "I think that's my affair, young lady. If you don't mind!"

"But I do mind. It was our bargain."

"I think you can trust me to do the right thing!"

"Will you call Jamey in the morning?"

"I shall do as I see fit!"

Amy's expression suddenly changed. The impassivity vanished from her features to be replaced by a look that was actually pleading. "Please, Cousin Dolly! The only sense that my life can still make is that I shouldn't have hurt Herman. Can't you see that? Can't you do that for me? I mean for him?"

Dolly did not answer, but she relished, anyway, the more vibrant note in Amy's tone. Whatever the tone of life that she had tried to establish in East 80th Street, it had nothing to do with the dull, the flat. If Amy and Herman had failed in contrast to Everett Chadbourne and the great Aldini, at least they could moan!

꧁ *13* ꧂

WHEN JAMEY LEARNED that his scheme had actually worked and that Amy had left Herman Fidler and returned to Dolly's apartment where, to the consternation of the Chadbourne relatives, she appeared to have been reinstated in her former duties, his state of mind was severely agitated. On the one hand he yearned to resume his habit of calling at Dolly's and to fuse the present with the past, smoothing over and obliterating the unhappy incident in the Village. On the other, he hankered to show Amy, by a disdainful absence, his contempt for her taste in lovers and the fact that he was fully aware that she had only done what she had done to preserve Herman's inheritance. But was this latter true? Had there not been a hint of disillusionment in the troubled stare with which she had faced him in the wretched room in Bank Street? And if this were so, was he not a fool not to forgive and forget?

Forgive? Forgive the public parade of her adultery, her contempt for everything that his world stood for? What was he thinking of? *Marrying* her? Marrying Herman Fidler's leavings? What would people say? Did he care? *Why* should he care? As he turned the idea feverently over in his mind, it fascinated him, pulled him ineluctably toward exotic images and salacious concepts. It was wild, heart thrilling, to imagine what Amy's gratitude might be, scooped up out of her sordid den of vice and placed beside him on a kind of throne of passion, ravished, adored, forgiven, cherished. Did he really want anything else as much anymore? Suppose, for example, for a feverish example, he had to choose between a night with Amy, a night of nakedness on a moonlit beach, and an appointment to the appellate division? Suppose . . .

One morning in his office, when he was still violently debating such questions, his father walked in.

"I understand Augie's case has been transferred to another judge. A woman."

"That's right. Dorothy Coxe."

"And what do you know of this Portia?"

"Very little. Except her reputation is good. She's supposed to be highly competent."

"Does the state senator to whom you spoke know of the change?"

"Lawson. I presume so. Why?"

"Because, my dear James, I have been doing your work for you. I learn that Judge Coxe has a reputation for extreme puritanism. It is bad enough for a man with Augie's playboy reputation to come before such a woman at all. It is a good deal worse if he comes before her under the shadow of a deal."

Jamey insisted that it had all been worked out with the district attorney of Nassau County, but he felt nonetheless an ugly little chill in the pit of his stomach. When his father had left, he tried to persuade himself that everything had been done that could be done, but it was futile. His mind, in a few moments' time, had become a long gray parade ground at dawn, shaking to the tread of marching feet and the gravelly shout, repeated from a thousand throats: "He's muffed it! Coates has muffed it!" He jumped up; he had to get out. He left his office and hurried down to Broadway to walk around the block. He reasoned desperately with himself, but his reasoning fell to pieces.

Without lunch, but after two shots of whiskey, he took the firm's limousine to pick up Augie to drive to court in Mineola. He was sure that he looked more like the defendant than did his cheerful client and brother, Augie, who had still the figure of a college athlete, betrayed only by the pockets under his merry dark eyes and the flicker of gray in his thick, shining black hair, the possible effects of dissipation.

"Why do you look so beat up?"

Jamey glanced to be sure that the window between them and the chauffeur was up. "I'm always nervous before going to court."

"You? I don't believe it. Anyway, I thought it was all fixed."

"Let us pray."

Augie gave him an affectionate cuff on the shoulder. "What's eating you, kid?"

"I just hope I've done the job for you I should have done."

"Of course, you have! But you're not fooling me. There's something on your mind."

"What?"

"A certain chick."

"Augie!" Jamey was so startled that for a moment he forgot his anxiety. "What on earth gave you that idea?"

"That old secretary of yours, Mrs. Glennan. The one who's so gone on you."

"You think I've got a thing about Mrs. Glennan!"

Augie laughed crudely. "I guess you're not reduced to that yet. But she's madly jealous. She told Dad you'd lost your head over Amy Hunt. She thinks you ought to be committed!"

"Mrs. Glennan told Dad that? I'll fire her tomorrow!"

"You'll be firing the best secretary anyone ever had then. Seriously, Jamey, she has your best interests at heart. She thinks you're going to ruin yourself over that girl. She went in tears to Dad. But she wasn't telling him anything he hadn't already suspected."

Jamey's mind reeled. "Dad? Suspected me? About Amy?"

"We all have, kid. Do you think we haven't heard about those dutiful visits to old Dolly? Getting her to sign papers she'd signed the day before? Telling her she'd used blue ink instead of black?"

"But Amy Hunt, Augie!"

"Well, what's wrong with Amy Hunt? I hear she's a real cute chick. Brown and tense and smart. A bright little wren. Just the kind for an old bachelor like you. What's getting you? Why wouldn't she be the perfect lawyer's wife?"

"My God, Augie, after what she's *done*?"

"You mean because she went off on a toot with Herman Fidler? So what? That's a reflection on her taste, not her morals. She's left him, hasn't she? She went back to that old lesbian, Dolly, didn't she?"

"You can't call Miss Chadbourne that!"

"Can't I? You've got to admit she looks like one. Anyway, the little Hunt certainly isn't. Why shouldn't she have a fling, poor creature? John Rappelye says old Dolly guarded her like a dragon. I bet she'd have gone off with *you* if you'd asked her."

"You think it's all right for a girl to commit adultery..." Jamey almost choked. "Just like *that?*"

"Well, what have you been up to on those dirty Paris trips of yours?"

"Not adultery, Augie!"

"How do you know it hasn't been adultery? What do you know about those girls?"

"Very little, I admit. But I'm a man. A nice girl is supposed to behave herself."

"Who decreed that? Do the girls we know? What about Naomi Fidler? I had her, before she was married. In the boathouse at the Harcourts' place in Dark Harbor during Alison's coming-out party."

"Augie! You didn't!"

"I did indeed. Would I lie about those things? To *you?*"

"All right, then, you did. But I don't like Naomi. I never did. It wouldn't surprise me in the least if she was unfaithful to Herman..."

"Your sacred Naomi!"

"But what did you just tell me?"

"Look, little brother. The fact that a girl gave *me* the green light doesn't mean she'll give it to everybody."

"Oh, of course, you're irresistible, I know."

"That's better. I like it when you snap. It's more like the old Jamey. I'd like to meet little Amy."

"But, Augie, she's a *whore!*"

"They all are, kid, they all are. Till they meet the guy they're going to stick with."

"Stick with? How could I ever think Amy would stick with me? How could I ever trust her?"

"I'll tell you that, fella. I'll tell you that after I get to know her. All I'm saying is that you mustn't judge her by one episode. Even if that episode is a stick like Herman Fidler."

Jamey grasped his brother's hand. "It's extraordinary our talking about Amy with what's hanging over you."

An hour later they stood up in the near-empty, paneled courtroom in Mineola before a pleasant, round-faced, gray-haired lady in a black robe.

"How plead you?" the clerk demanded.

"Guilty."

The judge's face at once darkened. "Are you ready then for sentencing, counsel?" she asked sharply.

"Ready, your honor," Jamey replied with misgiving. "I believe that your honor is familiar with the facts of the case. And with all the ameliorating circumstances."

The judge stared at him reprovingly. "I am aware that there have been discussions between counsel and the district attorney," she replied severely. "I am also aware that some very prominent persons have shown an interest in the disposition of the case." She paused to frown and shake her head. "But I cannot be moved by such considerations. The defendant has enjoyed every privilege in his life that our great nation can offer. His obligation to respect our laws and law enforcement officers is all the greater. Less than any other man should he be guilty of driving while intoxicated, resisting arrest and striking a policeman. What is the use of education and wealth if that is all he can show for it? I feel it my sad duty to make an example of him. I sentence him to three months in prison!"

Jamey at first could find no words. Then he managed, in a stuttering voice, to fix bail pending an appeal directed to the severity of the sentence. Augie had almost to support him out of the courtroom to the limousine.

his sister. Fortunately for you and him — fortunately for the family — I have higher standards."

"I think, Mother, that you should adapt your language to the facts. Amy Hunt may have deserved your scorn while she was cohabiting with Herman Fidler. But she has left him. She has gone back to Miss Chadbourne."

"And at whose suggestion? Do you think the whole world is your dupe, James? Do you think that I don't know that your mania for that woman has caused you to lose not only Augie's case but Naomi's?"

"Naomi's!"

"Certainly. It was your obvious duty to bring an action of divorce against Fidler on the grounds of adultery. Instead of which, fearing to brand Miss Hunt publicly with the name that all the world knows to be hers, you induced her to assume a virtue if she had it not. You persuaded her to hide behind the skirts of that old bawd, Dolly Chadbourne."

"But Naomi can still sue!"

"Is it possible that you haven't heard?"

"What?"

"My poor James, I see you haven't. As soon as Naomi learned that the concubine had departed, she threw her pride to the winds and rushed down to the Village. She spent the night with her husband in his studio, but she was still unable to persuade him to accompany her when she went home the next day. Of course, the only reason that the cad let her stay was that he wanted to prove condonation. So there goes her case!"

"She still has the ground of abandonment."

"But that's not as good, is it?"

"Perhaps not quite."

"You admit it's not as good? Well, that's something. And

do you admit that sending a state senator of less than unimpeachable morals to talk to a judge who has just been elected on a reform ticket was also not such a good idea?"

"I didn't know about Judge Coxe's morals."

"But *shouldn't* you have known? Wouldn't you have known had you not been so preoccupied with Herman Fidler's mistress?"

"Mother, you're being most unreasonable. I . . ."

"It is very dangerous for August to have you preoccupied, James. For then your natural antagonism and jealousy come out."

"You can't think I *wanted* Augie to go to jail!"

"The subconscious does strange things. And in that respect you had better watch your step where the concubine is involved."

"Mother, I wish you would not refer to Amy that way. It's not that I care what your moral judgment of her is. I know only too well that a woman who has done what she has done merits by your standards the epithet that you have used. But I hate hearing it from your lips. It doesn't become you. It is grotesque."

"You had better get used to it if you plan to have many further discussions of that female with me. Don't you know what it is that attracts you to her?"

"What?"

"Her very degradation! You have a complex that women do not care for you. It is perfectly apparent to all but yourself. Any number of women have tried to marry you, and you have barely noticed them. You think only a woman whom you raise up from the sewer will love you. But beware! She is just the one who won't! Never count on gratitude, my boy. We are more apt to hate those who do us favors."

"Mother, I see no point in going on with this."

"There *is* not point in going on with it!"

Jamey was able to control himself only by recalling Augie's admonition: that he go immediately to Amy after seeing his mother. But when he arrived at Dolly's, he found her alone in the living room without Amy, and he had to pretend that his call was on her. Dolly was in a grumbling mood. She plunged at once into her own problems.

"I did what you suggested, and Amy is with me again. She's probably hiding in her room, because you're Naomi's lawyer. You know it didn't work, I suppose. Herman has no idea of going back to his wife. And do you think any of the family appreciate what *I* did to bring about a reconciliation? Far from it! Naomi and her mother go on as if I were harboring a criminal. Even Roz takes the attitude that once Herman is safe, I should let her go. And as for Caroline Bayard and her sister, they refuse to have anything further to do with me and are screaming all over town that I'm running a disorderly house. Really and truly, Jamey, you don't know the mess you've got me into!"

"But surely, Miss Chadbourne, you've always prided yourself on your independence. You can weather a little storm like this one. It's bound to blow over."

"I'm getting old, Jamey. That's the long and short of it. Causes are for the young. All I want now is peace and quiet."

And indeed Dolly looked shockingly tired. Her eyes were watery and roved from side to side, and her breathing was heavy. But Jamey could not help thinking of all the years in which he had heard her declaim about the rights of the individual and the tyranny of the mob. And now at the first test . . .

"It isn't as if Amy and Herman had been Nelson and Lady Hamilton," she continued petulantly. "That might have been worth it, and the world well lost. But Bank Street, Jamey! Bank Street with Herman Fidler! Is it worthwhile to give up even Caroline Bayard for *that?*"

Amy appeared suddenly in the doorway wearing a white dress. She had the quiet demeanor of a trained nurse. "I'm sorry, Cousin Dolly. I could hear you from my room. You know what Doctor Jonas said about excitement. It's time for your rest before dinner. Will you excuse us, please, Mr. Coates?"

"You see how everybody orders me around," Dolly grumbled as she rose. Jamey rose too, but he lingered after they had left the room. In a few minutes Amy reappeared, looking for something, a book or paper. She started when she saw him.

"Oh, I'm sorry! I thought you'd gone."

"I stayed for a word with you. I wanted to say how glad I was you were back."

"Nobody else seems to be."

"Give them time."

"It hasn't worked, you know. Herman is still in Bank Street."

"Give *him* time."

Amy's pale mask was suddenly vivid. "Oh, Mr. Coates, can I ask you something?"

"Certainly. So long as you drop the 'Mr. Coates.' "

"I'm sorry, Jamey. I wasn't sure how we stood. But here's the thing. Cousin Dolly promised me that she would tear up that codicil if I came back. You know what I mean?"

"Do I?" Jamey had a sudden giddy sense of darkness and ice. "*Do* I know what you mean?"

"It's about disinheriting Herman. She shouldn't do it, Jamey. She ought to tear up that codicil right away. She's not at all well!"

"You seem very concerned about Herman."

"Why shouldn't I be?"

"May I point out that he's still living apart from his wife?"

"But that had nothing to do with my bargain with Cousin Dolly!"

Jamey sighed in the violence of giving in to his fury. He wetted his lips. "I think you misunderstood her. I think it had everything to do with it. I cannot allow my professional advice to a client to be influenced by your passion for Herman Fidler. It disgusts me. It revolts me! I wonder you're not ashamed to fling it in my face!"

Amy looked him over as if he were a madman. But when she finally spoke, she was the nurse again, controlled, controlling. "You totally misconceive me. My only wish is to put things back as they were. To undo as much damage as can be undone."

But Jamey was reckless. "I don't believe it!" Even in his wrath, however, he lowered his voice so that it would not carry down the corridor. "You're just waiting for her to die so you can go back to your filthy paramour!"

Amy's expression was almost one of awe. "Oh, Jamey, how can you? How can you be so wrong?"

But for answer he simply strode angrily to the front door. She did not follow, and he slammed it behind him.

≈ 14 ≈

ONE MORNING, WHEN Amy went to awaken Dolly, she found the big body of her employer sprawled in a heap by the toilet in the bathroom. Dolly was unconscious but breathing.

She had fallen from a sitting position. Amy rushed to get Nellie, and together they managed to haul the heavy woman to her bed. When the doctor came he pronounced it a massive and near fatal stroke. The apartment would have to be turned into a nursing home until the next one. There was no hope of recovery.

When Mrs. Fidler arrived, she showed all the brisk efficiency which old New York expected of its families in the presence of imminent death. She took Amy into the living room.

"There'll be no further need for you now, Miss Hunt," she said evenly. It had been "Miss Hunt" ever since Bank Street. "We'll have nurses round-the-clock."

"But I want to stay!"

"There'll be great expenses. I doubt we can justify your salary."

"I shan't need a salary. I'll take care of Cousin Dolly for nothing."

Mrs. Fidler's severe look was somewhat softened by this. "Well, I must say, that's handsome of you. But it won't be necessary."

"Oh, please, Mrs. Fidler! Let me look after her. I promise I'll never go out, never leave her. You can get a night nurse if you want, but that's all."

"It's a lot more than you undertook as a companion. It's hard work. Professional work, too."

"But don't you see, wanting to do it must be a part of the qualification? Cousin Dolly doesn't need any special services. Just someone to be near her, to help her. To love her!"

Mrs. Fidler closed her eyes, as if struggling with herself, and then, all of a sudden, reached over to put her hand on Amy's. "Very well, you shall stay. I mustn't let my feelings stand between Dolly and what is best for her. I'm sure she'd want

132

you here if she knew. And of course she never minded the thing with Herman the way I did."

"Oh, Mrs. Fidler, that's all quite over now."

Roz nodded, her lips tightly sealed. "I know that," she said with another effort. "And I know that I've been trying to fool myself into believing that you were solely responsible for what happened. But I can't. Of course Herman took advantage of you. I must learn to give you marks for leaving him."

"I did wrong in going to him. I acted precipitately without knowing myself. I caused great anguish to many persons. What I did may even have been a factor in Cousin Dolly's stroke. The least I can do is stay now and nurse her."

Roz sighed and then stood up, very erect. "I guess we must all forget about ourselves and pull together in this emergency. Thank you, Amy!"

Dolly regained the use of her limbs in a few days, but her mind and speech seemed gone. She was docile, but she had to be watched always, as she took to wandering about the apartment, opening and slamming doors and drawers. Amy would always guide her back to her bed or chair and try endlessly, futilely, to distract her. In the shockingly short time that it takes, she learned to accept her cousin's condition.

She had told Mrs. Fidler that Dolly would need someone to love her. But could she love a shell? And was the specter of Dolly really Dolly? In the long, dull, baffling days which followed, with no visitors, for Mrs. Fidler would allow none, being too proud, as she said, to let her sister be seen in this state, Amy had ample time to reflect on the question of whether she ever had really loved her. Certainly, since her return from Bank Street relations had been strained. Dolly had been cross and querulous and self-pitying, and Amy had deeply resented what she regarded as Dolly's duplicity about the codicil. Indeed, it had become a near obsession with her. It seemed at times the only bar to the restitution of the normalcy that she craved. If only Dolly would rescind it, the pre-Bank Street world might be reconstituted with something like its original quaintness and innocence. Life as it had been now appeared to Amy as a kind of lost paradise.

Another fantasy which began to haunt her was that in that reconstructed world, if it could ever be brought about, she and Jamey could start anew. He might repeat his proposal. Could she build a whole life on his seeming need of her? She thought it not impossible. It was a strange and moving experience to have a man who was so obviously fighting himself desire her so ardently. Like Darcy, in *Pride and Prejudice*. When she watched Dolly pounding aimlessly and horribly at the grand piano, she could only see in the wreck of the big old woman the wreck of her own life. Dolly had had a chance for happiness and rejected it. Amy had had her chance and not even seen it! What was the difference between them? They might as well both be dead.

Jamey dropped in occasionally, in the early morning or late afternoon, to see that things were under control. He spoke little to Amy and only about practical matters. It was clear that formality alone was permitted, after his last explosion, and that simply for Dolly's sake. He examined the mail and took away bills and notices. She dared not engage him in longer conversation, but watching him and listening to him, admiring his conciseness, his efficiency, she could not help contrasting him to Herman. Jamey seemed so in control of the life around him; Herman had eschewed the world and retreated to a seascape. She had been apt in the past to think of love as an emotion felt for a large man, at least one larger than Jamey. He was only her own height. But now she began to wonder if love might not be created by love alone. Certainly Jamey, if no Darcy, not even a Herman, was becoming each day more interesting. What was it? Was it just his large, shiny, brown eyes? Certainly they were part of it. Jamey's eyes seemed to take in everything, coldly, appraisingly, retentively, and yet to suggest at the same time that his clear gaze was also a veil, a screen which concealed all kinds of depths. His skin was very white and clean, with a sort of marble glow, and his features were fine. Indeed, if he only wouldn't have bustled so, if he only would have lost twenty pounds, if he only wouldn't have glared so comically as he ran a nervous left hand through his curly hair, if his voice had been less shrill, he would have been . . . a cupid? At *his* age? She imagined him dead, still, beautiful at last, a charming nude corpse of a boy by Daniel Chester French . . .

"And please don't forget, Miss Hunt, to telephone my secretary when the bill for the fire and theft insurance comes in. It should have been in a month ago, and we have to check it out and see if it's adequate — with all these medical people coming and going."

"I will."

"You mustn't wear yourself out. Be sure to get enough sleep. It may be a long haul." He paused and blushed. "Allow me to say you're doing a great job."

"Thank you."

What more could she say? Even if he were willing again to forgive her affair, as he had been before his last blowup, could she forgive herself? In her own mind it seemed to have contaminated her. Had she loved Herman as she now began to understand love, she might have tried to pardon herself, but to have lived with him as long as she had under so temperate a mutual attraction seemed unredeemably sluttish. That she and Herman, night after night . . . oh, it was repulsive! She would return after each of Jamey's visits to Cousin Dolly's side, frenetically anxious to take care of her, to coddle her, to make up for her own infinite inanity.

As Dolly could not articulate words, it was almost impossible to determine how much comprehension she had retained. She would sit in her big chair for a whole morning emitting at more or less regular intervals a sound which seemed to be the pronoun "who." At times she seemed to be attempting to form a sentence. At others she seemed to be just pointlessly hooting, like an owl. And indeed, with her large staring eyes and the way she wagged her head, she suggested an owl. When Amy put a question to her, asking if she wanted a drink or a pillow or a picture book, she would request her to shake her head or raise her hand if the answer were affirmative, but Dolly would simply stare back at her. Yet Amy often had the distinct impression that Dolly understood the question.

It was spooky. Once, on an impulse, she asked Dolly if there was a Picasso in the room, and Dolly pointed straight to his drawing of a clown over the bookcase. But when Amy asked the same question about Soutine, Dolly pointed to a chair. Had the first episode been a coincidence? Usually Dolly refused to point at all. She would sit at her desk for an hour at a time writing continuously. When Amy examined the scribbles she found them undecipherable. Yet in a curious way they looked like handwriting. They looked as if, with enough trouble, they could be read. At other times Dolly would simply fuss in seeming irritation with the papers on her desk, messing them about and sometimes tearing them up.

It was this last habit which gave Amy her idea about the codicil. She took it out of the drawer where she knew it was kept and held it up before Dolly.

"Don't you think you should destroy this now, Cousin Dolly? You know that you told me you would — if I left Herman and came back to you. And I have, haven't I? I haven't seen him once since, nor shall I, no matter what happens. That's all over. For good. I swear it!" Amy crossed her heart. "Oh, if you only knew how sincerely I meant it! And why should he be penalized for not going back to Naomi? You never liked her. You know you didn't! Don't you want to tear up the codicil, Cousin Dolly? *Don't* you?"

Dolly's stare was blank, curious, faintly shocked. Amy shook the document before her.

"Hoo," Dolly said.

"Look, I'll leave it right there. On the desk. If you feel like tearing it up, you can do so."

Amy left the room. Her heart was beating so violently that she was almost frightened. She went to her room and lay down on her bed. What was she doing but the right thing? And if one did the right thing, what was there to worry about? After twenty minutes she came back to the living room. She glanced at the desk. The codicil was still there, intact. Cousin Dolly was slumped in her chair, her mouth open.

By ten o'clock that night the body had already been removed to a funeral parlor. Jamey, more bustling than ever, seemed to be in every room of the apartment at once and always on the telephone. When he had sent Mrs. Fidler home and the weeping maids to bed, he at last mixed himself a dark whiskey and soda.

"You had best go to bed, too, Amy," he said peremptorily.

"Oh, I'm not tired. Or perhaps I'm so tired it doesn't matter. Anyhow, I doubt that I'll sleep."

"One last thing I should get before I go. The will. I'm the executor, so I'd better take it. I know just where it is. Miss Chadbourne insisted on keeping the original right here, in the apartment. It's in the cabinet in that closet. Do you mind if I get it out now?"

"Why should I? But can't it wait till tomorrow?"

"I'd like to check it tonight. When I get home."

As Amy watched, breathless, he went to the closet by the desk, opened the door and pulled out the top drawer of the steel file cabinet which filled most of the interior. He reached to the very end of the drawer and plucked out a fat document with a red ribbon. He glanced at it briskly, nodded, and then reached again into the compartment. He searched for several minutes through the drawer before he turned to her, faintly but unmistakably tense.

"There was a codicil. You knew about the codicil. Do you know where it is?"

"Yes."

"May I have it?"

She went to the desk and opened one of the small drawers on top, taking out a large envelope. The pieces are in here."

"The pieces?"

"She tore it up."

"When?"

"About a week ago. I don't remember exactly."

"She tore it up! But she was crazy, Amy! How did she get it?"

"I gave it to her."

"Why, in God's name?"

"Because she asked for it."

"Asked for it? She couldn't speak!"

"We communicated, she and I. She was not nearly as gone as people think. I was talking to her about Herman one day — I used to talk to her by the hour, about everything and everyone — when she pointed suddenly to the closet. For a long time I had no idea what she wanted, but she kept pointing, and I kept bringing her papers from the drawers, until I finally hit upon the codicil, and she nodded vigorously."

"So you handed it to her?"

"Yes. Why not? It was her property. I handed it to her, and she tore it into little bits. Quite violently. But she knew what she was doing. She knew she was revoking the codicil."

"You mean *you* knew what she was doing!"

"Of course, I knew."

Jamey's face was livid. "Do you think this will stand up in court?" he almost screamed. "Do you think I didn't know Miss Chadbourne's habit of tearing up papers? Everyone who's been here in the past two months has seen her do it. You, most of all! You simply put that codicil on her desk so that she would tear it up. Unless you did it yourself! Of course! You did it for your paramour! Well, if you think you'll get away with any such transparent fraud, you have another think coming, young lady! Not only will the surrogate admit *my* copy of the codicil to probate, he may very well turn the evidence of what you've done over to the district attorney!"

"What you say is true. Only I didn't do it for my paramour."

Amy, having hardly felt her knees buckle, simply knew that she was sitting now in Cousin Dolly's big chair. She felt very light and eerily comfortable. It was as if some giant hand had suddenly lifted the roof off the living room and all the miasma of a year's talk, solidly compacted in that chamber, were now rising to be lost in the suddenly revealed blue sky.

"Oh, of course, I did it!" she exclaimed with a kind of frenzy.

"I wanted to put things back! I wanted them to be the way they had been. I wanted to obliterate what I'd done with Herman. I would have obliterated myself with it if I could have. But what good would that have done?"

"But you wanted Herman to have the money!"

"Of course, I wanted him to have the money. It was I who had been the cause of his losing it. And then I could have started over. But how silly, one can never start over. That's the point of every tragedy, isn't it? However, I can go to jail. It might be almost as good."

"My God, Amy! Is it possible that you *don't* love Herman?"

"I don't love him at all! I never did. I've simply been an idiot. And now I'm not anymore. It's too late, but I like not being an idiot."

"Amy!" He came over to her now, very tense, his hands shaking, and sat down on the stool by her chair, looking up at her with a wild stare. "You won't have to tell anyone. We'll leave things just as they are. The partner who came with me to witness the codicil is on dozens of wills. He'll never ask what happened to it. He probably won't even know Miss Chadbourne's dead! I'll probate the will and forget all about the codicil. Who cares if Herman gets the money instead of his daughters? You're right — it's better that way. Miss Chadbourne never wanted to cut him off. Her sister talked her into it. And even her sister regrets it now. Oh, I won't have any trouble with *her!*"

Amy looked at him in dazed astonishment. "But suppose somebody *were* to find out?"

"I'll simply say that Miss Chadbourne tore it up. I'll even keep the pieces. Who is to say *when* she tore it up? We found it in an envelope with her will, destroyed."

"But isn't that wrong? I mean for you, Jamey. As a lawyer?"

"Very wrong." He reached up to take her hand. "Think of it, Amy! I'll be committing a crime. For you."

He rose now and pulled her to her feet. When he kissed her, she burst into tears. But then she flung her arms about his neck and clung to him. Even as she felt, with a bursting heart, that everything was going to be all right, that the bluebird was indeed at home, a loud, monstrous, frightening bluebird, beating with its wings against the bric-a-brac, the crowded cabinets of Cousin Dolly's cluttered parlor, threatening with the extraneous gift of undreamed-of happiness to knock the world down, shake the world up, even then she was aware of a little dark suspicion, fixed like a tiny malignant cancer in the very core of her euphoria, that she was buying this strange, this rather remarkable man at a high price.

PART II

JAMEY

❧ 1 ❧

TO ANY STUDENT of American social life Shoal Bay might
have seemed just another affluent Long Island village, like
Westbury or Locust Valley, characterized by Episcopalian com-
muters, country clubs and the Social Register. And, of course,
there was a degree of truth in this. It might have been difficult
to particularize it in 1938, say, to a resident of Tokyo or Singa-
pore. But to Fanny Lane, Shoal Bay was a last surviving outpost
of the New England-born culture of her childhood, a lonely
beacon light on a darkening plain dotted by such symbols of
worldliness as the villages just cited. Shoal Bay was moral; Shoal
Bay was public-spirited; Shoal Bay was good. Its hats were big-
ger; its limousines older; its brides lacier. On Saturday night, at
the Oyster Cove Club, there would be a square dance in which
the generations would mingle until late, yet everyone, or almost
everyone, would still be up for the eleven o'clock service at
Saint Luke's Church the following morning. If the smarter
young folk of Westbury and Locust Valley tended to dub
Shoal Bay as frumpy or dowdy, they nevertheless appeared at
its debutante parties and weddings. For Shoal Bay was never to
be disregarded. Shoal Bay was the summer seat of some of the
city's more important investment bankers and corporation law-

yers. A clever social climber, one aiming at a permanent altitude, would have been well advised to start there. As Fanny herself once put it: "It's usually easier for a newcomer to be dull than to be chic. Once he has put on the protective coloration of Shoal Bay, it's hard to tell him from the rest of us."

This remark was characteristic of Fanny. She had a habit of saying anything she pleased, of mocking anything she wished to mock. It was as if by the absolute conventionality of her own life she had purchased the right to a certain anarchy of spirit. She was a plump, plain, comfortable woman who wore low-heeled shoes and baggy dresses and never had her loose chestnut hair waved. She had a white round face with soft round cheeks, a sharp little beak of a nose and small, agate, piercing eyes. Her abrupt, aggressive pigeon-toed walk, her way of slumping on a sofa after any exertion and exuding breath with a loud "whoof!" her sharp, cackling laugh and the candor of her physical habits, her scratching and rubbing and throat-clearing, seemed at times almost a parody of Shoal Bay femininity, a defiance of all principles of sentiment and romance, a drop of spit aimed at the eye of the deity who had sought to distinguish between the sexes. And yet when she laughed hard enough and long enough at the ridiculousness of the world that she uncovered, when she threw back her head and closed her eyes and relapsed into mirthful silence, an air of sadness would seem to glide over her features, and there would be, at least to the discerning, the sense of a woman revealed, a helpless, a lonely woman, abandoned in a wood, or perhaps chained to a rock to wait for a monster at which she could only laugh.

The outer bay of Shoal Bay, small and snug, cluttered with pleasure craft (sailboats, of course; nobody but old Mr. Barnes owned a "stink pot") was surrounded by small hills on the tops of which sat the cottages of the leading citizens, usually in the shingle style but occasionally more pretentious, or in Shoal Bay parlance "fancy pants," with French or Georgian overtones, occupied only in summer and winter weekends, yet always "home." For it was in Shoal Bay, not New York, that one voted and had one's church. Fanny Lane, since the deaths of her husband and invalid son and the marriages of her four daughters, was one of the few who lived there the year round, and her big red and yellow shingle habitation, crowning the highest hill, was still considered the "dower house" of Coates, Lane & Coates. From her terrace she could peer down on the roofs of two of her sons-in-law, both junior partners in the firm, and on the newly constructed French pavilion of the Jamey Coates'. For when Jamey, the senior partner and Fanny's godson, had made his belated and unexpected marriage (how Fanny had deplored the failure of her oldest girl to take him!) he had largely made up for the oddness of his choice by bringing his bride for the summer to Shoal Bay and not to the worldly Southampton of his parents. Oh, he had rightly counted on his godmother! No tongue would wag against Amy in *her* hearing.

It was thus with a particular gratification that Fanny entertained Iris Coates on her terrace on a late June Sunday afternoon. The latter had motored up from Southampton to spend the day with her son and daughter-in-law and had discovered that a necessary part of even so limited a visit had to include croquet at Fanny Lane's. For forty years these two wives of law partners had eyed each other askance. Fanny had always suspected that Iris rather condescended to Coates, Lane & Coates, and it irritated her to consider in return that Iris must have viewed her own pride and joy in the firm as smacking of the parochial, the middle class. But Fanny could remind herself — and often did

— that Percy Coates was little more than the superannuated, if still ornamental, link between a brilliant dead father and a more brilliant living son. She and Iris now sat on wicker chairs watching the croquet match between Jamey and Fred Stiles and their wives.

"Oh, look, Jamey is going to whack Naomi's ball off the lawn!" Fanny cried. "Now we're in for it. She's such a rotten sport!"

"You don't think marriage to Mr. Stiles may have sweetened her?" Iris queried, her pinched smile supplying her own rebuttal. "Ah, now, there! Do you see? My boy, as usual, is acting the diplomat."

Jamey, with a stroke that fooled none but Naomi Stiles, contrived to knock her ball only a few feet off. Even so, Naomi's sharp exclamation of disgust carried to the terrace.

"I suppose you made that match, Fanny," Iris observed. "Hasn't Mr. Stiles always been your protégé?"

"Well, he was darling to my poor Gordon. That I can never forget. I don't know what you mean by 'protégé,' but I admit I have always taken an interest in the bachelors of the firm. Had he been a younger man, I shouldn't have dreamed of inviting him here so often with a divorcée. But Fred was thirty-six, and I was beginning to despair of him. And poor Naomi's divorce was no fault of her own, as you well know."

Iris shrugged, indifferent to the pointed reference. "She has money, doesn't she? And what they call social position? Your Mr. Stiles, I suppose, needed both."

Fanny bristled. Really, Iris was getting almost common in her old age. Nobody talked about "social position" in Shoal Bay. "Fred Stiles is one of the best trial lawyers in the firm," she retorted coolly. "He doesn't need Naomi's money. And even you must admit he *looks* like a gentleman."

Both women turned now to contemplate the subject of this speculation. Stiles was a tall, dark, tired-looking man, with thick short black hair, a strong, sharp nose, large, suspicious eyes too close together and a high forehead. Obviously bored with the game, he was still not the type that could lose easily.

"Why did he marry her then?" Iris pursued. "He's not so old as to be desperate."

"Would it never occur to you that he might be in love?"

"That's what social climbers call it to cover their calculation. Or rather their miscalculation." Iris, her eyes still on Stiles, was now amusing herself. "For that's what it is, you know. His judgment was off. And I wonder if he doesn't see it already. Oh, these poor, brilliant, insecure, self-made men! They have such terrible astigmatism. To a man like Stiles, Naomi probably seemed socially the cream of the cream. She took him in because she takes herself in. And now he finds that his princess is only one of many, and that almost any of the others would have had a better temper."

"Iris, you're such a cynic."

"No more than you are, Fanny, deep down. I simply don't coat it over with Shoal Bay sentimentality. I like my worldliness worldly, thank you. See the way Mr. Stiles is looking at Jamey right now. *Look* at him! Don't you sense the resentment lurking there? Poor man, the world is so unfair. Jamey, the son and grandson of partners, should, in Mr. Stiles' books, be a boob, or at least an incompetent. And yet he's head of the firm, on his own merits, too, while Mr. Stiles, the self-made man, must humbly follow. Oh, it's bitter tea, Fanny!"

"I don't see how you've made all that out," Fanny grumbled. She disliked the idea that Iris, so indifferent to the firm, might have divined something which had escaped her own notice. "Unless, of course, Jamey's been talking out of school."

"Jamey hasn't told me a thing. He never does. I've made it all out for myself. Sitting next to Mr. Stiles at lunch today. If there's one thing I know how to parse, it's the mind of an arriviste. They always make the mistake of assuming that society has standards. They can never get it into their heads that we make rules only to break them. Mr. Stiles, for example, assumes that my daughter-in-law, Amy — because she comes from a rather shabby branch of the Chadbourne family and because of that sordid episode with Herman Fidler — must be somehow déclassé. He can't take in that we only hold a woman's past against her when we dislike her anyway."

"He told *you* that Amy was déclassé?"

"No, dear, he's not so stupid. But I could tell by what he didn't say. A man like that, who does everything according to a plan, who never forgets a detail, cannot fathom how empty-headed, how giddy, society really is. Why, we forget everything. We haven't the courage of our own prejudices. Look at Naomi and Amy, so friendly now. Who would think that . . . ?"

"*I* don't forget everything, Iris."

"Oh, my dear, you're an elephant. You're from Boston. Enough said! Poor Amy would have been banned from Shoal Bay had she tried it under any auspices but yours! She'd have had to cross the island to my old Sodom and Gomorrah."

Fanny guessed that this was as close as Iris would ever come to a compliment, so she smiled. Too tactful herself to have brought up directly the subject of Amy's past, she was delighted, now that Iris herself had done so, to go into it.

"I hope you won't take it amiss if I say that we all think you've done a splendid job of your relationship with Amy. We know that it can't have been easy — starting as it did."

"On the contrary, that's just what made it easy. The only

direction that relationship could go was up. I'm a realist, Fanny. I made no bones of the fact that I detested Jamey's marriage, but when I saw that I was stuck with it, I made the best of a bad situation. And, of course, once Amy realized she did not have to *pretend* to like me, or I her, the path was smoothed. Now we get on very well."

"But I'd hate not to *love* my in-laws."

"You have very high family standards. So high that you'd invent a relationship if it didn't exist."

But Fanny had no intention of allowing the carefully woven tapestry of her Shoal Bay domesticity to be picked apart by those long nails. She reflected, with a little snort, that Amy had probably forgiven her mother-in-law all, simply for not being a possessive parent. Certainly, Iris seemed willing to let Amy have Jamey all to herself.

"You're lucky to have had sons, Iris." Then Fanny paused, wondering if Jamey's success was great enough to defend her remark from the charge of irony at Augie's expense. She hurried on: "Of course, I adore my girls, and I'm very proud of their husbands, but it's not what I might have felt had my Gordon lived and been a great lawyer like Jamey."

"Never undervalue the hand you were dealt, Fanny. Daughters can be trumps. You've done very well, and you know it. You and Thomas between you might have been too much for a grown-up son."

"What do you mean?"

"The pressure! Think of it. Gordon might have ended as an interior decorator. It's the old American story."

"Iris Coates, you don't mean . . . !"

"I don't mean anything, Fanny. Look. Here come the players. Who won?"

"The boys, of course," Naomi replied, tossing her mallet carelessly into the box. "They were too mean to give us a handicap."

Jamey instantly moved to arrange the mallets and correct her carelessness. "You didn't need one, Naomi. It was just that Amy may have been a bit tired. Are you all right, my dear?" He was moving solicitously toward his wife when his mother's sharp voice stopped him:

"Amy's baby is a year old now. Will you stop fussing over her as if she'd been confined yesterday and get me a rum punch?"

Fanny rose now to make two groups on the terrace. She placed Jamey and Naomi with Iris, while she took Fred Stiles and Amy over to the umbrella table.

"I know your mother-in-law will want to have a few words with Jamey before she goes back to Southampton," she explained tactfully to Amy.

"If she can get a word in with Naomi present!" Fred exclaimed with a jeering laugh. "My bride will be expatiating on the horrors of her second honeymoon."

"Now, Fred," Fanny reproved him, "you mustn't go on that way. We all know that you and Naomi are like two turtle doves. And, anyway, your honeymoon is six months back. You're settled married folk by now."

"Settled?" Fred smiled acidly at Amy. "Presumably our revered hostess means resigned. Do you know what an old married friend told me when he heard I was engaged? 'You're thinking perhaps of all those pesky little household chores which will be taken off your neck? Stand by for a shock, pal. You'll find they're exactly doubled!'"

"Well, if they have been, perhaps it's the purgatory you deserve for having stayed a bachelor so long," Fanny retorted severely. "You must learn to adapt yourself more gracefully to your state. Look at Jamey. He was a bachelor even longer than you, and he's taken to matrimony like the proverbial duck. I never saw a man so contented. Let him be your model!"

"Oh, Jamey, he's hopeless. He even likes the summer commuting. He says it gives him time to think out his day. That's Jamey all over, isn't it, Amy? Always putting every minute to work?"

"It's true that he wastes very few minutes," Amy admitted. "Sometimes I think it might do him good to waste a few more."

"Do I actually hear a criticism? A criticism of the god of Coates, Lane & Coates?" Fred raised his hands in mock horror. "How dare you, Amy? You and I are on sufferance here, you know. *We* didn't grow up in Shoal Bay. We didn't even spend our summers on Long Island. We try, but we never quite succeed, in talking the same language as our spouses. Look into our backgrounds and you may even find . . . a public school! But, Amy, despair not. If you learn to prefer last year's fashions, or even those further back; if you manage to disguise gossip as morality; if you can put Gilbert and Sullivan over Wagner and Mozart, there may yet be a chance for you in Shoal Bay!"

"You're being very silly today, Fred," Fanny scolded him. "After all, I was more of an outsider than either of you when I came to Shoal Bay. I was from Boston."

"Ah, but that was the source of Shoal Bay!" Fred exclaimed. "And, besides, you were a princess of Boston. An Opdycke! Everyone here has always deferred to you."

But Fanny was not pleased. There was a harshness beneath the banter in Fred's tone which made her think uncomfortably of what Iris had said. There was something inherently unassimilable about poor Gordon's law school roommate. Even in his moments of greatest emotional synthesis with her, when he had wept and called her his "real mother," Fanny had always been aware that there were two sides to this prickly young man: the gentle and sympathetic friend of poor Gordon, who had an uncanny way of reaching into one's deepest thoughts, and the sneering, defiant lawyer who was going to be tougher than the toughest opposition. Perhaps she had done wrong in asking him to the house so often with her oldest daughter's best friend, Naomi Fidler. But then he had seemed to like her, and he had shown so little interest in other younger women, and Naomi had seemed so much gentler, so much milder, under his attentions. Fanny felt that the sun had been suddenly obscured, and she turned, defensive, concerned, half-alarmed, to the young woman of the strange history who seemed, so oddly, to have made Jamey Coates happy at last.

"I hope you're not believing a word he's saying, Amy," Fanny broke out. "Certainly Shoal Bay has taken *you* into its very bosom."

"Oh, yes. I have no complaints."

"And you love it here, don't you?"

"Love it?" Amy's eyes ceased to smile. She seemed surprised by her own embarrassment. "Perhaps. Only I wonder if I don't find it . . . well . . . perhaps the least bit cruel."

2

AMY HAD NOT had to explain her epithet to Mrs. Lane — which she might have found difficult to do — because Naomi had abandoned Mrs. Coates at just that moment and come over to her hostess' table. She was obviously not going to risk a second husband to the clutches of the incomprehensible Amy. As soon as she and Fred had gone, Amy was able to leave with her husband, and for the next couple of days, at the Oyster Cove Club, she avoided Mrs. Lane, to avoid a return to the topic.

She did, however, ponder her own spontaneous choice of adjective. Why was Shoal Bay cruel? All she could think of was that so many things did not grow there. Nothing seemed to be permitted to grow, or even to be born, in Shoal Bay of which Jamey Coates and Mrs. Lane disapproved. That small marine community had become the symbol of the world which in the last two years appeared to have taken her over.

It was quite different in New York. Amy was acutely conscious, wheeling little August's perambulator down 72nd Street from their apartment to Central Park, or marketing on Madison and Lexington avenues, even in that affluent and restricted area of the city, of poverty, beggary, senility, abrasiveness. It seemed at times to her that the spirit of Theodore Dreiser hovered over the city. It was often unlovable, but it was certainly alive. Jamey's world existed in New York, but it was only a very small part of it. It was everything in Shoal Bay.

Why did she hold herself back from Mrs. Lane's questions? Did she not love her husband, and trust him, totally? Good Lord, she exclaimed to herself, if the emotion that so absorbed her and enveloped her and even almost subdued her, were not love, what else could it be? It seemed to her at times that she had lost control of her life, and it was certainly a question whether she had given it up of her own free will or whether it had been simply taken from her. She had a constant sense that

Jamey was watching her, even from downtown, to see if she needed something: a word of caution, a word of encouragement, a hint as to behavior — though always so tactful as to be difficult to disregard — a smile of sympathy, a kiss, a hug. Nobody had ever cared for her that way before, and now it had come all at once, soft, wonderful, overwhelming, but a bit smothering. It was like being rolled up on a cold night in a thick silk quilt of the very finest quality.

Well, if a question even existed that it was love, there was none at all that it was sex. Amy had reason to reflect that she might have been a virgin for all that her first lover had taught her to anticipate in her husband. Jamey made love to her so frequently and with so driving and sustained a passion that she began to wonder, in her dazed exhilaration, if those crude folk who maintained that *this* was what life was all about might not have hit upon an ultimate truth. Jamey had told her frankly, if in rather too lubricious detail, of his experiences with French whores. They had been for him, she gathered, more or less what Herman had been for her. There had been none of the exuberance, the glee which made him now glow, even in the company of others, with a new energy and confidence. Indeed, her sense of what marriage seemed to have done for her husband was almost as gratifying as the act of love itself.

Nor was the latter confined, as in Bank Street, to alternate nights. Sometimes Jamey would come uptown in the middle of the day to make love. Sometimes, perhaps acting out a fantasy, he would meet her for lunch at a Greenwich Village restaurant, unfrequented by their friends, as though they were having an adulterous affair. Waiting for him at the corner table that he had reserved, she would watch him come in and glance furtively about to see if he were recognized. Sitting down on the bench beside her, close to her, with only the gleam of a greeting, he would hold the menu with his left hand while the fingers of his right slid down her back. Once he even took her afterward to a hotel where they registered under false names. And if they visited his parents, he would be, if possible, even more uxorious. On one weekend in Southampton it seemed to her that they had spent most of their time in bed. It was as if he wished to throw his physical satisfaction in the teeth of his obviously disgusted old mother. Amy had been embarrassed.

Yet he never treated her as a mere accommodation to his appetite. He wanted her to be his partner in all things. He wanted to know everything that she did all day, and he was certainly free with the details of his own. This was not only occasionally fatiguing; it failed somehow, to her viewpoint, to provide the basis of a true communication. She would try to generalize their discussions, but when they turned to public topics they almost invariably disagreed. She admired the speed of his comprehension, the power of his analysis, yet it seemed to her that in the deepest things he was always wrong.

They had very few rows, for she usually let potential arguments go by default. But they had one over the notorious Richard Whitney case, involving embezzlement by a former stock exchange president. Amy maintained that the friends and relatives of Whitney who had loaned him money, knowing of his defalcations, were only a degree less guilty than he. Jamey conceded their legal wrongdoing but defended them morally.

"Suppose I had had the chance to rescue Whitney. Do you know that I should have been sorely tempted to do so? Who, after all, would have been hurt? Only myself. The loss, if any, would have fallen on me and not, as it did, on innocent creditors. And I should have had the satisfaction of knowing that I was protecting the financial community from being tarred and feathered because of one bad egg. Do you know what they're saying about Whitney now, Amy? That if he hadn't existed, the New Deal would have had to invent him!"

"But, Jamey, how would you have protected the public? He might have done it again."

"No chance. There are ways of arranging these things. The gentlemen who wanted to save Whitney could have retired him to an orange grove in California."

"Wouldn't that have been compounding a crime?"

"Of course it would. I'm talking about the *moral* issue. There may be times, you know, when it is morally right to break the law. Read *Antigone*."

"But there you had a despot and a cruel law. Here you're taking the responsibility on yourself to judge that Whitney is such a rarity in Wall Street that it's perfectly proper and safe to sweep him under the rug. What gives you that right?"

"My knowledge of the world I live in. Which is far greater than that of a lot of petty bureaucrats in Washington. And speaking of despots, what do you think you have down there? When they've got through passing all their rules and regulations, they'll have turned the financial game into cops and robbers. If you treat men as crooks long enough, they'll end by becoming so."

"But what can the public depend on but rules and regulations? You say that Whitney is such an exception, but now there's this Burden case, and . . ."

"The public can depend on character!" Jamey exclaimed, pounding the table at which they were having dinner. "That is all that anyone can depend on in the last analysis. I think Mr. Morgan pretty well laid down the gospel on the subject when he was asked by that snooping congressman what a banker's best security was: 'Character, sir! A borrower's character. That's your only real security!' "

Amy did not go on with it. What was the point? Jamey's faith in the financial hierarchy was almost mystical. As she gradually made out the world as he saw it, it took its shape as a pyramid in a medieval woodcut. At the bottom was the general population, sullen, lazy, easily agitated by politicians and trade unionists. On the next level were the proprietors of small businesses and farmers, and on the one above that, the leaders of industry. As she looked up from tier to tier she seemed to see in the faces and profiles of the individuals signs of greater probity and intellect — higher foreheads, sterner eyes, straighter noses. The top of the pyramid was devoted to finance and the lawyers of finance: brokers, then bankers, then investment bankers, then corporate counsel, and, on the summit, the very peak, with the wings of angels, the partners of the House of Morgan! It was ridiculous, and yet there were moments when she envied Jamey. It was something to have faith. For every angry moment when she yearned to disillusion him, there was a desperate one when she wanted to be converted.

What she could never get away from was the idea that, like Faust, he had bought her at the price of his own soul. For *her* sake he had violated what he deemed his holiest duty, and the bargain seemed to have bound them together for eternity. They never mentioned Dolly's codicil to each other, and Herman had long since collected his aunt's money, but Amy had an odd suspicion that Jamey's sense of his crime burned constantly within him, not as a pricking reminder of inconsistency, but as a kind of life-giving flame, a species of eerie magic. She found herself imagining her husband as a medieval priest, a mystic, who nonetheless reverted on certain old pagan feast days to the cult of disestablished gods. He had bought her, perhaps, from a sprite or devil, and he was actually proud of his purchase! It was something like this, at least, that she seemed to read in his passionate pride about her. Was she not a tribute to his own power? He, Jamey, had plucked a dishonored woman out of Greenwich Village and made her a queen in Shoal Bay! Bow, Shoal Bay! Remember that the title "Mrs. James Coates" is one that covers any past.

She had read that there were couples who sought relief from the intimacy of seeing each other too clearly in an exaggerated emphasis on the mechanics of life. But in their case this emphasis surely proceeded from Jamey's own fondness for precise detail. He loved to plan each weekend, each vacation, each dinner party. Despite all his hard labor downtown he found time to make lists of friends to be kept up with, of cousins and classmates to be remembered. Amy decided ultimately that she would have to resist his incessant projects to keep their life from becoming like the watch, quarter and station bill of a naval vessel. But the very first time that she did so, she was taken aback by the promptness of his acquiescence.

"You think we spend too much time on maintenance? You're probably right. Let's talk about something else. What shall it be?"

"Well . . . what about you and me? I don't mean just the things we do. What about all the things we think and feel? The *deep* things."

"I should like nothing better. Let's make it a rule to discuss ourselves every night when we have our cocktails. And if I'm working late, we'll double the time we do it the next night. As a matter of fact we could start right now. You go first."

"How do you mean?"

"Well, ask me a question."

"What sort of question?"

"Anything you want. But all right, I'll start. Tell me this, darling. Do you believe in God?"

"Well...I don't think I really know," she replied a bit faintly.

"Do you realize I've never asked you before? We live in a time when such questions are regarded as faintly indecent. And to think you're a minister's daughter!"

"Well, *he* didn't believe in God."

"He didn't? But now *that*'s interesting. I'd like to hear all about that."

By the time she had finished the discussion she was glad to get back to questions of maintenance. What she really had to figure out was not what Jamey thought or should think, what he did or what he might far better do, but what sort of a life *she* could make out of it. After all, he was satisfied, and if he was too satisfied, wasn't that her problem and not his?

When she added up what her "legal" life amounted to, it seemed to be mostly parties. Jamey believed very strongly in keeping up the esprit de corps of his firm, and he was convinced that social events were a vital part of this. There were dinners for the partners, dinners for the associates, dinners for both; there were receptions for the staff; there was an annual outing at the Oyster Cove Club. Then there were choicer parties for important clients, and the taking of tables at benefits for Legal Aid and bar association banquets. Jamey was quite capable of doing it all himself, down to the very selection of menus and the checking of caterers' bills, but he expected Amy to do her part, and when he delegated a function he was wise enough to delegate it completely. She found herself, indeed, under his never condescending encouragement, becoming almost as efficient as he.

Yet, however much he treated her as an equal, she never felt like one. Everything had run well before he had married her, and she was convinced that it would run as well were she to disappear. One afternoon she summoned up the courage to voice her doubts to Mrs. Lane.

"I know what you mean, dear," Fanny Lane told her, sitting on her terrace and working busily at her needlepoint. "I felt some of the same thing with Judge Lane. Lawyers are so darned self-sufficient. But I'll tell you a secret that I wouldn't tell many people. Because I know you're not only trustworthy but a true member of the team. Oh, yes, you are, Amy, whatever your doubts! We *all* have doubts. That is, if we have any intelligence. Which brings me to my secret." Here she put her needlepoint in her lap and leaned over to Amy, dropping her voice to a half-mocking, hoarse whisper. "This air of self-sufficiency — why do they put it on so? May it not cover some doubts on *their* part? All that high talk about the ideals of the bar, about seeking truth and justice and equity — would any profession be *quite* so fullsome unless it felt just a wee bit guilty?"

"Why, Mrs. Lane, you surprise me."

"Do I? Hasn't it ever occurred to you that they hate the idea that fundamentally, deep down, they're not their own masters? That they're even . . . mouthpieces?"

"That word from *you*? I can hardly believe it."

"Oh, we old Bostonians have a pretty shrewd idea of what's what. A man like Jamey is a great idealist. So was my husband. They have to keep dressing up their law practice to make it fit their ideals. They're like the old Southern slaveholders — the better ones, I mean — who were always poring through the Bible to find excuses for the peculiar institution."

"But you can feel that and not *mind?*"

"Men are strange beasts, Amy. They're not like us. They must have their illusions. The good ones, that is. So long as they have them and *try* to live up to them, we shouldn't complain. It is our function to keep them civilized. By bringing them gently down to earth when they fly too high. There, child, we'll say no more about it. I've told you *all*."

The weekend after Amy's talk with Mrs. Lane, she and Jamey went to Southampton to visit Mr. and Mrs. Coates. Amy, who had at first been intimidated both by her parents-in-law and by Southampton society, had now learned that she cut so little a figure in the eyes of either that she could afford to relax in her semianonymity and watch the show with detachment. It was difficult to believe, in that big, airy, silent house on the dunes, with its mat-covered floors, its faded prints, its white wicker furniture and its efficient, ancient, unspeaking housemaids, that the bustling world of Shoal Bay even existed. The values in Southampton were totally reversed. The heavy-faced bankers and brokers who came to the Coates', in brilliant sports jackets or immaculate evening white or black, strong drinkers who were never drunk, with their gruff talk of the golf course and the stock market, and their thin, brown-skinned, flat-chested, bejewelled wives, with their easy air of accepted boredom, would have scorned the morals and aspirations of Shoal Bay, had they even known them to exist.

Jamey, having been brought up in Southampton, was not in the least impressed by it. Dressing for his parents' dinner party on Saturday night, he pooh-poohed Amy's query if South-ampton might not actually be less snobbish than Shoal Bay.

"How could anyplace be more snobbish than Southampton?" he demanded.

"Well, I don't know." Combing her hair, she reflected that she should have had it set. "But you'll have to admit that your mother invites people to her house whom Mrs. Lane wouldn't have in hers. That society photographer at lunch, for example. And those two decorators."

"And I wonder if Mrs. Lane isn't right!" Jamey exclaimed with a snort. "But don't be taken in by Mother's liberalism. She'll ask anyone who amuses her and plays cards for her stakes. Anyone, in other words, who's in the crowd down here. But woe to the newcomer who doesn't respond to her two demand bid. Or who calls a curtain a 'drape.' Or who doesn't know who 'Lulu' or 'Ducky' or 'Big Pauline' are!"

"You mean your mother has no moral standards?"

"Oh, yes. Very stiff ones. For the poor and unfashionable."

"I remember. I came under that ban once."

But Jamey would never tolerate the least reference to that chapter in her life. "If I were in real trouble," he pursued with feeling, "and had to go to Mother or Mrs. Lane for help, you can guess which I'd pick!"

"But you never need help. You of all people, darling, can afford to pick your friends for their charm."

"And Southampton people have such charm?"

"No, but neither do . . ." She stopped.

"Neither do the Shoal Bay crowd? That's all right. You don't have to pretend with me. Hell, so far as I'm concerned, when I have you, I've got all the society I need. Do you ever feel that?"

"Well . . . yes."

"You don't at all!" He laughed good-naturedly and came over to reach his hands under her dressing gown. "Women crave a bit of society. Of course, they do!"

"Jamey, please! It's almost time for dinner." It shocked her how quickly he could arouse her. She caught one of his hands and rather desperately kissed it. "Unless you think we can be late. I don't care if you don't."

"No, no!" He pulled away, laughing. "I've got to mix the cocktails. But I'll make up for it later. Do you think it's too soon to drop the guards? How about starting a little brother for Augie tonight?"

"Or a little sister?"

He kissed the back of her neck. "I'll settle for twins."

But when she came down to the living room, ten minutes later, and saw Jamey already by the drink table, replacing the older butler, mixing cocktails for the first guests as efficiently as if he had been sent by a caterer, she felt obscurely as if she had sold out, as if he had purchased her submission with a slap and a tickle and knew that he could do so whenever he wished. It gave her such a silly thrill to know that in that little throng of sophisticates there was a man worth the lot of them who wanted nothing better than to take her upstairs and go to bed! It made up more than it should have for her isolation in the room, for her father-in-law's bland unawareness, for her mother-in-law's good-natured contempt. They and their guests sneered at her; they even sneered at Jamey. For them he was too fussy, too prissy, too legal — yes, she saw it! — but at least they recognized his brains and success. Oh, if it were a question of law or politics or of taxes, their dreaded taxes, how quickly they would listen to him! And she admired him for not being impressed by them. But was she not basely subjugated by this man? Was she not an odalisque — even if the sole one — in his harem? As she watched him now she wondered if she could not even visualize him in a fez, a busy, bustling, diminutive Mohammedan . . .

But this had to stop. This was madness. She saw that Mrs. Coates wanted her, and she joined her and Mrs. Fisher. Naomi's mother, a handsome septuagenarian, robust of feature, with a pearl gray countenance and the still suspicious gaze of a large aquatic bird, seemed to wish to demonstrate that she was subject to no normal taboos.

"Tell me what you think of my new son-in-law, Amy. You must see him and Naomi all the time in Shoal Bay. Naomi, in Shoal Bay — imagine! But *chacun à son goût*. Do you think a lawyer will suit her better than a stockbroker? At least he should be able to keep her out of trouble."

"Oh, we all think Fred is absolutely brilliant, Mrs. Fisher."

"Well, brilliance alone won't help him to understand women. My only fear is that he's been a bachelor too long."

"Maybe Herman Fidler wasn't a bachelor long enough!" Mrs. Coates exclaimed, and the two old girls cackled. Amy sensed behind their mirth a willingness to accept her on their terms, at least for that evening, because, for all her dimness and obscurity, she had succeeded, however unaccountably, in doing what she wanted with two of their men. She had deserted the son-in-law of one and "caught" the son of the other. Failure would have been followed by social annihilation, but success . . . well, that was something else again.

"They seem devoted to each other, anyway," Amy said lamely.

"I hope that having a son-in-law in Coates, Lane & Coates will reduce the fees I have to pay," Mrs. Fisher observed.

"There's this ghastly lawsuit, you know, Iris, against Fisher and Rappelye. Fred is in charge of defending us, and he seems sanguine about the outcome. But there's something rather glib about him, don't you think? And Naomi and I have an awful lot tied up in that case."

"Jamey, I know, has an absolute faith in Fred," Amy, now the senior partner's wife, replied. "He considers him one of the ablest litigators in the firm."

Mrs. Fisher's gaze was at first sharp, assessive, then reassured. "Well, I daresay things will work themselves out." She turned to Mrs. Coates. "Will Augie be coming down at all this summer?"

"Oh, no, Augie's become much too holy for Southampton. Ever since his . . . how does one put it? . . . his incarceration, he has devoted himself entirely to good works. This weekend, for example, he's taking his Scout troop on a bird watch in Jamaica Bay."

"How worthy. And is it true he's become a Catholic?"

"He has joined what he calls the true and only church. The word of God came to him, it seems, through a priest who visited his prison cell in Mineola. Curious, isn't it? Perhaps it bears out what Fanny Lane has always believed, that the Almighty favors the north shore of the island."

Amy hated it when her mother-in-law talked about Augie. Mrs. Coates told nothing but the truth about her older son: that he had been converted, that he had given up drinking and womanizing, that he had taken a small job in the Red Cross and worked with Boy Scouts on the weekends, but her tone had a hard chill. It was as if Augie had disgraced himself. What sort of love was it that ebbed when the recipient backed away from the suicidal cliff?

When Mrs. Fisher, who cared little for tales of redemption,

turned to address her approaching host, Amy could not forebear murmuring to her mother-in-law: "But don't you think Augie's happy? And maybe for the first time in his life?"

Mrs. Coates gave her a look which seemed to challenge her to notice its sudden, brief gleam of dislike. "What do you know about Augie's happiness? Don't talk about things you can't understand, child. Augie might better have died in the war. He would at least be remembered as someone beautiful and inspiring, like one of those golden English youths, a Rupert Brooke or a Julian Grenfell. But this way . . . I see you're shocked. Well, to me the whole thing is simply sordid. There's no point discussing it. Let us talk to our guests."

Amy wondered, as they both now rose, whether Jamey had benefited from his brother's fall from the maternal grace. She doubted it. Mrs. Coates was not going to change her standards. Like a ruffled old eagle on a high, bare rock, she scowled at the setting sun.

At dinner the civil war in Spain became the subject of general conversation, and Jamey, much exercised, took the lead. He was particularly emphatic in rejecting his father's rather languid suggestion that the United States should assist the Loyalists, if only to embarrass the Axis powers.

"I say a plague on both their houses!" he exclaimed. "There's not a pin to choose between them. The only fight worth fighting is one for freedom, and there's none of that anywhere in Spain. Communism, fascism, what's the difference? America stands for liberty! And what's more, she's the only country in the world that does. We can't afford to compromise with Moscow *or* Berlin. Come hell or high water!"

Amy was aware that her husband's emotional blend of a purist political idealism with something approaching jingoism was perfectly sincere. There was an element of the fanatic in Jamey, a spark which she had first noticed on the day when he had climbed up to Herman's loft to propose to her. At moments, particularly as now in his parents' house, she suspected that it might be informed, at least in part, by a need to show the two old materialists that he was just as much of a man as his brother Augie, and one, furthermore, who was dedicated to ideals far loftier than any which could have originated in *their* crass environment. But at other times she seemed to see past any such petty signposts of defiance and petulance to the beaten gold of a fine passion, a martyr's fury, and she would wonder almost in awe if everything might not still be all right, if she had not, after all, in touching her spark to his, ignited a blaze which would make the dusty hearth and grate of her "legal" life, of her social life, of Shoal Bay itself, seem merely useful, accommodating things.

The table tried now to shout Jamey down with the example of England, but he held to his guns. Great Britain, he insisted, had no constitution. The House of Commons could eliminate liberty tomorrow. Only in God's country was freedom guaranteed. Amy stifled her doubts. Who would not prefer the Jamey who hymned freedom to the one who hymned the House of Morgan?

After dinner Mrs. Coates, knowing that Amy's bridge was not up to the company's standards, suggested that she join the rather forlorn group of the noncardplayers on the terrace, but she pleaded that she was trying to learn the game by watching Jamey, and she was permitted to sit beside him as he played with Mrs. Fisher against his parents. She liked the deftness of his shuffling, the speed of his dealing; she shared the intensity of his concentration as she peered into the hand which he so quickly arranged. Jamey loved the game and played it expertly. When he set his mother three in a doubled contract, it was impossible not to suspect, in the way that he smartly snapped down each penalizing trick on the table before him, a small revenge for a lifetime of humiliations. There might even have been some of this in the abrupt way that he declined a third rubber.

"It's midnight, Ma. Amy and I are not used to Southampton hours. If you will kindly pay Mrs. Fisher the hundred and fifty you owe her, we'll go to bed. Dad, you can put mine on the cuff."

In their darkened room later, hearing the pound of the surf outside and the muffled murmur of voices and laughs from the parlor below, they made love without contraceptives for the first time since little Augie's birth. Amy, losing herself, or trying to lose herself in his embrace, wondered again if the point of life might not be simply in this. Listening to Jamey's satisfied snores beside her afterward, she hoped that she was pregnant.

3

WHEN JAMEY, in the two years that followed Dolly Chadbourne's death, thought, as he often did, of what he had done with the codicil to her will, it would strike him at first as incredible. If he were walking down a street, for instance, he would stop, as one does at the sudden recollection of a vivid and horrible dream, and then walk on in the quick relief of recognizing that it was, thank God, only a dream, and then pause again — frozen. Had *he,* James Coates, really done that? And then each time, he would go through the mental procedure of justifying his action, or at least of explaining it, to himself. But the little pantomime had to be repeated over and over. He had always to convince himself anew that there was nothing else in the world he could have done.

To begin with, there was his conscience, his moral conscience, to square. That was not so difficult. Some four hundred thousand dollars had been deflected from the pockets of two rich, spoiled little girls to their needy father who would presumably leave it to them when they were older and less spoiled. And the true intent of the testator had been implemented. For there was no question in Jamey's mind that Dolly Chadbourne would have revoked that codicil had she not lost her mind. She had only signed it, after all, at *his* instigation. What, in the last analysis, had he really accomplished but to right a wrong which *he* had done to Herman Fidler?

If, then, there was no moral wrong, and if it would never be discovered, surely there was nothing to worry about. But *would* it never be discovered? That was always the second question that had to be reviewed. Certainly there had been no hint of trouble so far. Nobody had raised any issue of a codicil when Jamey had offered the will for probate. Why should they have? What could have been more natural than that Dolly should have willed her trust to her only nephew? Why should anyone have even suspected that she might have preferred his daughters? Fred Stiles, the other witness to the codicil, had never asked a question. Was that so strange? He had witnessed dozens of wills and codicils, prepared by his partners, without having the least idea what they contained. And suppose he *had* remembered?

Suppose he had recalled that it was a codicil which he had witnessed at Dolly's apartment? Suppose, even less likely, that he had noticed that after her death he had never been called upon to prove his signature? Would not the obvious explanation have been that Dolly had revoked her codicil or replaced it with another? Were not old maids notorious for always drawing and redrawing their wills? Why in his wildest dreams would he have suspected Jamey of doing what he *had* done? Jamey had had, it was true, some nervous moments at the marriage of Fred and Naomi, a union which had converted the second witness to the suppressed codicil into the stepfather of its shorn beneficiaries, but still nothing had happened. And now what could?

But there was still a rub, his other conscience, the more delicate one, his conscience as a lawyer. Alas, there was no way of silencing this. He, an officer of the court, of the surrogate's court, had taken upon himself the prerogative of judging a testator's intent. Instead of submitting all the evidence to the court, he had submitted only Dolly's will, with the result that he, and not the surrogate, had determined who her real beneficiaries were. In this he had violated the canons of ethics; for this he deserved to be disbarred. He, James Coates, senior partner of Coates, Lane & Coates, and the member, past or present, of some dozen committees of the City Bar Association, a trustee of Legal Aid, a trustee and director of how many charitable institutions, deserved to be disbarred! It was a challenge, to say the least, to continue to live with such a burden on his mind and heart.

And then, each time, as the wheel of his recollections and ratiocinations came full circle, he would face what had been his alternative. Had he not done what he had done, he would have exposed Amy to certain agony and humiliation. She would have been obliged to testify in open court that she, and not Dolly, had destroyed the codicil. And she would have had to admit that she had done it for her paramour. Who would have ever believed that she had already broken with Herman and had been acting under a simple impulse to effect justice? The world would have assumed that there had been an atrocious plot between the lovers to defraud the semilunatic old maid, that Amy had been sent, ostensibly to nurse her but actually to ferret out and do away with the codicil by which the poor virtuous aunt had sought to chastise her adulterous nephew. Monstrous!

And then Jamey would be calm again. He would indeed be serene, happy. To save Amy from that he would have done it all again. And viewed in this light, as if filtered through a stained-glass window, his crime became something more dignified, something even commendable. Whatever others might think of it, *he* could cherish it, love it, for it was simply his love. It glowed there, under the light from the rose window, sitting on the high altar of his soul, the proof of his passion, of his vitality, of his manhood, a constant reassurance that he was alive. Its very secrecy was sacred, for it was something that could not be shared, not even with Amy, and he never mentioned it to her. He was like Lohengrin. He had his life and his love, so long as nobody asked him his name.

Amy was at all times perfectly conscious of the fact that her husband's silence about Dolly's codicil was intentional, and she respected it, sensing its importance to him. Not for anything would she have questioned him about whether the trust moneys had gone in fact to Herman or if anyone had noticed the substitution. She had placed the matter in his hands and it behooved her to trust him. He had taken risks, perhaps grave ones, for her sake, and it would be intolerable to reveal the smallest crack in her confidence. The least she could do for him was to be prepared to accept any consequences, or perhaps worse, the lack of consequences.

There were moments, of course, when she yearned to know more. Was it possible that there had been no crime at all, that Jamey, as Cousin Dolly's attorney, had had some kind of discretion as to her affairs? This she could hardly believe, but she knew little about the law and dared not ask. And then one day at the beach club she heard Naomi casually remark that Herman had refused, "typically enough," to raise the children's allowance, even though he was "now so much better off," and she gathered that the estate had been settled. It was over! They were safe.

But now she began to worry about Herman's daughters. For no matter what the moral equities, had she not in fact robbed them? And had she not done it for the totally inadequate reason that she had wanted to make up to Herman for the simple fact that she hadn't loved him? Was *that* the fault of his girls? Was there not some way that she could make it up to them? And then, quite fortuitously, at a dinner party given by Herman's mother at her summer house in Shoal Bay, she conceived what struck her as a brilliant project of reparation.

Mrs. Fidler had now accepted Amy as the family lawyer's wife. She, of course, never invited the Coateses to her house when her son was there, but she did ask them with Naomi, whose good will she continued to cultivate for the sake of her granddaughters. At these little gatherings she would always manage to slip Amy any good tidings of her son. It seemed that Herman was making definite progress in his painting and had already contributed to two group shows and even made a few sales. He had abandoned his small geometrical studies in favor of the human figure. He was now doing a series of what he called "dramatic monologues," portraits with backgrounds which told the observer something essential about the subject. One night before dinner, Mrs. Fidler made a little announcement to her guests.

"I want you all to know that I have just 'acquired,' as collectors say, a Herman Fidler. Believe it or not, I had to buy it. He wouldn't give it to me!" As the little group laughed, she continued: "Let me bring it in. No, you needn't help me, Jamey. It's not heavy. I *think* you'll all recognize who it is."

As Mrs. Fidler went out of the room, Amy felt a sudden absurd conviction that the picture would be Herman's study of her nude back. She held her breath as she turned away to watch Jamey watching their returning hostess. But she saw at once by his unchanged countenance that she was safe. How could she, even for a moment, have supposed Herman's mother capable of so coarse a joke? But, of course, she was always tense in that house.

The painting at which they all now gazed was a self-portrait. Herman, in a dark suit, was seen entering what was apparently a cocktail party. On either side of him, in the background, much diminished in size, were wraithlike figures in light colors whose outlines suggested persons laughing, flirting, drinking. They were caricatures, as opposed to Herman himself; they reminded Amy of the short-skirted flappers and beaux in straw hats and bell-bottomed trousers of the old cartoons of John Held, Jr. The artist and subject, looming forward into the picture, seemed about to join them, and presumably to drink with them, but his presence was somehow grave, and his eyes, sea-blue, sky-blue, were pools of detachment. Amy felt a little pang of something she could identify only as . . . envy?

"He's going to kill that party," Naomi observed tartly. "Trust old Herman!"

"But it's very good!" Amy protested, too warmly, and she felt Jamey's eye on her. Irrationally, she suddenly wished that the painting *had* been the one of herself.

Mrs. Fidler intervened to reprove Naomi. "He's not going to kill the party at all, dear. He's going to be very nice and correct to everyone, as Herman always is. It's only that his mind is now on higher things. That's what the painting says to me, anyway."

"Well, of course, *I* don't know anything about art."

"You needn't say that as if it were a virtue, Naomi," her husband retorted. "Let us hope that my stepdaughters will inherit their aesthetic sensibilities, if any, through the paternal line."

Naomi, immediately irate, glared about the little group for a target. Amy felt as she had felt back in Cousin Dolly's drawing room at a visit of the Bayard sisters.

"Let us hope, anyway, that Herman will paint enough pictures to make up to my poor girls for the art that went out of the family when Aunt Dolly died!"

This spiteful reference to the bequest to Amy of Dolly's modern art brought a quick change of subject from Mrs. Fidler. Nobody in that room was going to give Naomi the satisfaction of feeling that her reference had been so much as noticed. But Amy could think of nothing else during dinner and afterward. She loved the seven small paintings which had formed her bequest. They hung now in her living room in town: the

Braque village, the Picasso clown, the Utrillo Montmartre ...

"Naomi was odious tonight, of course, but I've been thinking it over," she said to Jamey in the car going home. "Maybe she has a point. Wouldn't it perhaps be a good thing if I gave Cousin Dolly's pictures to Herman's daughters? Mightn't it clear everything up?"

For several moments Jamey drove in silence. When he spoke, all the things that he didn't say — about her own love of the paintings and Naomi's meanness and that the Fidler girls were nothing to them — revealed how immediately he had grasped her principle of expiation.

"They're very valuable, you know. There'd be a considerable gift tax."

"But don't you think it might make for good feeling?"

"I suppose it would have to."

"The only thing that would make it impossible for me would be if Naomi were grateful. But she won't be."

"Because no gratitude is required?"

"No. Because she never is."

It was as near as they had ever come to speaking of the codicil.

"Shall I do it, then?" Amy pursued.

"If you wish. If it will make you happy, darling. Modern art means very little to me."

Only one thing bothered her now, and that quite suddenly, as she stared out the window into the black rainy night. Was she a criminal returning to the scene of her crime?

❧ 4 ❧

NAOMI STILES RARELY joined her husband for breakfast in the dining room of their rented summer cottage at Shoal Bay, but when she did, it was apt to be because she wanted something. On that hot August Monday morning a large sun blister on her lower lip had somehow the air of proclaiming itself the evidence of an obscure marital assault. Contemplating her sullen expression over his newspaper Fred sealed his lips and forced himself to consider that the days which she started badly she sometimes ended well and that by evening, when she had finished her second cocktail, she might be almost pleasant.

"Do you want the paper?"

"For what?" She never read the paper, except to glance at the society page.

"They say it's going to be ninety again today. Aren't you lucky you don't have to go into town? I wish *I* were a woman and could sit on the beach all day."

Naomi simply ignored this preposterous attempt to view her sex's long-established and well-deserved privileges as good luck. With a sigh Fred reopened the review, in what had already become a rather desperate mental habit, of the reasons that he had married her. He had done it because he was lonely. And he *had* been lonely, too, not only lonely but bored. He had done it to have a ready-made family: no diapers, no bawling. He had done it to be able to call the president of the Manhattan Bank

"Uncle Eben" and Mrs. Kip Van Rensselaer "Aunt Tootles." And he had done it to have regular sex. Naomi, like many bad-tempered women, loved sex. But . . . oh, never mind the buts! Yet how could he not mind them, when the tide of Naomi's bad moods filled up the brisk little rivulets of his own brighter ones? When her perpetual dissatisfaction with her life was eroding the foundation of his own, when her doubt that anything mattered besides his futile attempts to entertain her seemed to be placing in question not only the brilliance of Fred Stiles but his very identity?

"I thought I might drive down to Southampton to spend a couple of nights with Mother," Naomi said. "It's cooler there, and the girls like the surf bathing."

Fred very carefully concealed his relief. So that was all. She was putting herself in the wrong, by leaving him alone, and she knew it. But after only six months of marriage he had learned to give away no points. Naomi knew perfectly well that he would be delighted to be alone in New York, but that was all the more reason that she should be made to beg.

"And leave me alone here? In this weather? Thanks!"

"I thought you might like to stay in town and see the other summer bachelors. You know you like that."

"With the apartment closed? And no one to clean it?"

"I'll call Mrs. Askew and tell her to come in."

"I don't see why I shouldn't stay out here. Somebody ought to keep an eye on the place while you're off gadding. You needn't worry about me. I'll manage."

"And dine all alone? Don't be a martyr."

"I can always go to Jamey's."

"But Jamey spends at least two nights in town working."

"Well, Amy will be glad to have me."

"Not on your life, Buster!"

Fred smiled, pleased with his easy victory and at the prospect of his nights in town. "Are you afraid she'll get another husband away from you?"

"I'm not taking any chances."

"Very well. I'll avoid the siren. I'll stay in town and be a good boy."

"What has she got, Fred?" Naomi asked earnestly. "None of my friends could ever figure it out. Siren? She's more like a drowned rat."

"She has intensity."

"And I haven't?"

"I didn't say that." He could placate her now; she was going away. "There's really no one more intense than you. It may have been too much for Herman. But it's not too much for me. Not yet, anyway!"

Naomi, after a moment, seemed disposed to accept this as a compliment. "At any rate, she's beginning to show a conscience at last. She came to see me yesterday with a most curious proposition. About Aunt Dolly's legacy of those wacky modern paintings to her."

"Wacky? They're very fine and extremely valuable. What about them?"

"She wants to give them to my girls."

"To Lila and Sally? Why, in the name of God?"

"She says they were a kind of moral trust. That Aunt Dolly meant her to divide them with the girls when they were older, if they liked painting. She says that Jamey doesn't care for modern art."

"Well, grab them! They must be worth a hundred grand or more. And they're beauties, too. Can we hang them in the apartment till the girls get married?"

"But of course. That's the point. That the girls should be exposed to them. If they're actually so valuable, it's more appropriate for Aunt Dolly's great-nieces to have them than a distant cousin who was really only a kind of servant."

Fred could only marvel at the ease with which Naomi could convert the generosity of others into the mere expression of their duty toward herself. "I wonder that Jamey lets her do it."

"Jamey doesn't like her to have anything that he hasn't given her."

This was a shrewd observation, and Fred relapsed into silence to consider it. On the train to New York he sat, as usual, by Jamey and had the news confirmed.

"Amy feels that Miss Chadbourne left her the pictures only because she was hard up," Jamey explained. "Now that her situation has changed, she wants them to go back to the Chadbourne family."

Fred noted that this was a different explanation of Miss Chadbourne's motive, but he did not pursue the matter, as he had no wish to invite its reconsideration. He knew just how good the paintings were — he had seen them at the Coates' apartment in town — and he imagined himself already, as the gentlemen lingered over their brandy and cigars after dinner, pointing to the little Braque and telling, with amusing exaggeration, the bizarre story of the old maid collector.

At the office he found John Rappelye waiting for him. The case against the latter's investment firm for unloading a sour stock issue which they had underwritten into their customers' accounts was now on appeal in the federal second circuit. Fred had won in the lower court and was sanguine about his chances on appeal, but the potential liability for the partners of Fisher and Rappelye was very great, and the case had become a near obsession with John. He haunted the corridors of Coates, Lane

& Coates and was constantly looming up in Fred's doorway to demand bits of news or confirmations of rumors. The big man's hardened features seemed to have been undermined as by an inner leak: he had a damp, gray, decomposing look.

"I've been reading the opinion of Judge Gray on stockbrokers' liability," he started right off. "One of your young clerks gave me a stash of them. Do you realize how far left that crazy New Deal bastard has gone? He looks damn near red, from where I sit."

"Gray, of course, is the man we worry about. I've told you that, John. But he's only one of a three man court. Stephens and Oldenburg are more reliable."

"Can you be sure of that?"

"I'm not sure of anything. I'm a lawyer, John. I make what I think are reasonable estimates."

"But does your reasonable estimate tell you that if that court goes the limit, I could be wiped out?"

"Oh, come now, that's if the court decides against you on all three counts, which is unlikely, and picks the Delmore case liability rule, which is even more unlikely, and then is not reversed by the U.S. Supreme Court, which is most unlikely of all. Get hold of yourself, John."

"Yes, but it *could* happen. And it doesn't seem so unlikely to me. Gray will certainly opt for total liability, and how do you know he can't talk one of his brothers over? One is all he needs. And the Supreme Court has been pretty well stacked by King Franklin. Why wouldn't the easiest thing for them to do be to deny certiorari?"

"All right, John, have it your way. You haven't a chance. You're going to lose everything, right down the line."

"Damn it, Fred, don't talk like that! You're in this with us now. How will you look to Naomi if her mother loses half her fortune? She's a general partner, after all."

"I'd rather not think about that."

"Well, you'd better think about it, pretty boy. Can't you hear old Mamie Fisher shrieking like a banshee all over Long Island about how her son-in-law screwed up her case?"

"But what can I *do,* John, that I'm not doing?"

"I'll tell you what, my friend. I'll tell you just what." John walked deliberately to the door and closed it. Then he turned to stare blankly at his counsel, with half-closed eyes, for several silent seconds. "This Judge Stephens, what do you know about him?"

"He's able. Very able."

"I mean his character." Fred shrugged. "I hear he can be reached. That he even expects it."

"Are you suggesting bribery now, John?"

"Leave the definition to me, please. I hear — and on very good authority — that if a litigant before his court is able to arrange — tactfully, of course — an unsecured loan to one of the little holding companies that his honor uses for real estate speculations in Queens and Brooklyn, that he may expect a . . . shall we say, 'sympathetic' opinion?"

Fred watched his client with careful eyes. "I, too, have heard something of the sort."

"Well?"

"Well?"

"Damn it all, Fred, I consider it your duty as a lawyer to tell me a thing like that!"

"Your opinion as to my duty varies dramatically with that of the Ethics Committee at the City Bar Association."

"Don't fence with me. I maintain that you should acquaint

me with *all* the facts bearing on the outcome of my litigation. A corrupt judge is certainly one of those facts. The mere failure to oblige him may result in an adverse decision. I am not asking you to do anything that conflicts with your code of ethics. I simply suggest that you brief me precisely on the reputation and character of my judges and furnish me with the names of their clerks or other trusted agents. The rest can be left to me."

"You think that would not be cause for my disbarment? Why, if I even *knew* that you had improperly approached a judge — if I even had reasonable grounds to suspect it — it would be my duty to inform the court."

"Does the law require you to destroy a client?" John seemed about to shout, but then with an obvious effort, he managed to control himself. "Very well, Fred, I'll give you a day to think it over. I consider it my duty to my family and to my partners — my *solemn* duty, mind you — to take all steps necessary to ensure that litigation in matters vital to their welfare shall not be allowed to fail because of the spite of one disappointed jurist. I shall need to know precisely whom to deal with. One can afford no errors in such a case. I ask you to take no risk. Or to commit yourself to anything. All I ask is that you keep me from going to the wrong person. Tomorrow at noon I shall be here again. You will give me the name — orally, without witnesses, here in this room — of the man I should contact."

Fred's smile had withered to a crooked line. "And if I don't?"

"I don't threaten you, Fred. You know what's at stake. And you, of all people, should know whose side you're on!"

If John Rappelye did not know when to stay away from his lawyer's office, at least he knew when to leave. Fred, alone, wondered how many of his partners had been faced in the past with such a decision. He wondered how they had decided it.

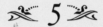

5

WHEN FRED STILES entered Yale as a freshman in the fall of 1922 he thought of himself as the hero of a Balzac novel coming up from the provinces to conquer the great world of Paris. He had an appearance appropriate to the times, as seen in so many silent films, long thin dark looks, a high forehead, thick black hair parted in the middle and eyes which he liked to imagine were capable of sudden softness and sudden menace, the eyes of a tense intellectual, a smouldering romantic youth embittered by manifold injustices and turned to a life of crime from which Lillian Gish would ultimately redeem him. The world was recovering at last from war: the sparks of Scott Fitzgerald already floated in the murky air. Fred Stiles was rather grimly determined to enjoy what he should conquer.

Because he had no neat pigeonhole in which to fit his social background, he decided that it would be well to choose one of his own making. His mother was a hopeless liability: a dreary, complaining, idle creature living alone in a nondescript middle-class house in Orange, New Jersey. She had been the daughter of an Irish Catholic druggist. What could one make of that? But something might be salvaged out of his father's past, so long as his father was kept out of sight. Frederic Stiles senior, an alcoholic, an ex-customer's man of a now defunct Wall Street house, who lived with a mistress in a gaudy, run-down West Side Manhattan hotel called the Lamballe, had nonetheless been the grandson of a New York judge, famous or infamous, depending on the point of view, for his purchased decisions in the railroad disputes of the past century. Stiles senior had started life with a certain dash and flare, with blond good looks and lusty appetites, but he had soured early after his shotgun wedding to the druggist's daughter and had soon abandoned her to dissipate his small inheritance in more colorful company. Fred had been brought up by his mother in Orange, living as best he could on an irregularly paid allowance, but he had taken charge of his life at an early age and had gone himself to his father to extract the money needed for an inexpensive but third-rate military school which would at least save him from what he imagined to be the social onus, when he went to Yale, of being a public school boy.

His father, who was a bit ashamed of his own conduct, went to some effort to help Fred have the proper clothes as well as the tuition for New Haven. Fred was careful not to ask what loans had been cadged, what desperate promises made, to effect his sartorial elegance. He had little bitterness against his father, but only because he had little time for bitterness. He knew the least that his father owed him, and he was careful to collect every penny of that. If his parents, between them, could just get him on his feet, if they could see him up to the starting line, well, at the sound of the gun he would be off, and there would be no need, moral or practical, to look back. Fred at Yale constructed a family past for his friends which bristled with politics, with corruption, with gleaming glints of ancient scandals. He was always tantalizingly brief, always interesting, always drawing curtains over things better left unsaid. His hearers were given the impression that the Stileses were people who had fallen from some precarious peak, that they must have been romantic, beautiful people, fatally embroiled with the powers of darkness.

If there had been weakness in Fred's background, there must have also been great charm. It was a legend of black and gold. The mother, of course, was totally excised from the fiction.

There was little disposition among Fred's new friends to question his unsolicited explanations, and as he had no witnesses from home or from the Southern military academy which he had attended, he had the advantage of not having to drop old friends or connections. He cultivated the social elite of his class, boys from such schools as Andover, Exeter, Choate, Hotchkiss and Groton, and he correctly divined that the richest and the most socially secure of these would be the least suspicious of false social claims. Anthon Phelps, whose mother was one of the richest women on the Eastern seaboard, and whose family's place on the north shore of Long Island comprised a thousand acres of rustic paradise, became his best friend. Through Anthon he was asked to the better debutante parties, and with his wit, his keen memory, his exact knowledge of who everybody was or ever had been, with his explosive good humor and sudden somber fits of seriousness, and, above all, with his remarkable insight into the nature of other people's worries, he was soon a popular guest in many great houses.

There were enemies, to be sure. Plenty of men at Yale, envious of Fred, spotted him as an adventurer. But Fred had a sure instinct as to which of these were potentially dangerous and which were not. The latter he simply ignored, while the former he cultivated with a flattering zeal which rarely failed. He also possessed a tool of particular value in an era when the affluent Yale undergraduate was prone to do little or no work. He could synthesize a lecture or a test in such a way as to pass on its kernel to a slower intellect with a minimum of struggle. As a "crammer" he not only made a tidy income; he knew when to make a gift of this talent to best advantage. Often a potential slanderer, a would-be investigator into the background of Fred Stiles, would be placated, enchanted, won over by an evening visit from his proposed victim with the cheerful proposition "I hear you're having some trouble with the Schleswig-Holstein question. I thought my notes might give you a hand." And the potential destroyer, not dreaming that Fred had any suspicion of his hostility, glibly now assuming that he must have misunderstood the once despised opportunist, would succumb to his visitor's charm.

If it had been a world of men, Fred might have easily prevailed, or even if he had chosen the right woman. If he had paid his attentions, for example, to Althea Phelps, the stout, good-hearted, but, alas, always perspiring sister of his friend Anthon. But no. Fred had to fly higher, and he was to meet the fate of Icarus. In a mad mood he decided that he would monopolize the attention of the most beautiful and popular debutante of the 1924 New York season, Dora Dunstan, whose career, thanks to a secret alliance between a scheming mother and a group of society reporters who saw the labor that could be saved in concentrating their columns on a single debutante, was achieving national news coverage. Dora, the stupid, rather sullen daughter of domineering parents, found quick relief in the company of an escort as clever and funny as Fred. He knew how to joke with reporters; he was relaxed before the camera, and he took advantage of the power of the press to take Dora to expensive restaurants and speakeasies at no charge to himself. She accepted Fred as she accepted the other accouterments of her fabulous nineteenth year, as her dresses, her headlines, the pop of flash bulbs, and she might even have accepted him as a hubsand had it not been for the intervention of a Yale classmate, Bayard Jones.

Jones was to Stiles as a weasel to a red squirrel, the one predator capable of following him up any tree, down any tunnel, to the death. He was one of those snooty, sneering, effete young men of exaggerated military carriage, who feel it their duty to guard the social citadel against all intruders, who join clubs made up of descendants of revolutionary officers and who would have preferred to ornament the shabby court of an exiled despot than to have been prime minister at home under a popular government. Jealous of Fred's success with Dora Dunstan whose money he coveted despite its origin in bathroom fixtures, he made it his business to investigate Fred's background and drove the bewildered Dora one Saturday afternoon to call on Mrs. Stiles in Orange on the insultingly transparent excuse that they had thought Fred was spending the weekend there. Mrs. Stiles was enchanted to meet the girl with whom she had seen her handsome son so often photographed and gave her and Jones a cup of tea while she prated on happily and innocently about Fred's boyhood, her family, her hardships and her hopes for Fred's ultimate rise in the world.

Now what was wrong about that? Only that it was so different from what Fred had so widely represented. Dora was terrified by this brush with lower middle class living, for which her mother, with bitter memories, had given her the greatest disgust, and even more terrified by Mrs. Stiles' air of possessive affection toward herself which seemed to imply some commitment which had never been made. When she came home she was determined to have nothing to do with Fred in the future. The next time that he telephoned, her mother went to the instrument to tell him not to call again.

It did not take Fred long to find out what had happened. Jones had spread the story throughout Yale. It had all the effectiveness of its venomous simplicity. Jones knew, either by instinct or induction, that complex stories do not travel well. All he needed was a tale in three steps: the boasts of Fred Stiles, the trip to Orange, the revenge of the Dunstans. Nemesis in the relation became nemesis in real life, and Fred found that almost over night he had become ridiculous. It did not last, of course, and he knew at the time that it would not last. But it lasted through the election to the senior societies, and Fred was mortified, standing with his classmates in the old campus, to find that he was not to receive the heartening tap on the shoulder and hear the stern order, "Go to your room!" which divided the elect from the nonelect.

He took it well. He studied hard in his senior year and won a scholarship to the law school. He devoted much time to reading and even cultivated some friends who offered him no social advantages. It began to be said that Fred Stiles was taking his medicine with very good grace, that he had become humbler, that his values had improved. The young are prone to forgive, and to young men especially there is something attractive about a fallen angel. Fred discovered that if he continued to be an object of suspicion to those classmates who belonged to the rich Manhattan group, he was nonetheless cultivated by some of the real college leaders: editors of the "News," or of the Yale "Lit," debaters, members of the Dramatic Society or even of Skull & Bones, so that his social position by graduation was actually superior to what it had been before his crisis. Furthermore, he enjoyed a truer popularity. His wit and his easy companionship made him a welcome visitor in many rooms in the relaxed weeks of the final semester. It was widely felt that Fred Stiles had developed into the kind of man one would wish to have as a "friend in life."

Fred noted all these developments with a caution and a care

which his relaxed attitude never betrayed. He was pleased with his new friends; there was a side of his nature which craved genuine affection. His ambition was by no means entirely vulgar. He aimed at the society of noble souls as well as the company of the rich and great. But he also saw that the greater rewards in life came with a judicious blend of the heart and mind. He realized that his earlier sights had been directed at a pinnacle which was not only too high for his climbing aptitudes but which would not have provided a very comfortable seat if attained. What he needed was a career that would satisfy his passionate curiosity and give opportunity for all his art: he wanted, too, a home life to fulfill his emotional needs. He wanted, in short, to be very happy and very successful. He was a greedy man who had learned at twenty-one that he must keep his greed under a strict discipline.

In the fall of 1927, in the beginning of his second year at the law school, he was already looking ahead to what his first job should be. It was not for reasons of friendship alone that he had selected for his roommate Gordon Lane, a semi-invalid. Gordon's father was Judge Lane, the senior partner of Coates, Lane & Coates in New York City, a firm which, according to Fred's shrewd faculty adviser, was "just the right size and age, neither too big nor too small, neither too old nor too new," in which a talented but unconnected young man might make his mark. Gordon Lane, a victim of rheumatic fever, did not expect to practice in New York, but in Arizona. His father might well have a job for a handsome roommate who was kind to his sickly son.

It all turned out even better than Fred had expected. Gordon Lane had a beautiful nature and a stimulating mind; he seemed to fathom the empty cisterns of his roommate's heart and to sense that they could only be filled by a gradual, persistent flow of affection and sympathy. With Gordon Fred began to think of law as something more than a ladder and of the Lanes as something more than a social convenience. He spent frequent weekends with the latter at Shoal Bay and came to be considered almost as a member of the family. When Gordon died of an attack of pneumonia in the winter of their final year in law school, Fred mourned him as a friend and foster brother. There was no question now about his eventual employment in Coates, Lane & Coates.

He was a success in the firm from the beginning. He found litigation perfectly suited to his abilities. He reveled in its technicalities, its inconsistencies, its anachronisms. He liked to soar with the glorious generalities of old judges, to explore the cerulean skies of Marshall's constitutional concepts and then drop to earth like a stooping falcon to pluck at a loophole in a tax statute. Judge Lane, and after his death, Jamey Coates, made him his principal assistant. Hard-working, driving, imaginative, he was a partner before his thirtieth birthday. But he found that he sorely missed the warm family atmosphere that he had enjoyed at the Lanes' in Gordon's lifetime. They were glad enough to see him, of course, when he called, but it was never the same thing. How could it be? Gordon was not there to bolster his fraternal status. But he was determined to become a Lane again, or at least a Lane-in-law.

And so it came about that he found himself, at a picnic in Shoal Bay, proposing to Edie, the youngest and prettiest of Gordon's sisters. Not surprisingly, he was turned down. Heartbroken, he persuaded himself that he had been passionately in love. And maybe he had been. But Edie, the healthiest and most normal of girls, must have suspected something faintly irregular in this attractive but unusual admirer's evident need to reach through her to greater domestic values than those represented by her person. She might have cherished, as did all the Lanes, the noisy entity of their intense family feeling, hemmed around as it was by shingle cottages and sailboats and guarded by the law in Wall Street and the church in Shoal Bay, but she didn't want to be married for it. It would have been like being married for one's money!

Fred did not take it that way. He felt the jerk of her pulling away, after the discovery of her undenied attraction to him, and he interpreted it, not as a nervous reaction to something insalubrious in his courtship, but as a snobbish rejection of his social insufficiency. Fred was too proud now to continue his intimacy with the Lanes, although he kept up with the Judge's widow. He took greater advantage of his bachelor status to dine out in more exalted social circles where a brilliant and unattached young lawyer was always welcome. He continued to work hard and to prosper, but on a summer weekend one was more apt to see him at the bridge table or the golf course at Piping Rock than at a square dance or a sailing race at Shoal Bay.

Yet it was at Shoal Bay, ironically enough, and not in these newer and smarter haunts, that Fred met his fate in Naomi Fidler. Mrs. Lane had been determined to find a "nice girl" for her poor son's friend, and Naomi, an old school friend of the Lane girls, a bit humbled by divorce, had found their summer colony a friendlier spot for a lonely, single woman than hard-boiled Southampton. Was she not just the bait to dangle before the more worldly Fred, when he paid his duty calls on the dowager of Coates, Lane & Coates?

It is said that all the world loves a lover, but it might be as true to say that all the world loves a match. Naomi, for the first time in her life, set herself out to attract a man. She had learned that a husband was essential to the only life that she had been trained for, and she was easily persuaded by Mrs. Lane that a partnership in Coates, Lane & Coates constituted a social rechristening. Fred, after all, was good-looking, witty and popular. All things considered — and those things certainly had to include Naomi's age and state of divorcement — he was a catch.

Fred was to reflect bitterly afterward that nobody had taken his side. Shoal Bay had united behind Naomi to present her as a woman uniquely trained in how to make even a confirmed bachelor comfortable. If she had had faults, as Jamey Coates gravely informed him, they had been "purged by the fire of her experience." If she had been extravagant, Mrs. Lane assured him, she had now learned to manage. Oh, the girl had been tried, tested! Of course, Fred had not been entirely taken in. Even at her best Naomi could not wholly conceal her bad temper. But he had allowed himself to fancy that it was part of an inner fire which was merging with her passion for himself.

It is easier to hate an individual than a whole community, and Fred, the disillusioned consort, found a degree of rather grim satisfaction in concentrating the thrust of his still concealed resentment on his own inner vision of the round bland face of Jamey Coates. What Fred could never forgive was that Jamey, the Fisher family lawyer, had known of Naomi's sterility and not told him.

"You don't think it was your duty to warn me?" he had asked him. "Your own partner?"

"I never dreamed she wouldn't tell you herself."

"You have great faith in women! Surely you could have at least hinted that I inquire."

"Why didn't you?"

"Because she had two children, damn it all! And she was only thirty-two. Why should I have suspected anything?"

"How was I to know you wanted children? You told me you liked the idea of a ready-made family. Don't you remember?"

"But that was just a joke. Of course I wanted a son. One son, anyway."

"Well, I'm sorry about it, Fred. Truly. But in any event I couldn't have told you. A client's confidences are sacred. But it so happens that we represent an excellent adoption agency that . . ."

"Thanks!"

What made it all a good deal worse was Jamey's evident happiness with Amy, a happiness, moreover, which had produced a son. It was another example of the cruel unfairness of New York life. By all the rules of the game a man of Jamey's appearance and background should have been a courtesy partner, shuffled off to the administration of a few old estates and married to an anemic debutante of more pride than vigor. Yet here he was, the big boss, and happy as a king with a lusty little slut who had caused a stinking scandal all over the East Side of Manhattan.

As the first year of his marriage drew to a close Fred began to recognize that there were certain factors in his life that were never going to change: the quality of his wife's temperament, the limited aspects of their social life, his position in the firm relative to the half dozen partners just ahead of him. He could only conclude that so far as success was concerned, he seemed to have arrived, and that *this* was the goal for which he had striven. He was like the man in the legend who is translated by death to what at first seems a heaven of beautiful women, music and wine, but which turns out, with his gradual sense of its dreary endlessness, to be the other place. And the worst of it all was looking up through a skylight to see Jamey Coates, lolling on a safe cloud with a naked Amy, strumming a golden harp and gazing fatuously at God!

6

ON A SATURDAY morning at the end of September, hot and muggy as only Shoal Bay could be in Indian summer, Amy begged her husband not to go to town.

"We have only another week out here, and you've hardly taken two Saturdays off all summer!"

"Sorry, sweetie, this is a must."

"Another reorganization?"

"No, it's no fun, actually. An internal thing, a firm matter. It could be very nasty."

"Oh, do tell me!"

"I can't. And you mustn't ask."

Amy sighed. Even when she and Jamey were at their most candid, they were like two well-bred children playing tag in a sunlit garden; they were never allowed to hide in the shrubbery or to jump out at each other from behind statuary.

"I only want to help, that's all."

"You do help. Just by being you."

"Oh, no, Jamey, that won't do. You're treating me like Nora

in *A Doll's House*. I want to share your life, your real life. Not just your bed and a lot of parties!"

"You mean you want to share the office?"

"Why not? If I'm not to have a career of my own, shouldn't I try to make one out of yours? And how can I do that unless you make me part of your secrets and worries?"

Jamey looked tried and perplexed, and for just a moment she felt sorry for him. What a bore it must have been to have to placate a nervous woman when one wanted to make one's train. Just because she had a headache, just because she had missed a period and was beginning to wonder if she were not a bit dizzy, did she have to be quite so unreasonable? So female? For that was what he was surely thinking. Why couldn't she tell him that she was probably pregnant and simply wanted him to stay home with her? He would be so pleased, so warm, so happy . . . but now his tone rejected her.

"It's not reasonable of you, Amy, to expect me to tell you secrets that aren't mine to tell."

She flared. "You don't trust me!"

"I trust you with all the things I ought to trust you with."

"Oh, of course! Lists of guests. Cocktails. Canapés. Flower arrangements. Nothing real. Nothing important."

"What's got into you today, darling?"

"I want you to show me that you really trust me. What is it at the office that may be so nasty?"

He sighed. "You make it very difficult."

"Can't you even give me a hint?"

"Well, suppose I have a suspicion that someone at the office has done something wrong. Really wrong. Just a suspicion, mind you. Is it fair to tell anyone, even you, until I've had a chance to investigate it?"

"Is it Fred?"

He became inscrutable. "Why do you say that?"

"Well, he was drinking rather heavily the other night at Mrs. Lane's."

"He's always been a party drinker."

"Yes, but this was worse. Is something wrong between him and Naomi?"

"Maybe we pushed that match too hard."

"You were all so sure she would knock that social chip off his shoulder!"

"The trouble with Naomi is that she knocks the shoulder off with the chip."

Amy looked at him shrewdly. "Of course, you're just trying to get me off the scent. It's not Naomi at all."

"Darling, I've got to go."

"It's not Naomi, is it?"

"I haven't even said it was Fred."

"But it is, isn't it? I'm right!"

"Amy, you are *not* going to get anything out of me, face it!"

"Oh, go ahead, then. Go to your office."

She turned away abruptly, half expecting that he would approach her from behind, turn her around and kiss her. When she heard instead the click of the front door — by him, not by her, not by Nora! — she burst into a fit of unreasonable sobs. Surely, she was pregnant.

When she had regained some of her equilibrium she reflected that she had not told him that at that dinner party, when they were table partners, Fred had been unusually sarcastic. He had always managed to package a sneer into his too fulsome praises of Jamey, but in the past the praises had had the edge. That night there had been a distinctly sharper note.

"He hates Jamey! He always has!" she whispered with conviction. She called Augie, as she had learned now to do when something particularly upset her. His deep, amused, friendly voice on the telephone always consoled her. He had become more like a brother than a brother-in-law; he seemed to have taken the place of the family that she no longer had. Yet she was aware that to him she was still primarily an in-law. He loved her because Jamey loved her and because he was convinced that she had made his brother happy.

"Jamey's quite right, you know," he cautioned her, when she had explained their altercation. "You shouldn't get into his office matters. You're not really interested in them, and he knows that. You just don't want him to have anything you don't have. That's a common disease in all your sex, honey. Don't think I didn't learn it the hard way. You'd better accept Jamey as he is. Let him have his old law. He's doing just fine."

"Sure he is. Why shouldn't he? He's got several wives. The law. His firm. His bar associations. And last and least — me."

"That's an American husband, baby."

"But, Augie, do you call that *love?*"

"What would you call it?"

"How about this: the satisfaction of owning another person?"

"What's the difference?"

"Isn't there any? Can't you see any? I hate that idea. I want Jamey's love to be something . . . well, something terrific."

"Like yours for him?"

"All right, I'm an idiot. I know."

"You've got everything a girl could want," Augie reproached her mildly. "Health, looks, money, a fine baby, a brilliant husband. Why, you even get on with your mother-in-law, in a most un-American way!"

"I'd get on with her a lot better if she were nicer about you. Really, Augie, does she have to be quite so mean?"

"Oh, I don't mind. I think it's even a relief. I always suspected there was a bit of alloy in Ma's extravagant praise of me. She knew I was an idle boozer, running after the gals, but I amused her. Now I bore her. So be it."

"Oh, Augie, you're so good! And you make me feel such a bitch."

"Get your animals straight. It's an ass you're in danger of being. Simmer down, sweetie. You'll find yourself, just as I did. Only in my case there wasn't so much to find."

When their conversation was over, and she went to get little Augie to take him to the beach club, she wondered fretfully if even her relationship with her brother-in-law was unselfish. Didn't she basically want Augie to put her ahead of Jamey in his heart? Didn't she begrudge her own husband the only love that he had ever really received from another human? Looking now at her son in his crib she reflected that his resemblance to Jamey was increasing. He was a peaceful child, who hardly cried at all, and it seemed to her in uneasy moments that he might be lacking in personality. She hoped that the next one would have more of Jamey's . . . fire. Or *was* that the quality?

The beach was not full — most of the Shoal Bay couples had moved back to town — but Amy spied Mrs. Lane under her umbrella, in a red bathing suit and a huge straw hat, working on her eternal needlepoint. When she had settled Augie with his nurse by the children's pool, she joined her.

"You're too passive with Jamey," Mrs. Lane reproached her when she had explained that Jamey was working. "You should insist that he take Saturdays off. That's your job, child."

"Don't you think Jamey's of an age to look after himself?"

"Is any man, ever?"

Amy would have made a little face had she dared. Instead, she tucked away the phrase for an imaginary compilation of

Shoal Bay aphorisms. "Of course, I'd like to think I could help him. Jamey is so self-sufficient."

"You've helped him enormously! We all think you've done a wonderful job of management there."

"Me? How can you say that, Mrs. Lane? Surely, if ever a wife was a poor dominated creature, I'm the one."

"But you arrange to be dominated, my dear. That's what's made Jamey a man."

Amy stared at her. "You mean he wasn't before?"

"Not really, no. Oh, I don't mean that he was lacking in virility, or anything stupid like that. I mean that he wasn't standing on his own two feet, as he is now. He was much too much concerned with other people and what they thought of him. His mother, for example."

"I thought the trouble with Mrs. Coates was that she didn't think of him at all."

"I'm afraid it was worse than that, Amy. She thought poorly of him. And Jamey spent his life trying to prove to her that she was wrong. It was pathetic. I know just how pathetic it was because he used to come to me as a boy to tell all the things he should have been telling her: his successes at school, his fights with other boys, the things he wanted to do when he was grown up."

"I know you were his real mother. He's practically told me that."

Mrs. Lane put down her needlepoint and rubbed her eyelids with her thumb and forefinger. It was her gesture of deepest perplexity. "But do you know something, Amy? I let him down. Oh, I did! I've wanted to tell you this for some time." She sighed, and her tone became actually personal. "I always kept him off. I was always too reserved. Oh, I let him be my little knight, sure. When he visited us, as he did when Iris and Percy were abroad, I always let him pull out my chair and run small errands for me. He knew he was a favorite. And, indeed I loved him — if for nothing else, because he loved me. But I had five children of my own, and it seemed to me that they made up most of my maternal duty. And then I was always afraid of encroaching on Iris' prerogatives, even if she didn't seem to care about them."

"Wouldn't any woman have felt that, in your position?"

"Well, I was wrong!" Mrs. Lane exclaimed sharply. "That boy was my responsibility! Responsibilities don't come in neat little postal packages marked 'mother-son' or 'mother-daughter.' That boy needed me, and I should have let him put his head in my lap and weep if he wanted. But oh, no! I had to play the half-severe, half-humorous sovereign, Queen Bess cuffing a favorite page, calling him to order, joking, snapping. And he wanted a heart, Amy!"

Amy felt suddenly oppressed. Why was it in Shoal Bay, on the rare occasions when people strayed beyond the picket fences of their public personalities, that one wanted them to go back?

"Perhaps what you gave him was enough."

"It wasn't! One had only to see what he made of it, as the years went on. It was fantastic. After my husband died, and Jamey began to take over the firm, he treated me as a kind of queen-dowager, to be consulted, to be flattered, to be given the place of honor on every occasion. And I loved it, old fool that I was!"

"But what was the harm of that?"

"The harm was that it wasn't the role God meant me to play. You see, Amy, we old Bostonians, we know precisely what God expects of us. Only sometimes we know it too late. Instead of romping about like the old Virgin Queen I should have had my eye on what was going on between him and my daughter Sally. But no, I wasn't the interfering type. Hands off! Let the young people work those things out for themselves!"

"Surely they should?"

"If they can! But Jamey was an emotional cripple. He didn't know how to go after Sally. She would have been all ready for him if he had. She waited long enough, God knows!"

"But he *did* propose, didn't he? He told me so."

"Yes, but how? In a way that any full-blooded girl was bound to refuse! And *I* knew just what was going on all the time. *I* could have made Jamey see it! I could have told him how, in a few easy lessons, to be the man Sally wanted. And to be the man he really was!"

Amy smiled, a bit dryly. "I don't suppose you expect me to regret that."

Mrs. Lane burst out laughing in a sudden realization of how far she had gone. "Bless you, child, how you lead one on! You must think I'm the most frightful ass. And, of course, what have I done but prove myself dead wrong? For all the while God may have kept me from interfering because he knew *you* were coming along!"

Amy left her now to go swimming. She yearned for the cold water to wash off Mrs. Lane's revelation. Jamey an emotional cripple! Did the lewd old bawd have to snatch at the last garment in her striptease, the poor little bangled G-string that she called romance?

She swam out vigorously to the deserted raft and back. The water was cold and revitalizing, but she could not rid herself of her sense of anxious apprehension. For if Jamey were really as insecure as Mrs. Lane implied, what was his life constructed upon but a passion which had been ignited by the sham of her own self-dramatization? Did he really know anything about her at all? Had he not first been dazzled by her dramatic outburst to Herman at the nightclub and then by her lurid behavior with Cousin Dolly's codicil? It seemed to her now as if she had come into a world stuffed wtih old dry things, with ancient silks and laces, with faded opera programs, with dusty books of law cases, with high shelves piled with files and records and dreary sums, and had lit it all into a blaze with a single match.

Coming out of the water, she saw that Mrs. Lane had gone, but she noted Fred Stiles sitting on the empty veranda by the outdoor bar. On Saturday the bar opened at eleven, but few of the members used it before lunchtime. For some reason Fred's posture struck her as meaning to emphasize more than usually that morning an alienation from the spirit of Shoal Bay. To begin with, he was not in bathing trunks or even in summer clothes. He was wearing a dark city suit and a white Panama hat, even though the wicker chair in which he was sitting was entirely in the shade. Secondly, he was holding a very dark drink which had a look of not being his first. He was gazing broodingly over the bright beach, on which the children played, and the many-colored umbrellas. Amy felt that his mood might fit her own.

"May I join you?" she called.

"I was just admiring your figure. By all means, join me. Can I order you a drink?"

"It's a bit early for me, thank you. I think I'll just sit." She pulled over a chair beside him.

"Do you seek to reproach me for my morning drink, little Amy? With your Victorian sobriety and your shiny wet sexy figure?"

Amy wondered how many drinks he had had. "I hope you tell Naomi nice things about *her* figure," she retorted, taking off her bathing cap and shaking out her hair.

"Naomi also has a good figure, but her breasts are too large. Yours are better. Rounder, tighter."

"If you're going to make personal remarks, I shall leave you. What would Jamey say if he heard you praising my breasts?"

"He would be astounded. But you and I come from a broader world."

"Am I supposed to take that as a compliment?"

"Unless you have lost your real self behind the protective coloration of Shoal Bay."

"But I *like* Shoal Bay, Fred!"

As his dark eyes mocked her, they seemed even closer together. "Do you know something, Amy? You're trying too hard to be Mrs. James Coates. Relax. Even he owes you a day off now and then."

"You've never liked Jamey, have you?" she said in a sharper tone. "I've always suspected that."

Fred threw up his hands. "How can you be so simplistic? One doesn't like or dislike such a man as Jamey. He's an institution, a way of life. He is to the practice of law what Saint Paul was to the Christian religion. He invented it!"

"You're making fun of him."

"I never make fun of Jamey. I am deadly serious about Jamey."

"But you always manage to imply that there's something a bit ridiculous about him."

"I think perhaps he's the only man in our world who is *not* ridiculous. He believes."

"In what?"

Fred spread his arms dramatically. "In all this. In Shoal Bay. In the law. Even in lawyers!"

But Amy was in a mood to be precise. "I understand about Shoal Bay. I can afford to differ with Jamey there. Shoal Bay doesn't matter. But law is different. What do you mean by Jamey believing in the law? Don't *you?*"

"Perhaps I should have said the practice of law. As exemplified by our own glorious firm."

"You mean to imply it's not glorious?"

Fred sighed. "You do pick one up, dear. All that I suppose I'm trying to say is that Jamey seems to see his partners as Knights of the Round Table and himself as King Arthur."

"I'm sorry to be so literal, but this is a subject in which I happen to be deeply concerned. I've been doing a lot of thinking about it. *Is* Jamey ridiculous? For thinking that he and his partners are public-spirited men of high moral character? Is that just poppycock to you? And would it be poppycock to the other partners?"

"They would not say so."

"What you're telling me, then, is not that Jamey is King Arthur, but that he's a kind of Parsifal. A naif. But doesn't that mean the rest of you are hypocrites? That you give only lip service to ethics?"

Fred's eyes showed a glimmer of impatience. "You're going too far."

"How much too far? I want to know. Seriously. It's important to me. Is it all right, according to you, to coach a witness to lie in court?"

"No, it would be crude. One must merely anticipate what he is likely to say."

"I am trying to find out what you conceive to be the moral

standards of the bar, if any. Would one of your partners bribe a tax auditor if he thought he could get away with it?"

"That would be stupid."

Amy found herself in her turn getting impatient. "Would any of them bribe a juror?"

She fancied that Fred looked at her strangely now. "Why do you ask that?"

"Because I want to find out why you sneer at Jamey. Is it because he professes to act by standards which govern you all, but which you for some reason find it poor taste to proclaim? Or is it because he professes to act by standards which really govern only himself? In other words, are you all good — so that he's a conceited ass to say so — or are none of you good — so that he's a stupid ass to say so?"

Fred seemed to give it up. "Maybe none of us is good."

"Even Jamey?" Fred shrugged in answer. "No, that won't do, Fred. I believe that Jamey *is* good. Very good. But he may still be naive in believing that others are like him. That you, for example, are like him."

"Oh, so I strike you as unscrupulous?"

Amy decided that they were getting shrill. "No. But you strike me as wishing to appear as more worldly wise, more sophisticated, than Jamey. And to imply that Jamey is to some extent living in a fool's paradise. How, then, can I help but wonder if some of his partners may not be doing things he wouldn't approve of?"

Fred looked at her now with eyes of unconcealed hostility. When he spoke, it was to change his tack. "Is Jamey really as good as all that?"

"You don't think so?"

"And was he always?"

"Since I've known him."

"Really? I should have thought that at least one time you might have had the occasion to observe him in a breach of ethics. That you might even have been grateful for it."

Amy felt an instant darkening in the atmosphere, as if a storm were announcing itself. In the suddenness of her alarm she looked out over the beach and was surprised to see that it was as hot and sunny as before. When she opened her lips to speak, her mouth was too dry for words. She coughed.

"You're wondering how I learned that," Fred continued in a now matter-of-fact tone. "It was when you gave those paintings to Naomi's daughters. I couldn't imagine your motive, unless it were involved with some kind of guilt. At first I thought it might be because you had taken Herman away from her. But no woman ever really feels guilty about a little thing like that. And then I recalled something. You had got those paintings through Miss Chadbourne's will. The word 'will' struck a bell. Hadn't there been a codicil? I distinctly remembered going with Jamey to act as witness to a codicil to Miss Chadbourne's will shortly before her death. Yet I could not for the life of me recall giving any testimony about it in the surrogate's court. How, then, had that codicil been probated?"

The fear that invaded her now was like some repulsive, clawing thing. She put one hand to her throat as if to elude its grasp. She wanted to jump up, to holler.

"There *was* a codicil," she managed to utter in a half-whisper. "But Cousin Dolly tore it up."

"That occurred to me, too, of course," the inexorable voice went on. "And knowing that Jamey would never destroy a record, even to cover a misfeasance, I went to the files myself. Sure enough, I found a copy of the codicil. It was no trifling matter, either. It simply switched the entire principal of Miss Chadbourne's trust from Herman to his daughters! And on it was penned a memorandum in Jamey's handwriting to the effect that Miss Chadbourne had destroyed the original and that the torn pieces were in an envelope in safe papers!"

Amy still did not look at him. After a pause of some seconds, she asked simply: "Well?"

"That raises no question in your mind? It does not seem to you that it might have been Jamey's duty, in view of Miss Chadbourne's mental condition at the time, to submit the pieces of the codicil to the surrogate, put all interested parties on notice and let the court decide if the instrument had been validly revoked?"

"I'm not a lawyer, Fred."

"No, but does it take a lawyer to smell fraud? Here are two innocent little girls calmly done out of a fortune without a chance to defend their rights."

"It wasn't all that great a fortune."

"I see we've changed our standards since we've become Mrs. James Coates! But is it even permissible to steal a small fortune?"

"It went to their father, anyway. He'll leave it to them."

"*If* he still has it! And if he hasn't married again and had other children. Come, Amy, you know all that has nothing to do with the price of eggs. Jamey suppressed that codicil for a reason. Why should he have cared whether Herman or the girls got the money? What was there in it for him to take the smallest risk over the matter? Obviously, he must have done it to protect somebody, and who could that somebody be but the person who had really destroyed the codicil? And who was that? Well, Herman Fidler was my obvious first suspect, but how was he to get his hands on his aunt's codicil? How? Why, obviously through the connivance of his aunt's companion, who happened to be his own mistress. It was clear as daylight! You, Amy, destroyed the codicil, and when Jamey discovered the pieces, he put the story together as quickly as I have. Only he demanded *you* as the price of his silence. You had to yield to his lustful importunity, but later, finding that you were pregnant, you forced him to marry you or be exposed as the seducer of the poor relative of a client. My God, it's like a Jacobean tragedy by Webster or Tourneur!"

Amy's terror had continued to mount as Fred, step by step, had paced out the truth of what had happened. But at his first false deduction a small tide of relief had begun to seep through her being.

"And what will you do with your theory?" she demanded more boldly now.

Fred laughed easily. "Suppose I were to hold it over you as Jamey did? Suppose I were to demand that you submit your white body to my lust?"

"Is that a threat?"

"No. Though any time you should be interested in that sort of thing, you would find me rather intensely willing. Indeed, it would give me a very special titillation to *tromper* my dear partner, Jamey. I think under such circumstances I might operate as a very potent lover indeed. You should try me, Amy."

"You forget. It's Jamey who sees the firm as the Round Table, not I. I have no intention of playing Guinevere to your shabby Lancelot. And, of course, you know your story's all nonsense. Jamey never threatened me with anything."

"He didn't?" Fred reached over to touch the upper part of her thigh with his forefinger. Then he ran the nail slowly down her leg. When she made no move he pushed his forefinger and thumb under the suit and pinched her buttock. "Well, then, he didn't. You have nothing to fear from me, little one. I shall not betray your codicil tearing. I wouldn't want to watch Naomi's satisfaction or see the zeal with which she'd go after Herman. Let him have the money, poor man. He needs it. And in the meantime I've had the mean little pleasure of scaring you shitless."

"Why do you think I'm so scared?"

"Because you let me pinch your sacred little Shoal Bay ass! And when there's fear, there's the beginning of attraction. I can wait, Amy. I can wait."

The repulsive part of it was that he was right. She *was* attracted, suddenly, violently.

"I think I will have that drink, after all. You'd better make it a double gin."

"To celebrate your immunity? Good girl. I'll get it."

When he returned, she drank the gin in slow, painful gulps, saying nothing and staring at the sea. There was a low appeal to her in his very weakness, his vileness, or maybe simply in her desire to be so appealed to. She was as bad, as rotten as he, and what had she done but drag a good man, an innocent man, after her, so that he was now at the mercy of this skunk? Oh, but she was a skunk, too, and belonged with skunks! And she wanted Fred now. She wanted to run down the beach with him and tear off her bathing suit and then strip the clothes off his long white bony body. She closed her eyes tightly as the gin made her temples throb. Salomé! Salomé with the long white body of the Baptist!

"I've decided that I don't want to owe you anything," she said at last. "I shan't even change into my clothes. I'll get a coat and put it over me. We can take your car and drive down the beach road. I know a spot. It's where we go for picnics." She rose. "Come on, Lancelot!"

He looked up at her, his mouth half open in a twisted smile, his eyes gleaming with something like fear. "Not if you're going to act like a white slave, my dear."

"Don't worry. Come on."

"Shouldn't we stop and get . . ."

"Never mind that. It's quite safe. I'm pregnant."

❧ 7 ❧

JAMEY, ALONE AT his desk the following Monday, waiting for John Rappelye, read and re-read the memorandum that he had received from the managing clerk. It implicated only John, to whom he had promptly sent a copy with the request that he come right over, but was it possible for John to be involved without Fred?

He had certainly noted changes in Fred's behavior in the past weeks. He had been coming to the office later and leaving earlier. He had not been in on a single Saturday. He had been so rough in his manner with one of the clerks that Jamey had been obliged to intervene to prevent his resignation. And at partners' lunches, after a second or third martini (the others never had but one) he had taken to making references to "our glorious senior" in a tone that was barely distinguishable from a sneer.

Of course, Jamey had always known that Fred envied and

resented him. But he had weighed the possible advantages and disadvantages to the firm of this and had long since concluded that it might operate as a desirable incentive, and, indeed, Fred had proved himself an active force in the litigation department of the reorganized firm. Jamey had come to think of their relationship as analogous to that of the headmaster of a New England church school and a brilliant agnostic teacher who was willing to attend chapel services and refrain from imparting his views to the students. Never before had he suspected Fred's essential loyalty.

Never before. But now there was this memorandum:

> *Following up the rumor which you mentioned to me, I made inquiries last night at the Reporters' Club. It seems that the U.S. Attorney's Office is looking into a series of loans made to Ajax Corp. Ajax is a real estate holding operation in Queens of which Judge Abel Stephens is a large stockholder. Some of the loans are said to have been made by parties to litigation pending in the second circuit. I am told that John Rappelye's name is on the list.*

Fred's reaction had been most unsatisfactory. When Jamey had showed him the memorandum he had merely shrugged.

"Yes, I've heard that. But I advise you not to get involved. These things can be dynamite. If John has been fiddling with justice, that's his lookout."

"But you won that case, Fred! Don't you care if your court was rigged?"

"I'm not the keeper of my client's conscience. I prepared and argued his brief to the best of my ability, and, naturally, I'd like to think it was my ingenuity that won it. But if John, who's been reduced to near insanity by this whole case, has chosen to adopt additional safeguards behind my back, I don't want to know about it. It's simply not our business."

"I can't understand that. Suppose John is indicted?"

"He won't be. They're after the judge. They'll be perfectly satisfied if they get his head. And from what I hear, they will."

"And will you represent John in the investigation?"

"Oh, no. He can get himself a criminal lawyer. I should suggest Nick Perez."

And that had been all he would say on the subject. Jamey had decided that it might be better if he had the first interview with John Rappelye alone.

When John came in, he seated himself almost insolently in the big armchair in the corner, refusing the smaller chair by Jamey's desk. A small, half-mocking smile relieved some of the rigor of his craggy countenance. He waved his copy of the memorandum at Jamey. "I've read this thing. It's all right."

"What's all right about it?"

"I made that loan to Ajax, sure. Why not? May I not make loans as I choose? I've made a good many odder than that."

"With the purpose of influencing a court's decision?"

"I don't see that my motives are your affair."

"When we represent you?"

"Does that mean I must open my books to you? The idea is impertinent, Jamey."

"It is highly pertinent to a litigator to know if his court has been purchased. Do you realize, John, that this could result in the retrial of your whole case?"

"That's hardly likely. After our victory in the second circuit we settled the matter most satisfactorily. Once that was done, and the breach healed, we found that we could do business very nicely with our erstwhile foes. As a matter of fact, when you called, I was about to call *you*. A merger is now under discussion. When we've ironed out the main points we'll be coming to you for the legal glue. Mergers are more your department than Fred's, aren't they?"

Jamey, fascinated, appalled, sat down and faced away from his client, as he thought this over. What was John saying but that the world of reality was *his* world? A world where litigants could make peace when they wished and continue their money-making under the benign rays of a purchased sun? And lawyers — what were lawyers but dolls, talking, squeaking, crying, dressed-up dolls whose purpose was to represent the rules and principles in which the true leaders of economic society did not even pretend to believe? He turned back to his visitor.

"Do you seriously believe that I'll continue to represent a client who admits to my face that he's bought a federal judge?"

John's smile disappeared at once. "I have admitted no such thing. I have made a loan, that's all. Part of my business is to make loans. Most of your clients have undoubtedly done things of which the sublime James Coates would disapprove. Do you seriously believe you'd have any practice at all if you only represented the Christers you pretend you do represent? Surely, even you, Jamey, must have moments of occasionally glimpsing the truth! You wouldn't be quite so sucecssful if you spent as much time in dreamland as you like to make out."

"Do you know you could go to jail?" Jamey almost shouted. "Unless the U.S. Attorney gives you immunity for your testimony?"

"There has already been some little talk of that," John retorted coolly. "I am not in the least concerned. I have been assured by Mr. Perez that I need anticipate no unpleasant consequences."

"Oh, you have retained Perez already?"

"Simply for this matter. It seemed the appropriate thing. I had no wish to embarrass you. You see how considerate I am?" John rose now and gazed calmly down at his angry host. "I trust that when you've had a chance to cool off and think this over, you'll come to your senses and stop this talk about severing an old and mutually profitable relationship."

"We cease to represent you and your firm as of *now!* And what is more, I don't even wish to see you again. Fred Stiles can take care of winding up any outstanding matters."

John stared at him for a moment with a nasty little smile, as if deliberating whether or not to say something indiscreet. The temptation, at any rate, was at last too great. "You think I pollute your atmosphere?"

"If you wish to put it that way."

"I suggest that Saint Jamey the hermit sniff around the cells of some of his sainted partners to see if the pollution comes entirely from without."

"What do you mean by that?"

"Simply that Fred Stiles was at all times aware of what I was doing — whatever *that* may have been. And that he even supplied me with a helpful name. But don't worry, Jamey. No one knows that little fact but Fred and me. And whatever you may think of my morals, nothing would induce me to betray Fred. Even for the admittedly great satisfaction of humiliating *you!*"

John with this strode from the office, and a stricken Jamey could do nothing but call out to Mrs. Glennan to tell Mr. Stiles to come at once.

"Close the door!" he exclaimed hoarsely when Fred appeared. "Tell me," he pursued, "is it true what John says? That you knew he had bribed Judge Stephens? And knew it when you argued that appeal? *Knew* that one of the judges you were trying to convince already had been? And that you told John how to get in touch with him?"

Fred, with a curious replica of the little smile that Jamey had already noted on John's face, seemed unperturbed. "No, it is not true," he replied softly.

"You deny it? He lied to me?"

"He lied to you. Evidently." Fred shrugged. "It's very odd, I grant. But I told you. He's gone dippy over this thing."

"Odd indeed! For whatever else John may be, he's a gentleman."

"Of course!" Fred retorted in a sneering tone. "He went to Groton with you, didn't he? How could a mere partner ever be trusted like a fellow Grottie?"

"But what possible motive had he?"

"Perhaps misery likes company. And then you're so smug, Jamey. He might have said it to take you down a peg."

"I don't believe it! Look here, Fred. If I decide this thing is true, do you know what I'll have to do? I'll have to go to the Grievance Committee and tell them what John has told me."

Fred seemed almost more perplexed than frightened. "And may I ask what proof you would offer for so slandering your poor partner?"

"None! They'd have to decide which of us to believe."

Fred now gaped. "You can't be such a fool, Jamey!"

"Do you think I'm going to continue to practice law with a man who's done what you've done?"

"What *I've* done?" Fred seemed to be struggling with an emotion that was choking him. Then, with a deep sigh, he regained control of himself. When he spoke, his tone was calm, almost weary. "All right, Jamey, look into the matter. I don't know how you're going to find out, but try. Just do one thing for me, will you? Before you do anything crazy, like going to the Grievance Committee, give me fair warning. Okay?"

Jamey did not even answer him. He simply walked to the door and opened it in a silent gesture of dismissal.

8

"You're a dear to come at such late notice. Olive Lester has a cold, and John's mother is such a stickler for a balanced table. But I feel I know you well enough to ask a favor. You're sure you don't mind coming without Jamey?"

"Oh, no. I rather like it, in fact. I miss him so when he goes on business trips, I need distraction."

"How sweet!" Sandra Rappelye, tall, fixedly smiling, in sky blue, standing in the double doorway to her parlor before a large statue of Hester Prynne fingering the marble letter on her breast, gazed at Amy as if she suspected something.

"I suppose that sounds fatuous," Amy added.

"Not at all, my dear, not at all. I feel just that way about my John. But have you heard about the row?" Sandra just glanced into the room where her husband and other dinner guests were standing. "John didn't see fit to mention it until I told him you were coming tonight."

"A row? You don't mean between him and Jamey?"

"I'm afraid so. I haven't the faintest idea what it's all about, but I'm sure it will be patched up. It needn't concern us wives, do you think?"

Amy reflected that her hostess' enamel cheer might survive any catastrophe. Moving away from her now into the parlor, she touched her finger to the front of her dress as though, like Hester, she were adjusting the scarlet letter.

Her host approached her with a smile too broad. "If I'd known Sandra was going to ask you, I'd have warned her! But you were good to come, Amy."

"I can't imagine why. Jamey hasn't said a word to me about anything."

"Well, I guess that's all right, then."

"Oh, I see your mother. How nice! Let me go and talk to her."

"She'll love that."

Amy moved to the alcove where old Mrs. Rappelye had just seated herself, away from the other guests, as though her great age might be an embarrassment to them. The dowager at once released a little plashing stream of compliments and comments.

"And where's your dear husband?" she interrupted herself to ask.

"On one of those tiresome business trips. How I hate them! I suppose it's wrong for a couple to be as self-sufficient as Jamey and I are."

For one terrible hour, on that Saturday night in Shoal Bay six weeks before, she had considered telling Jamey the truth. But when she had heard the sound of his wheels in the driveway and had gone out to greet him and seen how tired he looked — he who so rarely showed it — her heart had turned over. It was not only that he was a man and Fred Stiles a skunk; it was suddenly obvious that it was her duty to keep skunks away from him. Then and there, standing in the driveway, she had made the frantic resolution to treat what had happened as the mere climax of a past nervous crisis. And as she pretended now to listen to the prattle of her host's mother, she wondered if she were not learning to live with it.

"I think it's so wonderful when young people are happy together like that. It makes all the difference in life. My dear husband and I were never separated except when he went to Cuba with Colonel Roosevelt. And then he wrote me every day. Sometimes I would get a dozen letters in a single mail."

There were three paintings in the alcove where they were sitting, all, Amy supposed, by Gérôme, or at least in his style. They were lit brilliantly, and painted brilliantly; the only colors amid that dark rich blackness of the midnight mahogany, of ebony statuettes of deer and hounds, of Mrs. Rappelye's satin mourning. It struck Amy that their common subject was virtue embattled: Susanna, bold, ivory white, denouncing the hunched-over, cowering elders; Lucretia, disheveled, tearful, raising the knife that was to free her from shame; Theodora escaping from the brothel disguised as a Roman soldier. But hadn't the artist meant to convey, in the rounded white shoulder of the fiery virgin, in the exposed breast of the suicidal matron, in the bare legs of the flying princess, a hint of concupiscence, a snicker of sympathy for the lust which such glimpses inspired, a suggestion that the holy women themselves may have shared, deep down, subconsciously or even in partial awareness, the very urges that they denounced?

"I never stop counting my blessings," the old lady continued. "When I think, with all the divorces that you hear about today, of the happiness of my John and Sandra, it makes me humble indeed."

Did she mean it? Did she know nothing? Suppose Amy were to tell her that Herman Fidler had left this very house two years before to spend the night with her in the flat that John

Rappelye kept for his adulteries? Suppose she were to tell her that the same promiscuous female, only six weeks before, her bare back and buttocks scratched by the damp sand of a Long Island beach, had raised her knees and writhed in the heat of guilt to receive the clumsy, half-drunken thrust of the very man now appearing in the doorway? Surely, there was no common denominator between a woman like herself and Mrs. Rappelye; they had to live in worlds as different as Milton's heaven and Milton's hell!

"Sandra is so beautiful," she declared boldly. "And so noble. It's impossible even to imagine Sandra thinking of a man other than her husband."

"Oh, dear, yes — I mean no," Mrs. Rappelye murmured, embarrassed.

Fred Stiles, looking dark and a bit haggard, almost as if he hadn't shaved, although Amy could see, as he came up to them, that he had, bent down to speak loudly in the old lady's ear.

"I'm so sorry, Mrs. Rappelye. I have a rather important question to put to Amy. Would you mind terribly if I took her away for a minute?"

"Oh, dear boy, of course not. I have to go over to speak to Caroline Bayard, anyway. So you just sit right down here in my place."

Amy stared disgustedly at Stiles as he sat down next to her.

"What the devil do you think you're doing?" she asked, as Mrs. Rappelye hobbled away. "I have nothing to say to you. I thought I made that entirely clear. Our transaction was a simple matter of business. It's over."

"You put a lot of ardor into that business," he sneered.

"I had my reasons." She watched him coldly until the sneer had vanished. Then she paused to consider what she could say that would hurt him most. "It was a simple act of masturbation. *Now* will you leave me?"

"Not until I've said what I've come to say. I've phoned, but you wouldn't answer my calls."

"I told you that I would see you and talk to you only in public — and then only formally."

"Look, if you're afraid I'm going to suggest another . . . well, forget it. I feel the same way. But I've still got a hold on you, and now I'm afraid I'm going to have to use it."

"You mean you're going to welsh! You can't be such a filthy crook!"

"Hush up! Let's not have people looking over here. I never threatened you with anything, and I never promised you anything. All that talk about blackmail and ransom was *your* idea. But now I find myself in a fix, and I need your help. Will you just listen to me? For one minute?"

Amy began to realize that she was facing a desperate man. She let her silence be assent.

"I don't know if you've noticed, but your husband is a bit off his rocker these days. He's taken it into his crazy head that I helped John Rappelye bribe a federal judge."

Amy stared at him intently. So that was what was causing Jamey's worry. "And did you?"

"No. Oh, I may have given John the name of some guy on the judge's staff. Which he could have got from a dozen other people. It was nothing, really. And John would deny it, anyway."

"Then why are you so worried?"

"Because of Jamey! If Jamey goes blabbing his head off to the Grievance Committee, there's no telling what may happen!" Fred's voice rose into a kind of shrill squeak, and she saw that the yellow flecks in his eyes were panic. "After all, he oozes virtue. He has a big reputation. The committee might decide to question John under oath, and under oath . . . well, who knows?"

"He might even tell the truth?"

"Let's put it that he might say something embarrassing. So Jamey mustn't do it. You must keep him from doing it. You must save the firm."

"The firm? You mean save Fred Stiles?"

"Put it any way you want. But *do* it."

"And if I decline the honor?"

"Then I'll have to go to Jamey and tell him what I know about the codicil. And then I'll go to the surrogate."

"Why don't you tell him yourself, in the first place?"

"Because he gets so hysterical with me! He might be willing to cut off his snotty little nose to spite his pretty face. You're the only one to make him see reason. You're the one to make him see that if we both just hold our tongues, everything will be all right. Doesn't that make sense?"

"And suppose I say no? That it makes no sense?"

"Damn it, Amy, you drive me too far! Suppose I tell him about *us*?"

"Do you think for a minute he'd believe you?"

"Do you want to take the chance?"

Amy contemplated him scornfully. "It must be sad to be as mean a cad as you are."

"Is what I'm asking you so great a thing, for Christ's sake?"

"Get up. We're going in to dinner."

In the dining room, of course, she found that she was seated next to him. She talked to Bayard Jones, on her other side. He had detested Fred ever since their Yale days, and he now told her with relish of the rumor that the Stileses were about to separate. Amy, glancing down the table at Naomi and hearing her high, nervous laugh, decided that it might be true. The conversation turned.

"Have you decided if you'll do it?" Fred asked doggedly.

"When would I have to?"

"When does Jamey come home?"

"He should be back tomorrow night."

"Tomorrow night, then." Fred smiled faintly as he gulped the rest of his wine. "Isn't night the time for a lovely wife to ask a favor?"

"Don't be foul. And watch your drinking."

"Face it, Amy. You've got to do this little thing for me."

"Not if I'm prepared to face the consequences. And anyway, I don't think you'd dare tell Jamey about me. He might kill you."

Fred, in his obvious anxiety at the idea, actually signaled the waitress that he wanted more wine. Amy observed that Sandra, though impassive, had noted it. "Well, I'll just have to risk it!"

"*If* I decide to do what you ask, it'll be for Jamey's sake, not my own. And there'll be a condition. A stringent one."

"Do you think you're in a position to bargain?"

"One is always in a position to bargain. If one is reckless enough. And I'm reckless, Stiles. Believe me!"

"What's your condition?"

"That you resign from Coates, Lane & Coates."

Fred seemed at first almost more curious than surprised. "Why do you ask that?"

"Because I know that Jamey will insist on it. He'll never consent to practice law with you again — no matter what you threaten."

"Then *he* can resign."

"Ah, but he won't."

They were conscious now of one voice, a louder voice. The conversation at table had become general, and Bayard Jones was talking shrilly about the arrival in Paris from Spain of the survivors of the Abraham Lincoln Brigade. The American colony had been criticized for refusing them help.

"People say Americans should look after Americans, but I say nobody should look after communists. The Reds say their movement is international, that it transcends national lines. Well, so does ours! And I would refuse to feed or clothe or help in any way a communist, were he ten times an American!"

Miss Bayard, for once, supported her nephew. "I'm proud to hear you say it, Bayard!"

"I think he's a hundred percent right," John Rappelye agreed heartily. "We're facing a war to the finish between two ideologies, capitalism and communism. The greatest mistake America can make is to assume the Nazis are the enemy. Damn it all, they should be allies!"

"Dear me, how embattled we're getting," Sandra intervened. "You gentlemen are so fierce; I wonder what some of the other ladies think. What about you, Amy?"

"Oh, me," Amy replied calmly, looking around at the attentive faces with a detachment that surprised herself. "I care only for poor human beings. I'd be glad to help anyone who had fought in Spain. If a man is willing to put his life on the line for an ideal, well, the least I can do is bandage his wound."

Sandra at once turned to her neighbor to indicate that the conversation should return to particulars, and Amy smiled, grimly now, at Fred.

"You see what I dare," she told him.

"And I'm your man," he replied at once. "As for my resignation, it's already in the works. I'm going to be general counsel to John Rappelye's new merged firm."

"But you were hoping to stay with Jamey and make him swallow John as well, weren't you?"

Fred sighed, but there was a reluctant admiration in it. "You drive a hard bargain."

༥ 9 ༖

AMY WAS PLEASED with herself on the following day as she waited for Jamey to come home. It seemed to her that she was operating as his equal at last. She likened herself to Talleyrand, who had gone to the Congress of Vienna empty-handed and returned with his pockets full. She had risen to a dangerous challenge; she had worked out a peace with honor. No longer need the picture of a Jamey Coates who had married her in a moment of neurotic misapprehension be disturbing. Even if they both had their fantasies, they could still be a team.

He arrived late, almost at eleven, looking harassed and preoccupied. Amy, in a pink negligee, had placed a bottle of champagne in an ice bucket. When he noted it, he looked at first blank, then concerned.

"Oh, poor sweetie! Is it the anniversary of something? Have I forgotten?"

"No, no, it's just that I'm so glad to have you back!"

He relaxed and went to the bucket to uncork the bottle.

"Well, this will go to the right place, anyway." He poured two glasses and handed her one. "Here's to you!" He drank, but then suddenly frowned. "I was surprised, when I telephoned last night, to hear you'd gone to the Rappelyes. Of course, there's no reason you should have known it, but I've had a bad falling out with John. In fact, I've fired him as a client. I suppose he hadn't told Sandra."

"He hadn't. But I heard all about him and that judge from Fred Stiles."

Jamey's face darkened. "Oh, was he there, too?"

"He was there. And he told me that you suspect him of being mixed up in it."

"That is perfectly true." Jamey was now very grave.

"That he was mixed up in it or that you suspect him?"

"That I suspect him. It's John's word against his. But I can't imagine why John should lie to me."

"Darling, I have something very serious to tell you." She patted the sofa to indicate that he should sit beside her, but he went instead to the fireplace and faced her. His expression was halfway between a grimace and a grin, his habitual signal of defiance, or at least resistance, to rare ill fortune.

"You have bad news. Let me have it."

"Fred has pieced together the truth about Cousin Dolly's codicil. Or most of it. He knows it was torn up and that you kept the pieces. He will go to the surrogate if you go to the Grievance Committee. He says you can either both talk or both hold your tongues. That it's up to you."

In the silence that followed, as he took this solemnly in, she could only marvel at his impassiveness. He must have been waiting for this moment for two years!

"I see. Very well. It will not alter my decision."

"But, darling, wait! There's something else! I got him to promise to resign from the firm. *If* you don't talk."

"*You* did? Why?"

"Because I knew you'd never go on practicing law with someone you regard as a crook!"

"With a crook in my firm? I should hope not! But what about a crook at the bar? The man must be exposed, Amy! It's my duty!"

"And what will happen to you? If *he* talks?"

"I must abide the consequences."

She jumped up, clasping her hands to beseech him. "But, Jamey, that's horrible! When it was all my fault, too. Surely, there must be a way *I* can take the blame. What do I do? Go to court? Make a clean breast of it? I'm ready for anything. Oh, darling, you'll be proud of me!"

His eyes softened. "I'm that already. But fortunately, sweet, this thing is mine, all mine. You see, in law, the crime was not in tearing up the codicil. It was in suppressing the pieces. For that I was solely responsible."

"But you did it to shield me!"

"Is that an excuse? Listen, love. All I ask is that you be patient and brave while I do what I have to do. I shall start by going to the Grievance Committee and telling them what I've heard about Fred. I had some slight doubt about his guilt, but now none. Not after what he told *you*. I shall then go to the surrogate and make a full statement about the codicil. I'll tell him that you tore it up, under great provocation, in a moment of high tension, but that *I* concealed the pieces in my office safe. Let me take the blame that belongs to me, as a lawyer. Don't worry that none of it seems to fall on you. Time, I fear, will take care of that. You and I will have to bear the penalty together."

Amy began now to take in the full gravity of what was before them. It was not a case, as she had vaguely surmised, of simply restoring funds. "Oh, darling," she breathed, "will they disbar you?"

"Well, if they don't, they ought to!"

She looked at him with something like wonder. "But you seem . . . almost as if you were . . . relieved! Have you felt so guilty about it, all this time?"

"No, no. It's a hard thing to explain."

"And I thought it was my crime, my own crime, to confess, to expiate!" she moaned.

"But don't you see that this way it's easier for me? I couldn't bear it if it was you alone. What I did I did for you and only you and my love for you. I didn't hesitate. I wouldn't hesitate again! You were more important to me than all of morals and law and life. And I loved feeling that! But now that Fred's discovered it and thinks he can blackmail me, the game is up. I shall disbar him, even if I disbar myself. Don't look so sad, love. It's not the end of the world. We have some money. There are millions of things we can do. I've always envied Augie his year in the trenches. Well, now I'm going to have my own little war. Maybe I'll even like it!"

Amy went over to throw her arms around his neck and press her head against his chest. It seemed to her that they were closer at that moment than ever in their deepest physical union. She shut her eyes tightly as she hugged him. He was there, more there than ever before, not just the lawyer, the arranger, the fusser, the bitter son, the senior partner, the too constant lover, but, quite simply, the hero she had yearned for in all her crazy daydreams. The Brontë governess had found her Rochester! The novel had come true. But, ah, what had she become? Good God, what was *she*?

"Oh, darling," she murmured. "If you only *knew* how I admire you!"

"Do you think I'm in Augie's league yet?"

"Oh, beyond, beyond!"

Something in his tone made her slightly relax her hug. It was the faintest — oh, the very faintest — suggestion of a note of boyishness. But no, she wasn't going back to that. If he was immature, it was only the more reason that she should see what she could do! *Her* mind, at any rate, or so it seemed to her at that moment, had never been harder, more adult. The events of her life were pouring through the corridors of her memory like lines of soldiers trotting in close order drill, now pairing up, now separating, now proceeding down the main hall, four abreast . . .

"You must give me time," she murmured. "You must give me time to think. One doesn't destroy so many lives in a day."

Long after he had gone to sleep that night she lay awake thinking. That they should give up everything to bring Stiles to justice seemed to her beautiful beyond anything that she could imagine. But Fred would surely in his snarling downfall betray the scene on the beach. She might, of course, try to explain this as the price for his silence, as a degradation which she had incurred to save her husband, but wouldn't there be a lie in the very foundation that supported the beauty of what they were planning to do? And if she told Jamey the truth . . . well, it would be quite beyond him. He would be stripped at once of his love and his law practice; he would have nothing left.

Rising and roaming the apartment she sought desperately in the shadows for a solution. If there were only a way to acquit him of the codicil and leave him free to bring down Fred, it would not matter so much if she were lost to his love. He would still have his integrity; he would still have his firm. He would be, in short, as he had been when he had first met her. Ah, if she could only restore him to *that,* why should it be important what happened to her? The country cousin could go back to the country; it was where she belonged. And then, suddenly, she thought of the self-portrait of Herman Fidler entering the room where the silly cocktail party was going on . . .

❧ 10 ❧

ON THE FOLLOWING afternoon at six o'clock Amy met her husband at the Madison Avenue gallery that was exhibiting Herman Fidler's new show: "Vesuvius and the Bourbons." Herman had suggested that they come at closing time and see the pictures before discussing the matter that she had broached in a morning visit to him. Jamey had not been at all enthusiastic about being, even so briefly, the guest of his wife's former lover, but under the circumstances, as Amy had warmly urged, he was hardly in a position to decline.

All of the pictures in the exhibit had been painted during a six month visit by Herman to Naples. In the background of each large canvas could be seen a smoking volcano, sometimes as small and innocuous as a cigarette butt, sometimes black, ugly, menacing. All over the foregrounds was the yellow blue, green blue, gold blue of the Mediterranean, pulsating, iridescent, serene, soothing, menacing, sometimes rolling onto beaches, sometimes soaring into the sky, enveloping, cerulean. And looming out of the water or out of the clouds, sitting on chairs or thrones, standing stiffly in coronation robes or lolling about in what seemed to be nightgowns, or even rather desperately swimming, were the King and Queen of Naples, Ferdinand and Maria Carolina, with their myriad offspring, Nelson's royal family, Lady Hamilton's, with large, putty-white, scared, staring rabbity faces and big, haughty, reproachful, scared eyes.

Amy made a slow tour of the little gallery with Herman, while Jamey sat in a corner moodily reading the catalogue.

"I think they're fascinating," she commented, when they had finished. "Nobody has a chance. If the sea doesn't get them, the mountain will."

Herman smiled. "You don't think they can learn to swim?"

"Never. But I see you've done the queen three times. She reminds me of Naomi."

"Don't all queens?"

"Because they can't feel anything but pride and terror?"

"You do see it."

"But it must be rather exciting to feel nothing but pride and terror. Most of us feel only terror. Oh, Herman, honestly, I think they're very good! And to think I didn't even know you were having this show! Jamey and I live so remote from the art world — it's shocking, really. But I'm happy about your success. I'm even conceited enough to think I may have had a small part in it."

"Well, I shouldn't call myself a success, but whatever I am, you had a very definite part in it. Without you I might never have got out of my rut."

Amy glanced back at Jamey. But he couldn't hear them. "Watch out! I may claim a commission on what you sell. Amy, the rut-getter-out-of."

"Oh, I guess Mrs. James Coates has better things to do than pull people out of ruts."

"You'd be surprised."

"You mean you're going to get Jamey out of his?"

She flushed slightly. "Of course, you've really never appreciated Jamey. None of his old friends do."

"One can appreciate Jamey and still perceive the rut."

"If he's in one, he's just as capable of getting out of it as you were!"

"And if a certain matter isn't settled to the satisfaction of all concerned, he may find himself blasted out of it. Is that it? But we must find a way of avoiding that. Ah, there now, it's closing time."

The secretary was shutting the front door behind the last of the visitors. Now she crossed the gallery to the office. Herman proceeded to open a cabinet with bottles and glasses. Jamey rose and came over to them.

"I'd rather not drink, thank you, Herman. You told Amy you had a proposition to offer. I'd appreciate your telling us what it is."

Jamey's tone was clipped, if civil. Amy felt bound to protest. "Darling, don't rush him. We have plenty of time."

"Not at all. I'm glad to get on with it," Herman said easily, closing the cabinet and turning to Jamey. "Amy has told me her problem. That she wants you to be able to launch a criminal complaint against Fred Stiles without being subject to one yourself."

"Let me say at once, Herman . . ."

"I know," Herman interrupted him. "You don't care. You're perfectly willing to be damned so long as you can damn. Your integrity is complete! But I'm thinking of Amy. She did me a favor, I suppose, in tearing up Aunt Dolly's codicil. I don't know if a gentleman is supposed to thank a lady for tearing up codicils that disinherit him, but the money certainly came in handy at the time. And now that I'm better off — I had a windfall inheritance from a Fidler uncle last year — I'm glad to help Amy out. All I have to do is put what I got from Aunt Dolly into a trust for my girls. Is that right? As a matter of fact, I was thinking of doing it anyway. It makes a lot of sense, tax-wise. So that should shut up Naomi and Fred forever."

Jamey demurred. "He could still make a case against me on the legal ethics question."

"Could he? Be practical, Jamey. Wouldn't the bar association treat the whole thing as a family matter that was none of their business? You've got a nutty old lady and a torn codicil and a general mix-up. But when the smoke clears, the right parties have got the money. Who's going to go into that any further?"

Jamey shrugged. "Perhaps nobody."

"All right. So that's what I'm going to do for you. Or rather for Amy. It should certainly spare Amy considerable embarrassment not to have to testify in public about what she did. But in return I'm going to ask you to give up your vengeance. I ask it on behalf of my daughters. Fred Stiles is their stepfather, at least he is for the moment. It's possible, despite rumors, that he may continue to be. I don't want to have him disbarred or even threatened with disbarrment. My leaving Naomi and the divorce was hard enough on those girls. I want you to give up your case against him."

Amy and Jamey exchanged a long stare. "You mean that he is to be free to continue the practice of law?" Jamey demanded sharply.

"At least until he does something else that's wrong."

"You know what you're asking? You know he's a crook?"

"I'm not so sure of that. It seems a pretty strong word for what Amy tells me he's done. Of course, I'm not a lawyer, but lots of lawyers must have occasionally suspected their clients of greasing palms. So long as Fred didn't do it himself ..."

"But he told John Rappelye who to go to!"

"I suppose he gave him the name of some clerk. Oh, sure, it makes it worse. But I know from my years with Naomi and the Rappelyes what kind of pressure he must have been under. Poor bastard! Of course he was wrong, but what about you and Amy tearing up codicils? From where I sit, you're all a bit crazy. In this world there's art — and for me that's now everything — and there's happiness. Those are the two big things. If you're an artist, and I use that term very broadly so that it includes a lawyer like you, Jamey, you've got about all you're entitled to. It doesn't matter if you're happy. You ought to be! But for nonartists, for most people, for Amy and Fred and Naomi, happiness is it. And happiness, of course, must bow to a certain amount of morality — each generation decides the quantity — but not too much. Please, Jamey, not too much!"

Amy, looking from Herman to her husband, found herself suddenly resenting the former's condescension. "There's still a distinction between right and wrong, Herman. Jamey and I are absolutely agreed as to his duty in this matter."

To her surprise Herman turned on her with a flash of indignation in his eyes. "Has it ever occurred to you, Amy, that you might be too aggressive about life? When you were living with Aunt Dolly, you decided that none of us had any passion in our lives, and that it was up to you to supply it. Now you've decided we have no morals, so you must supply them, too."

"I'm proud of having married a man who has the guts to do the right thing! Even at the cost of his career!"

Herman shrugged. "You're like Samson. You're proud of pulling the temple down. But I don't want my daughters in the wreckage."

"Take it easy, Fidler. You have no license to insult Amy."

But this seemed only to anger Herman. "I'm trying to help her!" he replied hotly to Jamey. "How do you think she's going to feel if this business all comes out in court? How do you think she'll feel if you're disbarred? And disbarred because of something *she's* done? Is that what you call loving, Jamey?"

Jamey had turned very white. He stared hard at Amy, but he seemed unable to articulate a word.

"Darling, don't listen to him!" she cried. "I shall be bursting with pride!"

"You make me prefer terror," Herman retorted. "Anyway, those are my terms. Take them or leave them. You and Amy can have a great life, or you can throw it away."

"How can you say that?" Amy demanded resentfully. "If we go back to where we were, *you'll* be the only one who's escaped from the rut!"

Jamey, at this, gave her a long curious look. Then he turned to address himself to Herman. "You really expect me to close my eyes to the bribing of a federal judge?"

"I do. I'm perfectly clear about it. I can see that you will feel cheated out of a beautiful self-sacrifice, but I hope you will do it for Amy."

"You assume my morals are at Amy's disposal?"

"They were once. Why should they not be again?"

Jamey seemed to be making a great effort to control himself. "You're a hard man to answer."

"I'm trying to be. All I am suggesting is that you continue to its logical conclusion the cover-up that you started two years ago."

Jamey turned to his wife, his countenance suddenly blank, his eyes flashing but seemingly staring at nothing. "Darling, he's telling me he loved you more than I do!" he cried in a strange, cracked tone. "He's telling me I don't love you at all. He's telling me that I've got to leave this decision to you. And I must! He gives me no choice."

Oh, she had seen it coming! She turned to walk away from the two men and paused before one of the little princesses. It was evidently one who had died in infancy, for the child was shown with two seraphs precariously perched, high in the canvas, on what might have been the curve of a great billow or even a bluish cloud, her white little face and black panicky eyes comically resembling her mother's, as though she had gone to heaven bearing all the attributes of earth.

Herman's words sank slowly into her heart. Would it help her in the future to know that her disillusionment was not in the man she loved but in the life that had defeated him? For he was still a hero, and he loved her quite as much as she had ever dreamed of being loved. No, her comedy was not the ordinary one of a romantic vision not realized. Her vision had been. She had found all the courage and the passion that she had craved, and what had life done with them but make them ridiculous?

"Is it really up to me, then?" she asked, turning back to her husband. He nodded. "All right. Let us do as Herman suggests."

Jamey turned away from her quickly and plunged his hands in his pockets. "You have my word, Herman," he muttered in a strangled tone. "Stiles remains a member of the bar. God help us all!"

Herman strolled over to Amy and looked with her at the little princess. "Would you like her? She's yours."

"You're very kind, but she belongs with the others."

"I suppose they go together. Very well, I'll paint you something else. Or maybe give you the sketch of the next group I'm planning. It has a similar kind of common denominator. But instead of the Bourbons of Naples I think I'll use the Rappelyes, the Fidlers, the Coateses, of old New York."

"And what will be Vesuvius?"

"Well, I thought *you* might be." He looked back at Jamey, but he had wandered, hands still in pockets, to the far end of the gallery. "You were like a volcano erupting in our little midst that night at La Rue. Oh, it was something, Amy! I wonder if any of us have ever quite recovered."

Amy pointed to the faint line of smoke emerging from the crater in the background of the painting. "It seems quite extinct now."

Looking across the gallery at her husband's back, she knew that she could not fool herself. He would never learn about the scene on the beach with Stiles, but that was nothing now. The price that she would pay for his concession was simply a scar on his image of her, a scar which would ultimately travel from the image in his mind to the image in his heart and erode a portion of his love. Not all — no, no — but some. And what had been the imagined salvation of her married life but the very totality of that love?

So this was where she had come out. The little world that she had observed so carefully from Cousin Dolly's parlor and into which she had so wildly fancied that she could introduce some fire or light, had simply absorbed her, and by the process of its strong digestive juices had obliterated her differences and made her a homogeneous part of itself. The marriage of the Jamey Coateses would not now be individualized from the rest by any particular passion or any particular idealism. It would be quite good enough as a marriage, just as Jamey's law firm was quite good enough as a law firm, but . . .

She went across now to her husband. "Herman offered me one of his pictures. Wasn't that dear of him? Considering what we're costing *him*? But I said they had to be kept together."

He smiled faintly. "Suppose I buy them all? We could fill up the living room in Shoal Bay."

Glancing about the gallery, she shuddered. "Let's go home now, darling. It's been a long day."

Herman, smiling to hide the fact that he was relieved to see them go, opened the front door. She gave his hand a little squeeze. Was he really the only one to escape? She wondered as they drove away. Into art? Couldn't she do it, too? If she should write a novel, a novel about herself and what had happened to her? But then it would be fiction, and the only thing that was interesting in her story, its truth, would cease to be. She sighed. She was glad anyway that she was having the second baby. The poor child would have so much to make up for.